MW01659719

Guided Home

Guided Home

KARLA CHRISTIAN

WORD AFLAME PRESS

Guided Home

by Karla Christian

Cover design: Laura Jurek
Pictured on cover: Kevin Fluitt, Sharilyn Sheerin, Courtney Christian

Printed in United States of America

Printed by Word Aflame Press
8855 Dunn Road, Hazelwood, MO 63042
www.pentecostalpublishing.com

WORD AFLAME PRESS
8855 Dunn Road, Hazelwood, MO 63042
www.pentecostalpublishing.com

Library of Congress Cataloging-in-Publication Data

Christian, Karla, 1957–
Guided Home / by Karla Christian.
p. cm.
ISBN 978-1-56722-734-5
I. Title.
PS3603.H7457G85 2009
813'.6--dc22

2009014232

Acknowledgement

Special thanks to my awesome husband, my one and only, Mark Christian. Being with you has been wonderful! I thank God for blessing my life with you.

To my amazing daughters, Kara McCool, Courtney, and Kalee Christian. I have been blessed beyond measure by your love. Thank you for tolerating my "writing days" and even for providing ideas all along this writing journey. And to Bobby McCool, my son-in-law, who has been kindness personified.

To my wonderful mother, Wanda Smart. Thank you for your consistent efforts with proofing and for encouraging me along the way.

Thanks to the rest of my incredible family and to all the wonderful friends that have blessed the lives of the Christian family.

Contents

1

MEMORIES

Grant Hayes looked out the window of the passenger train staring at the swiftly passing scenery. He had mixed emotions concerning his pending visit home. It had been several years since he had ventured back to his hometown of Progress, Texas, and he was uncertain how he would feel once he got there. He had acclimated fully to the city life of Boston, and as much as he hated to admit it, he dreaded returning home.

He had enjoyed the city life and attending Boston University School of Medicine. Most of all, he was looking forward to his residency. Every time he entered the hospital corridors where his brother-in-law, Dr. Stephan Grant, served as chief of staff, he had such a feeling of exhilaration. It was the same feeling of exhilaration he experienced when he had made the decision to become a doctor.

Hearing the story of his birth for so many years influenced his decision to pursue a medical degree. Grant could not count the number of times his mother had related to him the story of his miracle birth, and as a small boy he never tired of hearing it. He leaned his head back against the seat and smiled as if he could hear the much-loved voice of his mother as she retold the story.

"Please, Mommy," begged young Grant. "Tell me one more time how I was borned. "

Kate Hayes laughed merrily. "Oh, Grant, honey," she said. "Do you ever get tired of hearing this story?" She ruffled his black, curly hair and continued, "I don't blame you, sweetie, because I never get tired of telling it." She tucked the covers about him tightly and said, "It was absolutely incredible. You see, I was about a month away from your due date when this ferocious storm called a tornado came to Progress. Since I was quite 'fat' with you . . . "

Kate paused as Grant giggled, covering his mouth with his chubby hands. "Dat is so funny, Mommy," he said.

"Yes, sweetie, it's funny," she agreed, "but I was indeed fat. Anyway, since I was so fat with you, I couldn't move as fast as I normally do and because of that I had trouble going down the stairs to the cellar. Since mommy was so slow, the bad storm made the cellar door slam on me. It knocked me out and I tumbled down the stairs into the cellar."

"What happened next?" little Grant asked, his blue eyes peering intently into her face.

Kate laughed. "You're a little ham, young man!" she tickled him. "You always act as if this is the first time you've heard this story." She paused. "I'll tell you what Clarissa and Margarita did, although I don't know how they accomplished it. Clarissa and Margarita loaded me in the wagon and Clarissa drove into town like a madman was chasing her. Grrr!"

"That's funny too," Grant said, "loading fat you in a wagon and a pretend madman chasing Clarissa."

"That's exactly what they did. They loaded fat me in the wagon and skedaddled to town."

"Do you remember 'daddling to town?" Grant asked, not for the first time.

"No, I was still knocked out and I slept for a long, long time," Kate explained.

"Did you dream about me whiles you was sleepin'?" Grant asked.

"Let me tell you something, little man," Kate said, tickling him again, "I dreamed about you a long time before you ever got here. Your daddy and I wanted you so badly we prayed and prayed that God would give us a little boy, just like you . . . "

"And He did!" Grant yelled before she could finish.

Kate laughed and hugged him close, "Yes, He did. Like I said, you know this story well enough you could tell it to me instead of me telling it to you."

"So what happened then?" Grant asked settling back down.

"Well, Clarissa almost ran Stephan Grant down as she came roaring into town, and that's how they first met," Kate answered. "Then Clarissa's Dr. Grant took care of me while I was sleeping in a coma."

"Mommy, is that 'coma' something like what Margarita says when she says, 'Cóma estás?' " Grant asked with his head tilted to one side.

"So I see we're still learning Spanish, are we?" Kate grinned at the boy. "No, I think Rita's 'cómo' actually means 'how are you.' It's quite different than the coma I was in."

"Oh," Grant answered, acting as if he understood. "And then I was borned?"

"Yes, Stephan had to perform a special surgery so you could be born," Kate explained. "That's when the miracle happened."

Grant clapped his hands gleefully. "I just love this part!' he exclaimed.

Kate laughed. "I know you do. Yes, you were my little miracle. You were born while I was sleeping. Many people in town were praying for me and for you. Stephan was very concerned that I might not get better. But then all of a sudden, I just woke up."

"Wow!" Grant exclaimed, bouncing on the bed in excitement. "Go on, go on! This is the bestest part."

"When I finally woke up, I saw the most beautiful curly haired little boy ever!" Kate finished, giving him a hug.

"And that was me!" Grant yelled, lifting his hands in the air.

"Yes, that was you!" Kate answered.

"And you loved me 'mediately?" he asked leadingly.

"Oh, yes! I did love you immediately," Kate agreed. "I tell you what, young man; you're too smart for your own good."

"Daddy says I'm 'posed to be smart 'cause I have two smart parents," Grant answered emphatically.

Kate laughed, "Your father has taught you well. Just you remember that when you get older."

"You remember what, Mommy?" Grant asked with a confused expression.

"Remember how smart your parents are when you get old enough to think for yourself," Kate answered.

Grant still looked confused. "But, Mommy, you and Daddy *are* smart. How could you ever quit being smart?"

Kate hugged him. "You dear, dear boy! I thank God every day for the joy you've brought to our lives. I love you so much."

"And I love you, Mommy," Grant said, hugging her back. "You will always be my smart Mommy."

Grant smiled at the memory. He knew beyond a shadow of a doubt that his parents loved him very much. His mother saw to his every need and his father always spent time with him, no matter how busy he was.

Because of the story his mother so often shared with him, Grant decided to become a doctor too, just like Stephan Grant. He knew that because of Stephan's efforts on his and his mother's behalf, he was named after the good doctor. He was so glad his adopted sister, Clarissa, won the heart of Stephan as well. Their romance was another good story his mother always loved to tell.

When Grant decided to study medicine, Stephan and Clarissa had offered to let him board with them in Boston, and Stephan worked diligently to impart his medical knowledge to the earnest young man. After college, Grant had completed all the requisite medical studies and was to begin his internship with Stephan in the fall. Since he had not been home in several years, his parents wanted him to at least come home for a little while before beginning the final grueling stage of his medical training.

It was difficult for him to pull away, but out of respect for their wishes he decided to journey home for a brief visit. He was looking forward to seeing them, but knew he would have to answer many sticky questions once he arrived.

He sighed and bent forward, resting his head in his hands. He knew his parents were godly people and they had placed a love for God in his heart as well. However, since moving to the city, he had not attended church as he should and knew it had become a great concern to Stephan and Clarissa. He also knew Clarissa had most likely let his parents know about their concerns.

Grant shook his head. *How will I explain myself to them?* he wondered. *I mean, I still believe in God. It's just not as important to my life as it is to theirs.* Going to Boston had opened up a whole new arena for him. He saw things in a totally different light. And once he met Tina—gorgeous, vivacious Tina—his entire perspective changed. He knew his mother would understand if he could just talk to her about it. Then he paused. *Or would she understand?*

2

First Impression of Boston

Ah, Tina, Grant thought. She seemed to fill his thoughts day and night—that is, when he wasn't studying. He remembered the first time he saw her. He had gone to a get-acquainted social on campus. Not knowing anyone, he walked in feeling a bit insecure. He had not wanted to go, but Clarissa insisted it would give him a chance to meet others and give him a good start in his new life.

Not usually one to be intimidated by anything, he hated to admit he felt just that. The big city was nothing like his hometown of Progress. There were so many things to see that he could not take it all in. It was, to say the least, a bit overwhelming. And the party overwhelmed him as well.

The decor of the administrative ballroom was quite elegant. He smiled, thinking about what his mother would say if she could see it. The red carpet, accented with various green plants and columns, was imposing. But even more ornate were the gold furnishings placed in strategic locations throughout the ballroom. It was beautiful but did not seem at all inviting. In fact, it seemed unwelcoming and somewhat foreboding.

Grant's perusal of the interior decorations was interrupted by tinkling laughter. His eyes followed the laughter and focused on a beautiful redhead in the midst of a covey of young gentleman. She worked the crowd quite well, seemingly giving each young man just the right portion of her attention to keep them all interested. For a moment, his eyes met hers, and the connection held until she turned away haughtily. *Oh, well*, he thought as he inched his way to the food table. *At least there's something nice about being here: free food.*

He was just picking up a plate and reaching for some delectable morsels when he sensed someone standing nearby. Grant glanced to his right and saw the laughing redhead also placing a few dainties on her plate.

"Hello" he said, nodding and smiling.

The redhead skewered him with a disdainful look and said, "Excuse me," as she swept back to her admirers.

Grant shook his head and commented to himself. "Nothing like a sweet encounter to build one's confidence. Oh, well, at least I still have the food." Then he chuckled as he found a place to sit.

He sat back in the chair, beginning to relax and eat. "Hey, there, my good fellow," said a voice. Grant looked up and found a nicely dressed young man extending his hand. "Welcome to Boston U."

Grant stood and met his friendly fellow student's handshake with a smile of his own. "Thank you," he acknowledged. "Is it so apparent that I'm a new guy?"

"I'm afraid so," the young man answered. "I'm Fred Thomas and I'm a soph. But I can well remember how I felt this time last year."

"Whew!' Grant said, smiling. "It's nice to know I'm not the only one who's felt like apologizing for being an inferior greenhorn."

"No, old chap," Fred said. "I can well relate. You see, I'm from England and everything here's different: bigger, more plentiful, more informal." He took a bite of seafood salad and continued. "At first I almost decided to go home, but then I remembered I was a tough Brit and I determined to master the ways of this foreign land and become a model solicitor to make my countrymen proud."

"Well, that's impressive. I'm glad you stayed, since you seem the only one polite enough to acknowledge my existence," Grant answered.

"Oh, don't worry, old boy," Fred encouraged. "Once you prove yourself to this snooty Boston society, they'll take you in just like one of their own. Do you have anything by which you can prove yourself?" he asked.

"Not to my knowledge," Grant said, "but I'll try to think of something."

"That's the spirit," Fred said, slapping him on the shoulder. "Take heart; I have a feeling you'll find your place here."

The rhythmic clacking of the train wheels on the track brought Grant back from his jaunt down memory lane as he reflected on that long-ago conversation. He thought, *It seems just a short time ago I attended that first social. And now, five years later, here I am returning home before internship. Keeping busy definitely makes time fly.*

He glanced out the window, enjoying the budding green trees. Spring was his favorite time of year. It gave one a feeling of renewal as the flowering plant life displayed its gradual rebirth and growth. But the foliage was becoming sparser as his journey westward progressed, indicating that he was indeed getting closer to home.

The conductor opened the door at the end of the passenger car and yelled, "Arriving in St. Louis, Missouri, in approximately one-half hour."

St. Louis. The first stop of his return journey. He had planned to stop for a short visit with his grandparents before going on to Progress. It was not often that Grant had the opportunity to see his aging grandparents, as they lived so far away.

He was looking forward to spending a few days in their company and knew they were anticipating his visit as well. His mother, Kate, was born and raised in St. Louis, and left that city following a heartbreaking experience. He had often heard how she chose to come to the Texas panhandle to escape all reminders of her lost love. *What a change it must have been for her*, Grant thought. *Ironic though! Mom moved from the big city to a small town and I've moved from the small town to the big city. And it's turned out quite well for both of us.* He smiled with satisfaction as thoughts of Tina again entered his mind and he remembered their second encounter . . .

"Hey, Grant," Stephan said, knocking on his bedroom door, "would you like to come along with me to the hospital this morning and on the way take a look around Boston's South End?"

Grant yawned and stretched lazily. "Sure, Stephan. Just give me a minute."

"Okay," Stephan answered. "I'm planning on leaving in about twenty minutes."

Grant quickly tossed aside the covers and hit the floor to work through a few sets of vigorous sit-ups and pushups. He usually started every morning with some type of exercise to get his blood pumping. He quickly showered and shaved and made his way down to the breakfast room.

Clarissa was sitting at the table supervising the breakfasts of her twin boys and little girl. "Good morning, Grant," she greeted him. "Come in and join the party."

Grant smiled at the youngsters. The boys seemed not the least bit interested in eating. Instead, they seemed to prefer playing with their food. He was amazed that his petite sister had birthed these two energetic boys who reflected so much of their father. The little girl was an exact replica of Clarissa with her huge blue eyes and jet black hair. She was probably about the same age as Clarissa was when her parents were killed. Grant's dad, Alexander Hayes, served as his niece's guardian from that point on. Then when Grant's parents married, they formally adopted Clarissa. Thus, she was his cousin as well as his sister.

"Good morning, mates," Grant said, as he sat down at the table laden with oatmeal, toast, milk, and jam. "What are you two up to today?"

"Ah, we gotta go get new school clothes," Conner answered.

"And that doesn't thrill us at all," said Cameron.

Courtney tossed her curls. "We can sure tell you two aren't girls; I *love* getting new clothes."

'Who'd want to be a girl!" Conner sneered.

"Well, now," Grant said, "What would you say if I told you I enjoy getting new clothes? They make me feel like a fine gentleman."

Both boys looked incredulously at him. "You like to *dress up*?!" Conner exclaimed.

"With a suit and tie and stiff shoes?!" added Cameron.

Grant laughed at their response. "Oh, you two just wait. When you get older that's all you'll think about: spiffing up to impress the girls."

"Not me!" Conner said emphatically.

"Girls—yuck!" Cameron added.

"Uncle Grant," Courtney asked shyly. "What are you going to do today?"

Grant smiled kindly at the little girl. "Well, Courtney, I'm going with your daddy to the hospital. He wants to show me around."

"Oh, I love going with my daddy," Courtney sighed. "It's so much fun."

Clarissa hid a smile and winked at Grant. "Yes, Courtney does like going to the hospital. Not many people look forward to it, but Courtney loves exploring the long halls and following her daddy around asking a zillion questions."

"Mom!" Courtney said, pink tingeing her cheeks. "I don't ask that many questions."

"Hey, it's all right to ask questions, Court," Grant said. "It makes one smarter than ever."

The young girl gave him a brilliant smile. "Really?" she asked.

"Oh, definitely," Grant answered. "I about drove your mother nuts with all my questions and look how smart I am."

"That's for sure," Clarissa agreed mischievously. "You had more questions than a dog has fleas, but as to how smart you are, that's questionable."

Grant gave her shoulder a playful push as the children laughed. “I shall prove you wrong, Clarissa dear!” he vowed.

Clarissa laughed merrily. “I’m sure you shall. Now, as to asking questions, how was the social last evening?

Grant shrugged, “Oh, nothing special. In fact, most of the people there seemed to think quite a lot of themselves.”

“Oh, I’m sorry, Grant. I hate to admit it, but the people here are rather standoffish. I guess it comes with their history and all,” Clarissa said. “I know that’s one reason my husband left here when he was younger. He wanted to get away from the highfalutin society.”

“I can understand,” Grant answered. “I did, however, meet a second year student who at least acknowledged my presence. His name’s Fred Thomas and he’s from England. He wants to be a solicitor. He seems friendly enough.”

“Well, that’s a good contact, don’t you think?” Clarissa said.

“Don’t worry, Clarissa,” Grant said reassuringly. “I’ll be fine. If I can survive in Progress with the hostility of the Johnsons, I can survive Boston.”

“That’s the spirit,” Clarissa said. “Really, I think this city will grow on you if you’ll just give it a chance.” She stood and started clearing the table. “Now hurry up, you three. We don’t have time to dally.”

“That’s for sure,” Stephan said, coming into the room, securing his cuff links. “Are you ready to go, Grant?”

“Yes, sir,” Grant responded, taking one last gulp of coffee.

“Well, we’ll see you all at dinner,” Stephan said, giving each child a hug and a kiss. “Be good for Mom and don’t give her any trouble. Is that understood?”

“Yes, sir!” they replied in unison.

“I’ll see ya’ll later as well,” Grant said. “And I want to see all the clothes you buy, okay?”

“Sure,” Conner said sarcastically. “I just know they will be absolutely wonderful.”

Everyone laughed at his doomed expressions.

“Now, cheer up, Conner. It’s not the end of the world,” Stephan said. Then he turned to Grant, “Ready?”

"Yes, sir," Grant said, opening the door for them to exit.

As they went down the steps Grant said, "What a lovely morning! I can already sense fall in the air."

Stephan nodded in agreement as they strode briskly down the sidewalk. "Yes, in this part of the country the seasons have a greater contrast than they do in Texas." Stephan changed the subject: "So, how was the social last night?"

"It was okay," Grant replied. "I just told Clarissa that everyone seemed to think a lot of themselves."

"Oh, yes," replied Stephan. "How well I remember! Just don't let these Bostonians intimidate you. It takes a bit longer to gain their trust than it does the Texas folks."

"Yes, sir. From what I saw last night they're not only standoffish; some are downright snooty," Grant replied.

"Don't worry; they're not all like that." Stephen answered. Then changing the subject, he commented, "I'm glad we decided to purchase a home not far from the hospital, it makes things much handier for me. I can walk to work and exercise the old legs while I'm at it."

"Yes, sir," Grant agreed. "It does make it nice, especially when the weather's as pleasant as it is today."

They walked along in companionable silence, enjoying the sounds of the morning. Before Grant realized it, they had arrived at the hospital.

The hospital was an imposing, red-brick building with several concrete stairs leading to the main entrance.

"Let's go around to the doctor's entrance. That way, I won't be stopped in case I run into some of my patients or staff," Stephan said. They followed a sidewalk around the building to a smaller entrance. It was obvious that someone had spent a good deal of time designing an inviting courtyard to this entrance. Stephan noticed Grant's examination and smiled. "This," he said, "was Clarissa's idea."

"Well, it was a good idea," Grant said. "However, do you have a problem with the doctors wanting to stay here instead of going inside?"

Stephan laughed. "Well, not a severe problem, but yes, they do enjoy this little alcove."

"I can see why," Grant said, as they entered the door.

The smell of cleanliness greeted their entrance. "This way," Stephan said as he led Grant down a long, white corridor.

"Wow!" Grant said in awe, "This is really something."

"Yes, it is," Stephan said. "I've spent many hours in this hospital from the time I was a young lad until now. My father was originally the chief surgeon here, and after he retired the board voted to offer me the position of chief of staff. I was honored to accept their offer."

"I can see why!" Grant said, still peering intently at everything in sight.

They had turned right and started down another corridor, when they almost ran headlong into another couple.

"Oh, Dr. Grant!" said an older man, "Sorry about that. Didn't mean to run you down. I was just on my way to show my daughter my new office decor."

Stephan smiled and patted the man on the shoulder, "Oh, that's quite all right, Dr. Hamilton. No harm done."

To Grant's amazement, he found himself face-to-face with the same captivating redhead from last evening's social.

3

Meeting Tina

The shocked expression on the young lady's face was quite evident. Grant's gaze did not waver as Stephan said, "Oh, Dr. Hamilton, let me introduce you to my brother-in-law, Grant Hayes. He's just arrived in the city and will be attending Boston U and eventually our School of Medicine."

Grant forced himself to avert his gaze from the girl and extend his hand to the older doctor. "It's nice to meet you, sir," he said, with a nod.

"May I also present my daughter, Tina, to you, Mr. Hayes?" Dr. Hamilton responded, indicating the young lady by his side.

Grant again turned his gaze to the young lady and nodded politely.

"How are you, Miss Hamilton?" he said. "Nice to see you again."

Both doctors appeared surprised at his statement. "Oh, you already know each other?" Dr. Hamilton asked.

"Not really, sir," Grant explained. "We saw each other at the social last night."

Tina's face turned a bright shade of red, but she remained silent. "Well," Stephan said. "I didn't realize you'd met already."

Tina still stood in silence as Grant explained, "Oh, we didn't formally meet. It was more of a . . . " he paused for words. "It was more of a passing acknowledgement."

"Are you all right, dear?" Dr. Hamilton asked, noticing his daughter's heightened color.

"Uh, yes, Father, I'm fine," Tina said, finding her voice. Smoothly she said, "It is indeed a pleasure to meet you, Mr. Hayes."

Grant nodded as Stephan said, "Well, it's nice to see you both. But I don't want to leave the impression with Grant here that we doctors have time to dally."

Dr. Hamilton immediately said, "Oh, yes, sir. I have a 'to do' list as long as my arm." Then he looked at Grant. "It was nice to meet you, Mr. Hayes. I trust Boston gives you a genial welcome."

"Thank you, sir," Grant said, looking at Tina. "Perhaps it will." Tina's face again suffused with color.

Stephan and Grant turned and continued their trek down the corridor. Stephan punched Grant playfully and asked, "What was that all about?"

Grant chuckled and said, "You're quite observant, Doctor."

Stephan laughed as well. "As a doctor should be. Of course, it would've been difficult not to sense the tension in the air."

"Well, I tried to make an acquaintance with that young lady last evening and I received the brush-off of the century," Grant explained.

"Oh, I see," Stephan drawled. "Did the young lady perhaps surmise you were not worthy of her status?"

"Something like that," Grant said.

"Hmmm," Stephan said. "Too bad! Perhaps things will change now."

"You think so?" Grant asked.

"Oh, definitely so," Stephan said. "Dr. Hamilton is a good man and a good doctor as well. But he was affronted when the Board of Directors asked me to take the reins as chief of staff instead of him. Status and power matter a great deal to him. He's always been kind and cordial on the surface, but I know it hurt him deeply that a younger man was offered the position instead of him. I've always tried to be as kind as I can to him, but I can sense his negative feelings just under the surface."

Grant shook his head, "That's too bad. I know it was a disappointment to him, but it was a board decision and they knew you'd be the best choice."

"I don't know about that," Stephan said, "but I do appreciate your kindness. I've always loved this hospital and know it like the back of my hand since my dad discussed so much of the protocol and problems he encountered here. For that reason I think the board believed I had a little more insight into things than Dr. Hamilton. But whatever the case, our main priority should not be who's in charge, but making this hospital the best medical facility in Boston."

"Yes, sir," Grant agreed. "You're right." Then smiling slightly, he added, "Perhaps the reason my folks agreed to let me come here is because of the wisdom you just imparted."

Stephan laughed. "Uh-oh. I see there was a predominate influence in your life, most likely your mother." He grabbed Grant around his shoulders and said. "I can tell I'm definitely going to enjoy having you around."

Grant placed his arm around Stephen companionably as well. "I think with you and Clarissa by my side, I can conquer Boston."

The two talked and laughed as they made their way to Stephan's office.

"Arriving at Union Station, St. Louis, Missouri," shouted the conductor.

Grant stood and stretched as the train came to a halt. He located his bag from underneath the seat and made his way down the aisle to the outside door. Just as he descended the stairs, he heard, "Grant, Grant, dear! We're over here!" He turned to see his beloved grandparents standing nearby. His grandmother was waving her handkerchief, so he quickly hurried to join them.

"Grandmama!" He exclaimed, scooping her up in his strong arms. "You are still as beautiful as ever."

She swatted him playfully, "Oh, now, Grant, you silly boy. You know your mama taught you not to lie."

He gently put her down and reached for his grandfather, "Grandpapa, how are you?" he asked.

"I'm fine, my boy!" he replied. "And you've grown into a fine young man." He clapped him on the shoulder. "So good of you to stop and see us old folks."

"I wouldn't miss this for the world," Grant replied. "I'm going to have to look quite intently at both of you because I know Mom will want to know every little detail and will also probably ask my medical opinion of both of you."

"Well, what she doesn't know won't hurt her," bellowed the older man. "Mama and I are in fine form and there's nothing wrong with either of us but old age creeping up. And, I'm running as fast as I can to get away from it."

Stephan laughed. "Well, if anyone can outrun old age, Grandpapa, it's you."

"Pshaw!" Grandpapa Jenkins replied. "Now come along and let's get some sustenance so I can outrun that age factor."

The three laughed and talked all the way to the buggy and continued while Grant loaded his luggage into the back. Finally, all three were settled and as they made their way along the streets of St. Louis, Grant reminisced about past visits to the city.

"I can remember when I came here as a child how excited I was to see the Mississippi River. I couldn't believe there was so much water anywhere in the world. There are few rivers in the Texas panhandle and very few lakes. A body of water is something to be admired with wonder. And the trees! I couldn't believe all the trees," Grant said. "If you saw a tree in the Panhandle, you wanted to go over and hug it."

His grandparents laughed. "Oh, yes," his grandmother said. "I can remember some of the letters I received from your mother when she arrived in Texas. She always mentioned you could see for miles and miles."

"Yes, ma'am," Grant replied "We could see our neighbors' house even though it was miles away."

"So how are your neighbors, the Johnsons, doing these days?" his grandfather asked.

"Oh, things have been a bit quiet from their side, at least that's what Mom said," Grant explained.

"They just aren't very sociable people, are they?" his grandmother inserted.

"Well, I know they've been unkind to my family for a number of years. I think it's because they've always wanted to join our lands and thought marriage was the ideal way," Grant said. "I know Clarissa could have been killed by their maneuvers, even though they'd only intended to cause a rift between Clarissa and Stephan to further their own cause."

"Tsk, tsk," his grandmother clucked. "I don't know what their problem is."

"I don't know either. However," Grant said, frowning a bit, "the Johnson girl named Danielle seemed different from the rest of them. Her mother was the granddaughter of Ezra Smith who owned the mercantile in Progress. When we were in school, Danielle was kind and sweet to everyone. Her brother used to get mad at her because she wouldn't lord it over everyone like he did. In fact, she'd go against him when he mistreated anyone."

"Hmmm," his grandmother mused. "So there's some good in that family. That's interesting. I just don't know what made them turn out the way they did."

"Well, I think perhaps they felt slighted because my grandfather was one of the first to settle there and that always gave him status with the community. From what Dad said, people in the community would come to Grandfather if there was a problem instead of allowing the Johnsons to rule the roost in Progress," Grant said.

"It's sad when you can't be happy," his grandmother said. "The Bible said we should be content in whatever state we are in."

Mischievously, Grant asked, "Does that mean if we live in Texas, Missouri, or even Massachusetts, God wants us to be happy?"

"You silly boy!" the grandmother said, slapping him playfully on the arm. "You know what it means: God wants us to be happy and not always desire something we can't have."

"I'm glad you know your Bible, Grandmama," Grant said.

"I intend to know my Bible so I can always remind you of things in it when you aren't doing right," she said. "By the way, have you been going to church like you should?"

"Now, Grandmama," Grant began. "I've been busy."

"That's no excuse, boy," Grandpapa Jenkins said. "If you're too busy to go to church, you're too busy."

"I know," Grant agreed. "It should be much better now that I've finished all my undergraduate requirements and graduated from medical school."

"I certainly hope so," said Grandpapa. "It would break your mother's heart if you let go of God just to further your career."

"Grandmama!" Grant exclaimed. "I've no intention of letting go of God. I could never do that, after all the teaching I received."

"Well, that's a relief, at least," Grandma said, nodding emphatically.

"Now, since I have only a short time here, could we just enjoy being together and leave the lectures up to my parents?" Grant said. "After all, grandparents are supposed to always take up for the grandkids."

The Jenkinses laughed. "That's true, son," said Grandpapa. "That is, with everything but serving God."

"Okay, okay, you win!" Grant said throwing up his hands in surrender. "I'll get my act together."

"Don't be upset, Grant dear," his grandmother said, leaning her head on his shoulder. "We just wanted to prepare the way for you when you get a stern reprimand from your parents. Our intentions are good."

Grant laughed and hugged her tightly. "I really do have a great family," he said.

4

An Enjoyable Visit

Grant softly closed the door to his bedroom, took off his coat, and laid it on a chair. He flopped down on the bed and folded his arms behind his head. He had enjoyed a delightful few days with his grandparents and chuckled as he thought of their various conversations. They never failed to provide lots of entertainment with their anecdotes and opinions.

Grandpapa and Grandmama Jenkins were the only grandparents he had known. He usually saw his grandparents only once a year. They came to Progress to visit every other year, and he and his mother would visit St. Louis the corresponding years. Grant had many wonderful memories of those visits to St. Louis. His grandfather took him around town to various places: walks as well as paddleboat rides along the Mississippi, and picnics in the parks. But his favorite visit had been when he was eighteen just before he started at the university. His grandparents took him to the 1904 St. Louis World's Fair. He had marveled at the 'palaces' that displayed people and things from other lands, but especially enjoyed riding the gigantic Ferris wheel. Even though he had now reached the ripe old age of twenty-three, being with his grandparents made him feel like a little boy again. Their love gave him a solid, secure feeling.

Grandfather Hayes, Alexander Hayes's father, had died of a massive stroke before Grant was born, so all he knew of him was what his parents, Kate and Alexander, had told him. He knew his grandfather had been a great man. His dad often told him of how his mother, Kate, had cajoled and beleaguered the elder Hayes until, as his dad put it, "she coaxed him into the kingdom." It seemed his mother had a gift for coaxing people. Although he dreaded the prospect of returning home, he was looking forward to seeing his family once again. He felt blessed to have such a wonderful family.

Grant was also looking forward to getting reacquainted with his baby sister. Gabrielle had been so small when Grant left for Boston. His mom and dad had been resigned to the fact that the Lord was going to bless them with only one child when to their surprise, Gabrielle came along. Grant had enjoyed holding her and helping care for her but was afraid she wouldn't remember him since he had left when she was so young. It was nice to know he had a sibling and intended to spend as much time with her as possible.

He yawned and got up to prepare for bed. He laid out his clothes for the following day, just as his mother had taught him. "If you have everything ready, son," she would say, "it takes a lot of the stress out of the morning and helps you arrive where you are going in a much better state of mind." Grant smiled, thinking of her admonition. *I don't think she'll ever leave me or forsake me*, he thought, smiling. *She's a lot like the Lord.*

He winced, thinking of what she would say to him when he arrived home. Grant knew she was disappointed in his lack of church involvement, but he had promised himself he would make it up while he was home. *That should make her happy*, he thought. He completed his preparations for his continued journey home the next day and folded back the bedcovers.

As he lay down, thoughts of Tina again entered his mind. Amazingly, he had not thought of her much at all since he arrived in St. Louis. But now that he was again on his own, he remembered everything about her.

Grant strode across the campus, in a hurry to reach his next class. He was still trying to adjust to the locations of his classes, and found it a challenge to reach each one in the time specified by his schedule. Intent on his mission, he strode into class searching for an empty desk.

"Hey, Mr. Hayes," said a voice. "This desk is empty."

He looked up in surprise at the now-familiar redhead. Grant paused, not certain why she was speaking to him since she had totally ignored him at the social. However, he made his way to the desk next to hers.

He nodded in greeting as he sat down. "Miss Hamilton," he said.

Tina also nodded, "Mr. Hayes. So how has your first day been?"

Still surprised that she was actually speaking to him, he answered, "Uh, I think it's going pretty well. Just trying to locate all my classes."

'Yes," she answered silkily, "that is a challenge. I well remember my first day last year and it was difficult. If you ever need any help, please don't hesitate to ask me. I'll be glad to help you."

Grant frowned a bit at her offer and answered, "Uh, sure. I appreciate it."

At that point, the professor entered the room and began the class session. For over an hour, he told them what was required and what he expected of them. Grant wrote furiously, trying to make certain he got everything down. Several times he glanced in Tina's direction and found her eyes on him. He smiled slightly and continued his note taking.

Following class, Grant was gathering up his books when he found Tina standing at his side. "Would you like to walk out together?" she asked.

Grant shrugged and answered, "Okay."

They made light conversation as they exited the building into the sunlight. Grant was still in awe at the change in Tina's attitude. Although he was puzzled by the difference, he decided to just enjoy her companionship and think about it later.

"I had best get to my next class," she said, "But please remember, if you need anything, just let me know."

"Okay," Grant said, "thank you."

Tina was walking away when she turned back, "By the way, Mr. Hayes," she said, "You can call me Tina."

"Sure, uh, Tina," Grant replied. "And my name is Grant."

She waved airily and said, "I'll see you soon, Grant."

Grant simply stood and nodded.

"Hey, there, my good man," Fred said, slapping him on the shoulder. "How goes it?"

"Hello there, Fred," Grant responded. "I'm doing pretty well for my first day I think."

Fred jabbed him in the side, "Looks to me like, good fellow, you did something to prove yourself."

"I'm sorry?" Grant said.

"I'm making reference to our conversation at the social. You weren't feeling quite comfortable and I assured you that the Bostonians would be your friends once you proved yourself to them," he reiterated. "And from the looks of things with you and Miss Tina Hamilton, you've proved yourself."

Grant glanced at Fred as they walked along. "The thing is, Fred, I'm not quite certain what I did to warrant her attention."

"Well, if you think on it awhile, my man," Fred said, "I'm sure you'll eventually figure it out. And, when you do, please let me in on the secret because I've been here a year and haven't even warranted a glance from the uppity lady."

"Hmmm. That's interesting," Grant said, frowning. "She wouldn't even speak to me at the social, and then when I was with my brother-in-law at the hospital, we ran into her and her father, and she seemed different somehow."

"Your brother-in-law?" Fred questioned. "Who's your brother-in-law?"

"Dr. Stephan Grant," Grant answered.

"Really?" Fred asked in astonishment. "The Dr. Grant who is the chief of staff at the hospital?"

"Yes," Grant answered.

Fred threw back his head and laughed. "So that's it!" he said. "You, my good man, have achieved status. That's why the elusive Tina has changed her tactics."

Grant looked at Fred in confusion. "What d'you mean?"

"Oh, now, come, come, my friend. I haven't known you very long, but I do know you're a smart man," Fred said, clapping him on the back. "Your brother-in-law is a well-known figure here in Boston. His family name goes back several generations. And, he's the youngest surgeon in the history of the hospital to achieve the position of chief of staff." Fred chuckled. "Why wouldn't the supercilious Tina suddenly become friendly?"

Grant looked disbelievingly at Fred. "Oh, I don't think that's the case at all," he said emphatically.

"Oh, yes, my good man. Old Fred has it all figured out," he said insistently. "I tell you what, friend. I've learned something from this experience as well. It pays to be friendly because you never know who you're befriending. After all, look how my status has jumped simply by being nice to *you*." Fred stood in an exaggerated fashion with his hand placed across his heart. "I, Fred Thomas, after sauntering nonchalantly along, wondering if I would ever be accepted, have now found a friendship that will benefit me profoundly. I vow to my new-found friend, Grant Hayes, that I solemnly swear to stand by your side in sickness and in health, in sorrow and despair, when rejected and lovelorn . . . "

Grant interrupted, "Oh, stop it!" he said sternly. "I think you're wrong about Tina. I think she's just shy."

"We shall see," Fred said knowingly. "But can I still be your friend?"

Grant laughed. "How could I say no to that? After all, you were the first one to welcome me. Even though you're being ridiculous about this whole situation, I'd still like to be friends."

"That's great!" Fred said, raising his fist exuberantly. "Let's go, my friend, into the future with hope in our hearts."

"You're something else," Grant said, shaking his head. "Now we better get to class before we're expelled on our first day. I've had about all the oratories I can take from you in one day."

Sunlight streaming through the window and a tantalizing aroma of bacon and fresh-ground coffee drifting past his nose woke Grant Hayes the next morning. He smiled and stretched lazily before rising. He jumped out of bed and carried out his morning regimen. Then dressing quickly and gathering up his last few belongings, he hurried downstairs.

Grandpapa Jenkins sat at the table reading the paper and drinking coffee. He peered at Grant over the top of his reading glasses. "Well, nice to see you up and at it, young man," he said jokingly. "I thought I might have to oust you out of bed before the day was far spent."

Grant laughed and sat down at the table. "Good morning, Grandpapa and Grandmama," he said. "Sure smells good in here."

Grandmama Jenkins laughed. "I knew the smell of cooking would make you get out of that bed," she said jokingly. "Now just sit yourself down and I'll get you started."

They spent a good hour talking and laughing together, and all too soon it was time to leave for the station.

"I appreciate you stopping by to see your grandmother and me," Mr. Jenkins said as he helped Grant with his luggage. "We've so enjoyed the last few days."

"I wouldn't have missed stopping by," Grant said, hugging his Grandmama. "It was so nice to get the chance to spend some time with the greatest grandparents in the world."

"Pshaw!" his grandmother said. "Listen to him go on. Now, you take care of yourself and give your mama and Gabrielle a great big hug from me."

"I'll do that, ma'am," Grant said, taking his grandfather's hand in farewell. "Take care of yourselves."

"We will, son," his grandfather said. "In case we haven't told you before, we're very proud of you."

Grant took a few moments to contain his emotions before answering, "Thank you, sir," he said. "I hope I won't disappoint you."

"I doubt that will ever happen," Grandmama said as Grant started for the train. "Take care now!"

Grant waved once more before stepping up into the passenger car. He took a seat and quickly turned to wave one more time to his beloved grandparents.

"Well, I declare!" said a soft, feminine voice. "Whatever are you doing on this train, Mr. Alexander Grant Hayes?"

5

A Surprise Passenger

Hearing his name, Grant turned and looked down into the face of an attractive blond young lady who occupied the seat opposite him. Not recognizing her, he said, "I'm sorry. Do I know you?"

The young lady's merry laughter permeated the whole atmosphere. "Well, I should hope you know me. I usually don't make a habit of addressing handsome young men unless I do know them," she said. Then mischievously she said, "Take a close look and see if you can figure out who I am. I'll give you a little hint. We're from the same town."

Grant peered closely at her, and then exclaimed, "Danielle? Danielle Johnson? Is it really you?"

Again she laughed merrily. "Oh, you get a brownie button indeed," she smiled. "Yes, I'm the one and only Danielle Johnson of the Texas plains."

"What in the world are you doing here?" Grant asked, settling into his seat as the train started its departure.

"Well, I've been attending St. Louis University here in St. Louis. I just graduated, and . . . " Danielle started.

"Congratulations!" Grant said.

"Why, thank you!" Danielle said graciously.

Grant smiled, "I'm sorry. I didn't mean to interrupt."

"Oh, that's okay," Danielle said, "I prefer not to talk about myself anyway. I gladly accept any interruption when that's the case."

"But I did ask what you were doing so it's okay to talk about yourself," Grant said.

"You're right!" she said, and then mischievously added, "I knew you were always one of the smartest guys in school."

"Oh, now," Grant said with evident embarrassment. "I'm not too sure about that."

"Aw, just accept the compliment, mister," Danielle teased. "You know it's the truth."

Grant looked up and encountered her teasing smile. A smile gradually spread across his countenance and he said with fake humility, "Well, okay, if you insist."

Their laughter erupted spontaneously.

"So back to your previous explanation before I so rudely interrupted," Grant said. "What degree did you receive upon graduation?"

"I received a degree in nursing," Danielle said.

"Really?" Grant said, and then added. "Isn't that something? What made you decide to pursue nursing?"

Danielle paused only a second before saying, "Well, really, I thought the nurse's cap would look nice among my blond curls."

Grant stared unbelievingly at her. After several seconds, she again broke into laughter. "I'm kidding, Grant," she said. "Don't look so stern."

Slowly a smile appeared, "Whew!" he said. "You got me again. I couldn't believe that would be your reason. I was thinking you had a long row to plow if it was."

"Seriously, I've always wanted to be able to help others," she explained, "and since it's so difficult for a woman to become a doctor, I chose the next best thing, nursing."

"I see," he said. "I assume you aren't planning on settling in Progress then?"

"Well, just think about it, Grant. Have we ever had a nurse in Progress?" Danielle asked.

Grant paused, shook his head, and responded, "No, I don't recall ever having a nurse in Progress."

"Well, then, enough said," Danielle said with a determined nod. "Seriously, I'm not certain what I plan to do. Right now

I'm just going home to enjoy a much-needed rest. These last few years have been a bit difficult."

"I can imagine," Grant said.

"So what about you, Mr. Hayes, or is it Dr. Hayes now?" Danielle asked.

Grant looked incredulously at her. "I can't believe you remember my plans to become a doctor," he said. "That was a long time ago."

Danielle suddenly appeared shy and answered quietly, "I kept up with lots of information about you, Grant."

A silence followed her statement. "Really?" he asked.

"Yes," she said, smiling. "You made quite an impression on me, whether you know it or not. Your focused attention on medicine also impacted me as well. I remember in school you were so intent on your goal that you didn't notice much of anything else or anyone else for that matter."

"Man," he said peering at her, "You make me sound like an uncaring individual."

"Oh, I'm sorry," she quickly said. "I didn't mean that at all. If anything you cared too much. I just know that many of the kids used you as an example of how to pursue their dreams."

"Well, whether you believe it or not," Grant said, "I did notice you. I noticed how kind you were to people." Then he snapped his fingers. "In fact, just yesterday, I mentioned that fact to my grandparents during my visit with them."

"You did?" Danielle asked incredulously.

"Ironic, isn't it?" Grant replied.

"Yes, it is," Danielle said softly. "I didn't think you knew I existed." Then quickly covering her statements, she added jokingly, "Thanks for noticing me!"

Grant looked taken aback, and again noticed her teasing smile. "You're something else. I don't quite know when you're serious or when you're joking with me," he said.

"Then perhaps I'll be an enigma to you. I would so love to be a lady of mystery," she said, with a dreamy look in her eyes. "I've heard that is quite attractive to young men."

"You've heard that, have you?" Grant asked, peering curiously at her. "I wouldn't know since I'm much more mature than the average young man."

"Well, I say," she responded laughingly. "I was hoping to receive a little insight from such an eligible bachelor as you."

"Oh, well, then, let me expostulate some on that. Mystery is definitely attractive to us young men," he said grinning.

"Thank you," Danielle said, nodding her head in a manner of acknowledgement. "That will give me something to work toward in my pursuit of a husband. I'll appear mysterious and aloof."

Grant quickly added, "I didn't say anything about aloof."

"Yes, sir, I realize that," Danielle said drawing her shawl around her in a condescending manner. "But I've heard that young men do like a challenge in their pursuit of the opposite sex, so what better way to appear as a challenge than to appear aloof as well." She raised her chin haughtily and asked, "How am I doing?"

Grant chuckled impulsively and answered, "You're doing a fine job with the aloofness, but to be perfectly honest, I prefer the openness I saw when you first called my name."

Silence prevailed for a few minutes and then Danielle sighed. "All right then, Dr. Hayes, I'll take your advice and just be myself."

"A good decision indeed," he said smiling at her. He glanced out the window and then back at Danielle and said, "I'm very glad we're on the same train, Miss Johnson."

Danielle smiled back and responded, "So am I, Mr. Hayes. So am I."

He leaned back and added smilingly, "This could prove to be a much more interesting journey than I originally thought."

Grant enjoyed exchanging pleasantries with Danielle as they journeyed toward Progress. She was an agreeable young lady and did not seem at all self-centered, which was quite interesting to Grant. The time he spent with Tina required a good bit of attending to the young lady's needs and wants. Not that Grant minded, of course, since he was the envy of the gentlemen on campus. He sensed that his mother would not approve of Tina and dreaded telling his parents of his attachment to her. He had rehearsed several times how he would approach the subject, but could not seem to find the exact words to say. However, he would think about all of that later and simply enjoy this refreshing time of sitting and visiting with a young lady who did not require much "catering to."

"So did your family leave early from your graduation ceremony?" Grant asked.

A shadow crossed Danielle's features. "Unfortunately, my family was unable to come," she said.

'Really?" Grant asked in disbelief. "What happened?"

"Oh, you know," Danielle explained, "things are quite busy this time of year and they just couldn't seem to find the time to leave the ranch." Noticing the frown on Grant's face, she quickly added. "Oh, it's okay. I understand. My mom really wanted to come, but Dad didn't want her traveling by herself since she's never traveled before."

"I'm sorry, Danielle," Grant said sympathetically. "I know you were probably disappointed."

"Yes, I was," Danielle said, and then added brightly. "But it's not the end of the world. I mean, who cares about a silly old graduation anyway? It's just wearing a funny cap and walking across the stage, and I'm uncomfortable when people are staring at me anyway. So it all turned out just fine."

Grant was amazed at her attitude. He didn't think he would be handling the situation quite as positively as Danielle if his parents did not show up for his graduation. In fact, he knew he wouldn't.

"Do you always find something good in spite of being disappointed?" Grant asked.

Danielle looked taken aback. "Well, I never really thought about it, but I guess I do. It seems when I look for something good, it helps me handle disappointments." She paused and then brightened, "After all, the Bible tells us to be content no matter what state we're in. So, that's what I try to do."

Noticing Grant's incredulous look, she asked uncertainly, "Did I say or do something wrong?"

Grant laughed. "No, no, you didn't say or do anything wrong. I'm just marveling about coincidences."

Still looking puzzled, she asked, "What coincidences?"

"Well," Grant said, rubbing his chin thoughtfully, "first I mentioned you to my grandparents in a discussion yesterday, and you show up on the same train. Then, when my grandmama was giving me a lecture about finding true happiness, she mentioned that same Scripture verse about whatsoever state I'm in to be content." He shook his head, and then continued, "It's just interesting that two such incidents occurred so close together."

Danielle leaned over and whispered conspiratorially, "It could be a sign."

Grant looked into her eyes. "Pardon?" he asked.

Then she laughed merrily, and said, "Got you again."

Grant paused and then as her soft laughter melted his confusion, he joined her laughter. "Yes, I guess you did," he agreed. "You got me again. I see I'm going to have to keep my wits about me when I'm around you."

Then she giggled charmingly. "Yes, Dr. Hayes, you certainly are."

6

A View of Home

The landscape was beginning to take on a different aura. It had passed through several phases since Grant Hayes's departure from the city of Boston, Massachusetts. The green hills and tree-lined avenues, which Grant never tired of seeing, were now only visions in his mind. He leaned his head against the window pane as the train rolled onto the red clay of the State of Oklahoma. Grant knew that he was not far from the flat plains of his west Texas home.

He sighed and looked across at Danielle, his pleasant travel companion. Her blond head was leaning against the window, but instead of peering out at the landscape like Grant, she was enjoying a nap. Even in sleep, she appeared content. Grant smiled at her sleeping form and took advantage of her slumber to study her unobserved.

The short time he had spent with Danielle had been an unexpected surprise. She was quite a proficient young lady. Their conversational interludes had been pleasant encounters. He could not remember talking to a young lady and enjoying it as much as he had while talking with Danielle. She was not only intelligent, but pleasant and humorous as well. Grant shook his head, wondering why he had not taken special notice of her before. Of course, they were both quite young and at their time of past acquaintance did not move in the same social circles. If you could say Progress had social circles. He chuckled quietly at that thought.

Grant also remembered some of the stories his mother had told him about the Johnsons. His Hayes heritage often made him want to confront Butch Johnson and give him the "what for" because of his hostile behavior toward his family. He remembered his mother relating how surprised everyone was in the town of Progress when Susie Smith married Butch Johnson. Susie was the granddaughter of the much-loved Ezra Smith who owned the mercantile. He could not remember the details of how it all came about, but he knew it created quite a sensation in their small town.

Thus, Danielle was the daughter of Butch and Susie Johnson. Even though as a child he had not cared for her brother, Daniel, he did remember a little blond girl with a sunny disposition. He had often heard his mother comment, "Well, thankfully that sweet little girl inherited the goodness of the Smith family." And spending the last few hours with the young lady reinforced his memory that she was indeed a pleasant sort of person.

So intent was he on his thoughts that he was unaware that her startling green eyes were no longer closed until she asked hesitantly, "Uh, Grant, is something wrong? Am I drooling or something?"

Grant laughed. "Oh, no," he quickly answered. "I'm sorry. I didn't realize I was staring. I was so lost in thought I forgot you were there."

"Well," she responded, "now that you put it that way, I feel much better. You're so good for a girl's ego."

Grant slapped his head. "Oh, no, I didn't mean it that way." He shook his head in frustration. "I just can't seem to say or do the right thing with you."

Danielle looked peeved for as long as she could and then tried to stifle the giggle that burst forth. "Oh, I so wished I could've made you believe I was upset. But the laughter always gives me away." She smiled at him, and said, "I was rather enjoying the stare and thought you were actually finding me to be mysterious and aloof. But alas," she said, putting her hand dramatically to her forehead, "that wasn't the case. It's times like this when I remember that Scripture verse that goes something like, 'When you think you stand, take heed lest you fall.' "

Grant shook his head, "I'm sorry, Danielle. I didn't mean to offend you at all."

"Oh, you silly thing," she said, "I'm not offended in the least. I'm just teasing with you."

"Whew! That's a relief. It seems I may need to lighten up some if I'm going to be around you. You know those city folks I've been living amongst are so staid and uppity that I may have forgotten how to take teasing."

"Perhaps you do need some respite from the city life, Dr. Hayes. You need to take some time and just enjoy life. You've probably been so intense with your studies that you need a break as much as I do," Danielle said.

"You're so right!" Grant agreed.

"Let's make a pact, Dr. Hayes," Danielle said, extending her hand for a friendly handshake. "Let's agree to have fun when we're around each other and remember that we don't have to 'put on airs' when we're together. We can just be ourselves."

Grant extended his hand to meet hers. "Sounds good to me," he agreed. "I'll probably need a friend like you when I get home."

"Well, whenever you need a friend, Grant, just look me up," Danielle said brightly.

"That I'll do," Grant said as they shook on their pact.

Grant felt a gentle shake and heard a soft voice, "Grant, Grant," Danielle said, "you might want to wake up. We're about thirty minutes from Progress."

Grant came instantly awake and sat up abruptly. "Whoa!" Danielle said. "You don't have to scare the whole train! We're not being held up by despicable bandits or attacked by Indians!"

Grant smiled sheepishly. "Sorry. I guess it's just a habit of mine because I'm usually awakened because of an emergency of some sort."

"That's okay," Danielle said. "I just didn't want you or anyone else getting hurt."

Grant ran his fingers through his hair in an effort to cover his embarrassment. "I guess you're right, Danielle. I do need to lighten up a bit."

Danielle smiled. "Perhaps in the next few months, you can at least gain a much-needed rest and just enjoy being home."

Grant smiled sideways at her. "You really are little Miss Sunshine, aren't you?"

Danielle blushed unexpectedly. "I'm sorry. I don't realize sometimes how hard I work to make everything seem better than perhaps it is."

Grant smiled kindly. "Well, I for one really need your positive attitude. I was dreading going home, but you've made me enjoy the trip. And now I even feel excited about getting home and seeing my folks and baby sister."

"Well," Danielle said laughingly "At least I'm good for something." Then she sobered. "I guess I've learned some things the hard way being raised in my family. You know, my dad is somewhat . . . different. I don't know why he seems so difficult to get along with sometimes, but I'm always afraid he's going to offend or hurt someone, so I guess I try to overcompensate for his unkindness." Then she paused. "I know there's a lot of history I probably don't know about, but I do know my dad isn't very well thought of, and you know, that sometimes hurts."

Grant nodded sympathetically. "I can imagine."

Then Danielle brightened. "But I know that everyone thinks well of my mother and that my Grandfather Smith was loved by many."

"Yes," agreed Grant, "I remember my mom telling me how kind he was to her when she first came to Progress. He's a wonderful man, and your mother seems nice as well. I do know that a lot of things must have happened through the years, especially before my sister, Clarissa, married. But like you, I don't know the details. Whatever the case, Miss Johnson, it shouldn't affect our friendship."

Danielle smiled becomingly. "Yes, Dr. Hayes, you're certainly correct there. It shouldn't affect us being friends."

Suddenly, Grant exclaimed. "Look! There's my house. We're almost home, Miss Johnson."

Danielle smiled and followed his gaze. "Yes, indeed we are, Mr. Hayes! Indeed we are."

7

Home Again

The train arrived at the station, blowing steam as it slowed to a stop. Several residents were on the plank platform awaiting the arrival of their guests, or perhaps the return of loved ones and friends. Grant stood and bowed slightly. "Well, here we are, my lady," he said dramatically to Danielle.

"Yes, my lord," she replied in kind. "It seems our arrival is awaited by many."

"Right!" Grant answered sarcastically. "I'm sure the town has turned out en masse, just knowing that I, the well-known Alexander Grant Hayes, is returning."

Danielle pouted prettily. "But I thought they were all here for me!" she exclaimed.

"Of course, my dear, how could I have been so wrong? I might have known they were here for the newly graduated nurse," Grant corrected.

"Right!" Danielle in turn answered sarcastically.

"Tell you what," Grant said, reaching for his bag. "Why don't we exit together and wow the crowd at the same time."

"An excellent idea!" Danielle agreed.

"Shall we?" Grant said, offering her his arm.

Danielle giggled and took the proffered arm.

When they arrived at the door, Grant stepped down, and turned to assist Danielle. Just as Danielle stepped to the ground, Grant heard, "Oh, Grant! You're finally home!" Before he could turn to bid Danielle good-bye, he was surrounded by his parents' hugs and pats on the back.

"Mom! Dad! It's great to see you!" he exclaimed, returning their affection.

Then noticing the small auburn-haired girl standing by his mother, he knelt down. "And who is this lovely young lady with you?" he asked.

Gabrielle, his little sister smiled happily at his attention. "You're turning into quite a beauty," he said. "I'm glad I came home when I did to ward off the advances of all the young men!"

Gabrielle laughed and said, "Oh, sure!"

"How about a hug for your big brother?" he asked.

Instantly the child jumped into his arms. Smiling mischievously, he looked up at his father. "Hmmm," he mused. "Seems like she's a lot like her mother."

Kate Hayes swatted at him playfully. "That will be enough of that, young man," she said. "Hardly home five minutes and already acting as if you know everything!"

Alexander Hayes seemed to enjoy his son's humor for he responded, "Couldn't have said it better myself."

"All right, you two, let's get a move on. Enough analysis about the mother. I guess I don't have a chance: a lawyer husband and now a doctor son," Kate said. Then looking dramatically towards the heavens, said, "Lord, please hear my cry and grant me grace!"

The family laughed together as they went to retrieve Grant's luggage. As they walked along the platform, Grant looked around for Danielle. He spotted her to the side, talking to her mother, with her father standing sullenly by, evidently unhappy that he had to be there. A feeling of sadness overwhelmed Grant, and at that precise moment, Danielle caught his eye. With a quick look in her father's direction, she waved a hesitant hand in farewell. Grant responded with a wave as well and gave her an encouraging smile. Instantly her features were transformed into a smile.

"Who are you waving at?" Gabrielle asked.

"Oh, just a friend I met on the train," Grant responded.

"And who might that be?" his mother asked.

"I rode home with Danielle Johnson, Mom," Grant explained. "She took the train from St. Louis to here."

Kate stilled for just a moment before saying, "She seems a nice enough girl. It's a shame she had to be born into the Johnson family."

"Now, Katie," Alexander admonished.

"Oh, I know, dear. I shouldn't talk about her. But her father has become meaner and ornerier as the years pass. I don't know how sweet Susie ever ended up with him. She hasn't mellowed him at all," Kate said.

"And thankfully, he hasn't soured her either," Alexander added emphatically.

"Yes, that's true!" Kate said. "She's as kind as always. There just seems to be some bad blood in that family for some reason."

"Well," Alexander said, "let's forget about the Johnsons for the moment and get this boy home!"

Gabrielle clapped her hands in excitement. "Yes, let's go!"

The Hayeses laughed and talked all the way to the Hayes estate, catching up on each other's news. Much to his surprise, emotion overwhelmed Grant as they started down the lane to his home. Kate noticing his sudden quietness, said, "There's much truth to the statement, 'There's no place like home,' huh, son?" Grant nodded silently. "Well, we're so happy you're home for a nice long visit, Grant," Kate said. "I've missed you more than you know."

"And she has reminded me daily of your absence, son," Alexander added jokingly. "At least she has Gabrielle to lessen the pain of your absence."

Grant turned to look at his little sister. "Thanks for helping me out, Gabby," he said kindly.

Still somewhat in awe of her big brother, she covered her mouth and giggled.

Alexander slowed the horses to a stop in front of the house and jumped to the ground. He turned to assist Kate's descent and looked across the buggy to smile at his son. "Welcome home, son," he said.

Grant returned his smile and said, "Thanks, Dad."

Gabrielle jumped down and grabbed his hand, "Come on, Grant. Hurry and come inside 'cause I'm really hungry."

Grant chuckled as the little girl pulled him toward the house.

"Qué bueno! Mi hijo está aquí!" Running to meet Grant was Margarita, the Spanish housekeeper. Grant opened his arms as the woman rushed into them. She kept exclaiming in broken English, "So happy, so happy!"

Grant smiled as she kept muttering. "It's nice to see you, Rita. Did you miss me?"

Swatting playfully at him, she declared, "You silly boy. Payaso!"

Grant threw his head back and laughed. "Yes, Margarita. I'm still a clown. But please don't tell my Boston friends that because I have them fooled for the moment."

"Hurry, Grant," Gabrielle said, pulling on his arm again. "Come see what we have for you."

Grant entered the foyer and savored the familiar scene. *Yes, it's good to be home*, he thought.

"Venga, venga!" Margarita said, pushing him toward the dining room. "Must eat now or it get cold."

"Now that would be a travesty, wouldn't it?" Grant said jokingly.

Margarita scowled threateningly at him. "Okay, okay," Grant said lifting his hands in surrender. "Just let me wash up and I'll be right there."

He stepped quickly into the downstairs powder room to wash up and glanced in the mirror. His hair was disheveled and he felt a bit travel worn. However, he knew that the important thing for restoring a body, according to Margarita, was food. The rest could be accomplished later. He washed his hands, took a washcloth and moistened it with cool water, and washed his face. Then he finger combed his unruly locks and nodded at himself in the mirror. *That'll have to do for now.*

As he exited the room, he saw his mother descending the stairs. "Grant, dear, are you ready to eat?"

"Yes, Mother, I better be or I'll infuriate Margarita on my first day home," he answered.

Kate took his arm and smiled in agreement. "Yes, she's prepared quite a feast in your honor—all your favorites." Then squeezing his arm, she said, "I'm so glad you're home!"

He placed his hand on top of hers and answered, "I'm glad too, Mom."

An extravagant feast met them as they entered the dining room. Margarita was scurrying about, setting the last few dishes on the table.

"Come, come!" she said, indicating the chairs. "Sit, por favor. Everything is ready!"

"Thank you, Margarita," Alexander said. "It looks lovely! Come, son, have a seat."

"Thanks, Dad," Grant said, as he watched his dad pull out a chair for his mother. It never ceased to amaze him at the love he saw between the two of them. He had always hoped he would be able to find the same kind of love when he chose a mate for life.

His mother looked across the table at him and smiled contentedly. "Now this is nice!" she said. "It's wonderful to be together as a family again. I couldn't be happier than I am right now." She sighed and then leaned forward. "Grant, dear, why don't you offer thanks tonight?"

Grant gave his mom a startled look.

8

Catching Up

A tense silence filled the atmosphere. Alexander, realizing his son was uncomfortable with the request, cleared his throat and said, "Now, Kate. Give the boy a chance to get his bearings. After all, he just got home after a very long and rigorous train ride. I'm sure he can barely stay awake, much less offer the thanks due this incredible meal."

Kate laughed, and the atmosphere cleared. "Of course," she agreed. "What was I thinking? My dear husband, you always seem to know everything, as much as I hate to admit it. I apologize, Grant, for being so inconsiderate." She smiled at him.

Grant returned her smile. "It's okay, Mom, but I've looked forward for many months to hearing Dad offer thanks. He always seems to know just what to say, and I think this time is no different."

Alexander reached for his wife's and his son's hands. Kate reached for Gabrielle's hand to complete the family union and they all bowed their heads.

"Dear Father, what a wonderful day this is for the Hayes family. Our beloved son has returned home safely, for which we are thankful. We thank You for the goodness we see in him and for making sure his future rests in You. Now, we thank You for the wonderful food set before us and although I have much more to thank You for, I think it best to delay it until another time so my family will be able to focus better without smelling all these delectable dishes. I'll suffice it to simply say, thank You, from the bottom of my heart for everything. Amen!"

Light laughter followed his prayer. Grant smiled at his father, and extended his hand. "See, what did I tell you? No one can pray like my dad."

"That's for certain," Kate agreed then added as an afterthought, "of course, it must be remembered that I taught him to pray in the first place."

Laughter followed her comment. "Now that," Alexander responded, "we must never forget. Your dear mother loves to remind me she's the reason I have hopes of making it into the kingdom." Then he continued, "So, son, tell us about things in Boston."

Grant politely finished chewing before he answered. "Well, Dad, I can honestly say that I love living in Boston. I wish I could exactly describe my feelings, but suffice it to say, it's one great city."

"I'm so glad you're happy there, Grant," Kate said.

"I am too, son," Alexander agreed. "So you're enjoying your studies then?

"Oh, yes, sir," Grant responded. "And my favorite times are being at the hospital with Stephan. Every time I enter the facility I experience such a feeling of exhilaration."

Kate sighed sadly, and both men looked at her questioningly.

"What's wrong, Kate?" Alexander asked with concern.

"Oh, nothing," she said with sad countenance. "It's just that it's hard to believe my baby boy has grown up so quickly. He's so intent on becoming a doctor and seems content to live in far-away Boston."

Grant chuckled and said, "But, mother, don't you want me to grow up and pursue my life's work? I mean, after all, Clarissa left here."

"I know," Kate said somewhat despondently. "I was just hoping you'd stay here and be content to settle somewhere close by so I could see you all the time instead of having to be so far away like Clarissa and her family."

Grant smilingly shook his head. "Oh, Mom, I don't mean to make you sad, but I do love my city life. Anyway, how do you think Grandpapa and Grandmama felt when you settled clear across the country from them?"

"Okay, okay!" Kate said raising her hand, as if admitting defeat. "You're right."

Alexander smiled and leaned toward her. "One thing you can't deny, my dear, is that the boy definitely learned how to respond in a persuasive manner." He rubbed his chin thoughtfully. "I wonder where he got that from."

Kate playfully swatted his arm. "Well, now, I certainly wouldn't know the answer to that. After all, I'm not the lawyer in the family."

"Well, you should've been," Grant interjected.

"Vale, vale!" Margarita said, entering the room. "Do we eat or just laugh?"

"Well, I think we're doing a little of both, Margarita," Grant said. "But let me tell you I fully intend to take advantage of this wonderful meal. Boston has plenty of seafood, but there's one thing I can't get in Boston and that is Margarita's delicious cooking!"

"Bobo muchacho," Margarita responded, patting his shoulder, "You haven't changed a bit. Un momento. Let's see, how you say? Oh, si: You could flutter the butterfly with no wings."

For one moment silence reigned, then more laughter ensued. "I think you mean I could flatter the wings off of a butterfly," Grant said.

Margarita shrugged, "Well, you know what I mean. Los frases de los americanos. I just can't seem to get your American sayings right."

"Don't you worry a bit about that," Grant said. "You just keep cooking like this and we won't notice anything else."

Margarita raised her head proudly. "Claro que si! At least I can do that!" she said, marching determinedly out of the room to the chuckles of the family.

"I'm so glad you hired Margarita all those years ago, Alexander," Kate said. "She's been such a godsend."

"Yes, she has," Alexander agreed. "She's become a part of our family. I couldn't have done without her when Clarissa first came into the house after her parents' accident." He paused in his eating and looked at Grant, "By the way, how are Clarissa and Stephan?"

"They're doing great, Dad," Grant answered. "Cameron and Conner are quite the duo. It's so hard for me to believe ladylike Clarissa bore such two robust boys. Courtney, on the other hand, is an exact replica of her small mother."

"So Stephan's work at the hospital is going well then?" Alexander asked.

"Yes, sir," Grant answered. "To be the youngest physician on the hospital staff and the chief of staff at that, well, that's a marvel. But if anyone deserves the honor, it's Stephan. He always seems to know exactly what to do. He's good at managing the rest of the staff, and never fails to show them respect." He paused thoughtfully and smiled. "Yes, I've learned a great deal from him and I'm sure I'll learn even more."

"I think it's wonderful that you have him to look up to as an example," Kate interjected. "And what an added bonus that he's a member of our family as well."

"Oh, well, Stephan doesn't show partiality even though we're family," Grant explained. "And I'm glad about that. He entrusts me only with the cases he thinks I can handle. I wouldn't want the staff to become resentful of me and think Stephan is partial to me. That wouldn't be good at all."

"You're right there, son," Alexander said. "I don't think that would benefit your medical career at all if everyone thought you'd gotten recognition only because of your connection to Stephan." He paused and said dramatically, "I'm glad to know that I'm related to such intelligent people." A silence followed his statement. Alexander looked up and chuckled at their startled expressions. "Got you both," he said mischievously.

"Dad!" Grant groaned. "I didn't quite know how to take you. I'm not used to your teasing. I know Mom always picks on people, but I didn't know you'd taken up her habits."

"Well, I've been fortunate to be around this beautiful, feisty lady so long I've picked up several of her habits," he said.

"Humph," Kate pouted. "My habits, indeed. If anything, I've been a positive influence on you, and you know that's the truth."

"Yes," Alexander agreed, winking at Gabrielle. "I believe you've created lots of positive things around here."

Gabrielle, quiet until this moment, looked across the table at Grant and asked innocently, "Do you have a girlfriend in Boston, Grant?"

Grant stared uncertainly at his little sister, finding it difficult to believe she had asked the question he so dreaded hearing. He looked up and found both of his parents peering intently at him.

9

AN UNEXPECTED CONFRONTATION

"Uh, well, uh ..." he stammered. "I, uh, well, I do have someone special I've been seeing."

"Really?" Gabrielle asked excitedly.

Swallowing, he continued, "Uh, yes. She's a beautiful and intelligent young lady."

Kate leaned slowly forward, placing her elbow on the table and resting her fist against her chin. "Really?" she asked.

Grant looked at his father, hoping to see some sign of encouragement or support in his eyes, but instead he saw questions in his gaze.

"Uh, yes. Her name's Tina Hamilton and her father is on staff at Stephan's hospital. He is a well-known doctor in Boston as well." He paused, hoping they would say something, but since there was no response, he continued defensively. "The Hamiltons are a fine, upstanding family."

"So you met her at church?" Kate asked.

"Uh, no, ma'am. We met at a get-acquainted social when I first arrived at the university." He laughed uncomfortably. "It was funny, really. When I spoke to her she looked at me, stuck her nose in the air, and walked away without saying anything." No response. "So, anyway," he continued, "the following day Stephan and I were at the hospital and ran into her and her father. She was rather embarrassed by her treatment of me and went out of her way to make up for it. And that's kind of how it all started."

"I see," Kate said, frowning slightly. "Sounds very interesting. So you began socializing perhaps following church services?"

"Well, no, not really," Grant explained, looking uncomfortable. "We didn't actually attend church together because the Hamiltons aren't really faithful churchgoers."

"Is that so?" Kate said, her voice sounding strained.

"Oh, we did attend one service together at their church," he quickly added. "It was quite formal and very subdued, but I didn't mind since I had the chance to be with Tina."

"Oh, I get it," Kate said. "Being with Tina matters more than being at church."

Grant quickly backpedaled. "No, I didn't mean it that way."

"Well, it certainly sounded like that's what you meant," Kate answered, her temper surfacing. "Look, Grant, we didn't raise you to slough off church as if it were some inconvenience. Your dad and I both taught you to love God with all your heart and all your soul. We taught you that God should be number one in your life and that nothing else matters but Him."

"I still love God, Mom," Grant interjected.

"But from the sound of things, I would question that statement," Kate continued, her cheeks infusing with color.

Alexander reached out to her, trying to calm her. "Kate, sweetheart, I think we can talk about this without getting upset."

"I don't know if I can or not, Alexander," Kate said. "Our son is interested in a young lady who, from the sound of things, has no regard for God, nor evidently does she care about attending church. Isn't that the way it sounds to you?"

She looked at her husband closely and at his, "Now, sweetheart . . . " she continued, "Yes, well, that is what it sounds like to me. Some pretty little girl has influenced our son to neglect God and instead focus on her, doing her bidding and meeting her needs." She paused, shaking her head in disbelief. "Oh, my, my! I'm so disappointed! A lifetime of teaching is cast aside because some pretty girl has caught your eye."

"Mom, please!" Grant implored. "It's not that way at all."

"Okay, then, so what church did your regularly attend while you were in Boston?" Kate asked.

"Well, I really didn't have time . . . " Grant began.

Kate interrupted and threw her hands in the air, "See, that's what I thought." She rose from the table and went to look out the window. Her husband looked sadly at Grant and shook his head. Kate turned from the window, her eyes filled with tears.

"Mom, please try to understand," Grant begged. "When you meet Tina, you'll understand. I plan on introducing her to God, but I don't think she's quite ready."

"Oh, Grant," Kate said tearfully, "Sadly, son, you're the one that doesn't understand. We've taught you to seek companionship inside the realm of church, not outside the boundaries of God's will."

Grant answered a bit sarcastically, "Well, if my memory serves me correctly, I don't think Dad was in church when you met him."

"Okay, son, that's enough," Alexander said sternly. "You're not to speak to your mother in that tone of voice."

Sheepishly, Grant looked down and mumbled, "I'm sorry."

Kate sighed and took a deep breath. "Yes, Grant, you're right. Dad wasn't in the church when we first met. However, I returned to St. Louis because I felt there would never be a future for us. Thankfully, he was interested in finding God and did so before approaching me about his feelings."

"Well, there you go," Grant said.

"Whoa, son, hold it right there. Perhaps you better simmer down a bit. Your mother never stopped attending church, nor did she turn away from God because she was trying to impress me," Alexander admonished. "In fact, she was so involved with church and God that I didn't think she even knew I existed. I think there's a big difference in the situations."

"I really believe Tina will come to know God," Grant insisted. "I have strong feelings for her and she cares about me as well. I really think this will work. If I just approach it slowly and give her time, I believe she'll learn to love God just as I do."

Kate stood very still with her arms folded about her for comfort. She remained silent as Alexander stood and came to her side. "Kate, sweetheart, let's not ruin Grant's first evening home. I really feel as if the boy believes what he's saying. And I don't believe he has evil intent." He hugged her close and motioned for Grant as well. "Let's make a pact to pray about this together and allow God to lead us, okay?" He looked from his handsome, strong son to his beautiful, sad wife. "Can we do that? God can help us with this."

Kate hesitantly nodded. Then Alexander looked at his son and said, "I want you to promise me, son, that you'll pray for God's will to be accomplished instead of just praying for what you want. Will you do that?"

Grant hesitated for only a moment and then humbly nodded his head. "Okay, then." Alexander said encouragingly. "This is a good start, don't you think? Now can we hug and make up?"

Grant immediately reached for his mother and she went into his arms. Against her hair, Grant said, "Mom, I'd never willingly do anything to hurt you and I'm so sorry that I've done so. I love you and Dad, and Gabrielle so very much and want our family to always be close. I promise I'll pray for God's will."

Kate sighed, and said softly against his shoulder. "That's all we ask, Grant. I believe you'll do just that."

Gabrielle ran to them and inched her way inside the circle of their embrace. "Please," she said quietly. "Can't we all just love each other?"

Immediately, laughter filled the tense environment. "I don't think you need to worry about that, little one," Alexander said, reaching to lift her up. "If there's one thing this family has it's love for each other."

10

A Trip to Town

The sun was already making its way to a prominent position in the sky when Grant finally awoke. He stretched slowly and rolled onto his stomach to peer out the window. The quietness that surrounded him was quite different from the sounds of the bustling city he had grown accustomed to each morning. He leaned his chin on his folded arms and grimaced as the events of the previous evening came charging into his memory. He had been so troubled by his parents' reaction that he had not fallen asleep until the early morning hours.

Grant knew his mom and dad had very strong beliefs about God, but had felt certain he could talk them around to understanding and accepting how he felt. However, that was not the case at all. He didn't think he had ever seen his mother so upset nor so unmoved by his explanations. In fact, she was completely unyielding on all accounts. Even though they reached some sort of truce, Grant was disturbed about the whole situation.

In Boston he felt very confident about his plans and his feelings for Tina. But now that he had left the city, he was surprised at how unsure he felt. Grant shook his head slowly back and forth in disbelief. How could he, a grown man of twenty-three, suddenly be thrust into such confusion? How could one feel so certain one minute and the next minute wonder if he had made the right decision after all?

His thoughts were interrupted by a soft knock on the door.

"Grant?" his dad queried. "Are you awake, son?"

Grant rolled onto his side and answered, "Yes, sir, I'm awake. You can come on in."

The door opened slowly and his father entered the room.

"Well, good morning," Alexander said, and then smiled slightly. "We thought perhaps you'd returned to Boston after last night."

Grant gave him a lopsided grin. "The thought did enter my mind," he responded. "But I knew if I did so, Mom would be right behind me, so I decided to save her the trip."

Alexander chuckled. "Yes, you're probably right." Then he paused. "Grant, just don't forget that we love you dearly and only want the best for you. I regret we became embroiled in such an unpleasant conversation, especially on your first night home. But I guess your mom and I were surprised about the status of things."

"I know, Dad," Grant answered. "I think I delayed saying anything because I knew in the back of my mind you wouldn't approve. Even though I'm supposedly a grown man, I still desire your approval."

"And for that we're very thankful, son," Alexander quickly acknowledged. "Tell you what. Let's just forget about everything for a while. Why don't you and I ride into town for some lunch and just enjoy your being home, hmmm?"

Grant looked up into his father's kind eyes and gave him a ready smile. "That sounds like a winner to me," he responded. "But before I cause a riot in the town perhaps I ought to do something about my attire."

Alexander returned his smile and said, "Yes, perhaps that would be the best decision." He stood up and continued, "I'll be waiting for you downstairs while you prepare to astound the town."

Alexander gave a small wave as he left the room and descended the stairs. He was relieved that his son's good humor seemed to have been somewhat restored, which was a good indication that things were not lost as yet.

Alexander and Kate had been very concerned when they returned to their room the previous evening following their conversation with Grant. They discussed the letters they had received from Clarissa, which indicated Grant was not attending church as faithfully as he should. She had also mentioned that he had been spending some time with the daughter of one of Stephan's colleagues. But it was not until last night that they had discovered exactly what had been transpiring in their son's life. And this knowledge was unsettling.

They had prayed together and asked for God's wisdom and guidance in how to best handle the situation. So, it had been with much trepidation that Alexander approached his son's bedroom this morning. He was very uncertain how he would be received and prayed he would be met with at least some semblance of civility, which thankfully proved to be the case.

He sighed with relief. It was obvious Grant was Kate's son. How often through the years of their marriage had he encountered her flares of emotion only to find her the next moment humble and contrite, expressing her apology by words and actions. At least they both seemed to have the personality that did not hold grudges for indefinite periods of time.

Alexander walked into the parlor and met his wife's anxious gaze as she carefully placed her teacup on the side table.

"Well?" she asked anxiously.

"My dear, I'm not certain if we'll enjoy Grant's visit as much as we had anticipated," he said seriously.

"So he's still upset then?" she prompted.

Alexander rubbed his chin as if in deep thought. "Well, I wouldn't exactly call it upset," he stated. "He did smile at me."

"Oh?" Kate said excitedly. "Well, that's a good sign, don't you think?"

Unable to tease his lovely wife any longer, he laughed. "Oh, Kate," he said, "You never change. Worry is the main word in your vocabulary. Now, you can just relax, as I think our son's going to be just fine."

"Oh, you!" she huffed, unable to express what her heart was feeling. "You had me all in a stew. Making me think he was cold and unyielding. Oh, I could just, just . . . "

"Yes?" Alexander teased.

"Oh, what does it matter?" Kate sighed. "I'm just so glad that he at least talked to you that I'll let your misleading ways go for now. However," she said, shaking her finger at him, "I'll not hesitate to get retribution at a later date."

"Of that I can be sure," he said, coming to sit by her on the settee. "Seriously, my love, he's agreed to go into town with me for lunch, and even seemed quite amiable."

"Oh, thank God!" Kate said clasping her hands together. She reached for Alexander's hand and said, "We'll just pray and pray until we receive an answer."

"I think that's an excellent idea," he agreed. "Now let's talk about something else, just in case the boy comes in."

"I'm glad we decided to ride the horses into town," Grant said, bending over to pat the horse's neck.

"Yes, it's such a beautiful day," his father agreed.

This June morning in the Texas panhandle was a bit cool, making the ride quite refreshing. The dry air and the slight breeze could almost have been a paradise if it wasn't for the surrounding flatland and the occasional tumbleweeds floating across their path.

They rode along in companionable silence, savoring the morning atmosphere. Several jackrabbits bounded across the plains and flying geese formed a V in their flight overhead. An owl hooted and the call of a crow echoed on the wind.

"Well, I see the Panhandle is still making its own music," Grant commented.

'Yes, it is," Alexander agreed.

"I remember hearing the hoot owls as a kid, wondering if anyone ever answered their questions," Grant reminisced. "And I used to worry about all the animals thinking they might not have a home."

Alexander smiled, "Yes, I remember you finding little rabbits and contriving shoebox homes for them."

"And you made me take them back to where I found them so their mom would find them," Grant said. "I couldn't imagine a mother leaving her kids right out there in the open."

Alexander laughed heartily. "I imagine you couldn't. Not having the mother you had, that's for sure."

Grant smiled indulgently. "Yes, she was a bit overprotective. There were times it drove me absolutely bonkers, but at other times I was very glad she cared so deeply."

"Yes, your mom is quite a woman, Grant," Alexander said, "and believe me, she's more worried about you right now than I've ever seen her."

Grant worked his jaw back and forth. "Dad, I know that. But you and mom need to realize that I'm a grown man now and more than capable of making my own decisions."

"Yes, son, I'm well aware of that," Alexander said, "but even though you're grown it doesn't mean your decisions are necessarily the correct ones."

"Dad," he said tightly, "you and mom are just going to have to trust me. I really care about Tina, but I promised you all last night I would pray about it. Can you just trust me to do that?"

"Yes, son, I can," Alexander said. "I really didn't intend to bring the subject up again. I'm sorry. We're just concerned, that's all. So, let's just enjoy being together today, okay?"

"Sounds like a winner to me, Dad," Grant said, glancing at his father, as they rode into the outskirts of town. "Well, it looks like Progress hasn't progressed all that much." He paused, "some things remain constant in spite of all the changes in this world."

"In spite of appearances, it might surprise you how we're trying to progress."

"Sorry, Dad, I shouldn't have said anything derogatory. Made me sound like a snooty city slicker, didn't it?" Grant asked sheepishly.

"Yes, as a matter of fact, it did," Alexander said. "Just remember your roots, son. No matter how well educated we become, nor how informed we may be, we're still just mud balls."

"Well," Grant said, chuckling. "That should make me feel better."

"My father told me that one time when I had returned from law school feeling a bit 'full of myself,' Alexander said, joining in his laughter. "I'm just passing on his advice."

"I'll remember that for sure," Grant said, looking around. "Hmmm, it looks like there've been some changes after all. Fresh paint, new businesses, and sidewalks instead of the old boardwalks. I'm impressed with the progress."

"Yes, the people are trying to make our town more presentable," Alexander said. "Of course, we don't have a city government like Boston, so everyone's responsible for their own improvements. We don't have access to taxes to fund our projects."

"I hadn't thought of that, Dad," Grant acknowledged. "Perhaps that's why you're a lawyer and I'm a doctor."

"Perhaps," Alexander answered. "Now how about getting some lunch at Tabor's? My stomach is growling so loudly I'm certain the whole town can hear it."

"Well, I certainly can," Grant said. "I may need to give you a checkup the way you're sounding."

"No need for that," Alexander quickly assured him. "I never make a medical appointment unless it's absolutely necessary."

Grant laughed. "Well, that's normal. The greatest percentage of all males refuses to go to any doctor, unless they're dying. It seems you're no exception."

"Most doctors just find more things wrong if you do go," Alexander argued. "And that's one thing I don't need."

"Now, I take exception to your statement, sir," Grant said adamantly. "You're insulting my medical profession."

"Well, that makes us even, since you insulted my town," Alexander returned. The two continued sparring as they crossed the street to Tabor Hotel and Restaurant.

Upon entering, they took a few minutes to adjust their eyes from the bright sunlight to the dimmer interior. Jed Tabor rushed forward, gushing, "Come in, come in, gentleman." Then seeing Grant, he added. "Oh, my goodness! Look at little Grant Hayes. What an honor it is to see you, all grown up and standing right here in my restaurant."

Grant laughed and he shook the old man's hand. "I'd take exception to the 'little,' but since you immediately acknowledged that I'm grown up, I'll let it go this time."

Mr. Tubur chuckled and said, "Now, that's just my age speaking. I usually keep it quiet, but sometimes it takes over my young body."

"Oh, I see," Grant said.

"Come, come, let me show you to a table," he said leading them to one by the window. "I bet you're happy to see your young'un, Mr. Hayes."

"I certainly am, Jed," agreed Alexander. "He's been gone too long, that's for sure Mr. Tubur."

"What can I bring you while you look at the menu?" he asked.

"I'll take a cup of coffee," said Alexander.

"Make that two," added Grant.

Alexander looked across the table and winked at his son. "Isn't it nice to be home and have people putting you in your place?" he asked.

"You know, I really don't mind," Grant said. "I know the people around here care about me and don't mean any harm."

"You're right, son," Alexander said, "they certainly don't. In fact, they're very proud of you."

"Yes, sir," Grant said humbly.

Suddenly, someone slapped him on the shoulder and stated, "Well goodness gracious! Who do we have here? Don't tell me the prodigal has returned."

11

An Innocent Walk

Not accustomed to being greeted in such a manner, Grant stiffened. His father seeing his strained expression quickly gave him a reassuring look.

"Pastor Russell!" he exclaimed. "Yes, we're so happy our son has returned home."

Grant quickly recovered and rose to greet Kent Russell and saw that he had a beautiful young woman in tow.

"Hello, sir," he acknowledged with respect. "It's been quite some time since I've seen you, much to my regret."

"I hope you know I'm just picking at you," he said amiably, slapping him on the shoulder again. "I know you're not the prodigal. You'd never treat your parents in such a manner as the biblical prodigal son did."

Grant shook his head and said, "No, sir. I certainly hope not."

"That's my boy!" the pastor said heartily. Then he quickly said, "Oh, I'm sorry. Grant, I'm sure you remember Sharon, my daughter?"

Grant's glance settled on the demure brunette. For a moment, he was caught totally off guard. "Sharon?" he ventured. "Sharon Russell? Oh, my, you've changed!"

"I certainly hope so," the young lady answered with a twinkle in her eyes. "I'd hate to think I looked like the same gangly girl you last saw when you left Progress."

Recovering his manners, he quickly said, "I only meant it's been a long time since my last visit. Perhaps we can start over." Standing tall and bowing slightly, he said, "Good morning, Miss Russell. May I say how charming you look?"

Sharon blushed. "Oh, please. Seriously, Grant, it's good to see you."

"And you," Grant agreed.

"Well," Reverend Russell said jovially, "since we didn't intend to interrupt your lunch, we'll leave you be as I know you deserve some father-son time. I merely wanted to welcome you home, Grant. Now, come along, dear." Kent Russell gently took his daughter's elbow and led her to another table.

"Thank you for your kind welcome," Grant said graciously. "It was a pleasure to see you both." Just as he was about to sit down, Sharon came back to their table.

"Uh, one more thing, Grant," she said quietly. "The church is having a youth social this Friday night, and we'd be honored if you'd come. It might give you a chance to renew some old acquaintances."

"Why, thank you for the invitation, Sharon. That sounds fine," Grant answered.

A beautiful smile illuminated the girl's features. "Great!" she said enthusiastically. "It begins at 7:00 PM."

"Okay, then," Grant responded. "I'll look forward to it." He remained standing as she again joined her father across the room. Then he slowly turned and sat down, meeting the questioning gaze of his father.

"What?" he asked.

"Oh, nothing," his father answered innocently. "I was just listening."

Grant peered sternly at his father. "I'm sure you were. If I didn't know any better, I'd think you were doing a bit of conniving."

"What, me?" his father asked. "Whatever gave you that idea?"

"Perhaps it was something in your actions," Grant retorted.

"Well, she's a lovely young lady," Alexander insisted.

"Yes, she is," Grant answered. "But, you must remember, Dad. I'm interested in someone else at the moment."

"Just because you're on a diet doesn't mean you can't look at the menu," his father quoted.

"Oh, really?" Grant asked. Then shaking his finger at his father, he added, "I think you've taken on *too many* of mom's characteristics."

Alexander laughed. "Yes, that woman has had quite an influence on me."

"I think if I were you," Grant continued, "I'd try to focus on her good characteristics instead of her less desirable ones."

"Ah, but your mother doesn't have any less desirable characteristics. She's perfect in my eyes," Alexander said knowingly.

Grant shook his head and chuckled. "I give up on you two. The love between you after all these years is quite amazing."

"Yes, son, it is special," Alexander said. Then he leaned forward and looked deeply into his son's eyes. "We hope and pray that you'll find someone with whom you can have the same type of relationship."

"I'm working on that, Dad," Grant said in frustration. "Believe me, I want to find the right companion. However, the one I desire as a companion may not necessarily be the same as the one you and mom might pick."

Alexander leaned back in his chair and softly said, "Just be careful in your pursuit of a lifetime companion, son. And most of all, pray that God will help you in your pursuit."

Quickly Grant changed the subject. "So, enough about that. How about that lunch you promised me?" he said, looking intently at the menu.

Alexander shrugged and also began looking at the menu.

The rest of the week passed at a leisurely pace. Grant enjoyed sleeping much later than his usual schedule allowed and was amazed every time he opened his eyes to find the sun making cheerful progress on its journey across the clear blue sky. His mother enjoyed kidding him about his lazy ways, but quickly assured him he was only catching up on the sleep he must have lost while keeping up with his arduous schedule.

Kate always saved breakfast for him and seemed to savor the time they spent chatting at the kitchen table, just the two of them. Grant visited with his father mainly during the evening meal and they often exchanged political and social conversation until late in the night.

However, the highlight of his week had been spent in the company of his little sister, Gabrielle. He so enjoyed being around her. Since she'd been a toddler when he left home, he hadn't had the opportunity to get acquainted with her. The child had a wonderful capability of finding something positive about most everything and seemed to wear a continual smile. She was a miniature replica of Kate, and she unconsciously portrayed Kate's mannerisms, which was quite endearing.

One afternoon Grant had invited her to take a walk and it became a daily ritual. He found he could talk to her much easier than to his parents, especially since they'd shown such uncertainty about his relationship with Tina. Gabrielle asked dozens of questions about his life in Boston and would listen intently as he described various things about the city. She was especially fascinated by Grant's description of seeing his first Model T, since Progress was still in the horse-and-buggy era. She never hesitated to ask about Tina and how they met or what she looked like. She seemed to be unaware of her parents' feelings about his relationship with her. Because of her openness, he spoke freely of what he considered Tina's attributes.

One afternoon as they were taking their stroll, Grant talked about a certain social event they attended one Sunday. "The people were gathered around the pond, sipping their drinks and talking about the state of the nation. All of a sudden, a downpour came unexpectedly. It was fun to watch everyone scramble for cover in an effort to protect their elegant clothing," Grant said. "They spilled their drinks everywhere as the ladies squealed and the gentlemen offered their assistance in the best way they could in the unexpected deluge." Grant grinned, remembering the event. "It was unusual for it to rain on Sunday morning, as most of the showers come in the afternoon."

Gabrielle looked up at him and asked, "So you went to this party on Sunday morning?"

"Oh, yes! Sunday is a perfect time for these gatherings," Grant said enthusiastically.

Then the child asked incredulously, "But what about Sunday school? Did you miss church to go to this party?"

Grant started as he realized what he had done. "Well, uh, yes, Gabrielle. Most of the parties are scheduled for Sunday because the rest of the week is so busy."

Still confused, she asked, "But when are the church services?"

Grant walked for several seconds at a loss for words. Quickly trying to recover, he said, "Oh, church services are held everywhere in Boston, Gabrielle."

But the child persisted, "But if you're at a party, you aren't at church."

Knowing the child had caught him and not wanting to mislead her, he quietly said, "No, Gabby, I wasn't a good boy that Sunday. I did miss church."

Then as if they were surrounded by other people, she whispered, "Does Mommy know?"

He smiled involuntarily and answered, "No, Gabby, Mommy doesn't know. But I fully intend to try to explain it to her."

"Oh, she'll be so mad!" Gabrielle declared.

Grant stifled a laugh and answered, "I know. That's why I haven't told her." Then he quickly added, "Don't do like your big brother, Gabrielle. Always make certain you don't miss church for something as silly as a party."

They walked along in silence for a few seconds and then the child said with uncanny wisdom, "If I'd missed church to attend a party, I couldn't have enjoyed it because I'd know I was doing something wrong."

Grant sadly realized the child had innocently brought conviction to his heart. "You know, you're right. The party wasn't as much fun as it could have been because I missed church. I should try not to let that happen again, shouldn't I?"

Gabrielle reached up and took his hand. "Oh, you don't have to worry, Grant," she said confidently. "All you have to do is ask God to forgive you and that'll make everything all right again."

"Is that so?" Grant asked.

"Oh, yes," Gabrielle said emphatically. "Whenever I act badly, I hurt right here." She patted her heart. "Then when I pray and ask God to forgive me, it quits hurting." Then she paused and looked at him in confusion. "Didn't Mommy and Daddy teach you that?"

Grant squeezed her hand and said, "Yes, Gabby, Mom and Dad did teach me that. But sometimes it takes someone special like you to remind me of what I seem to have forgotten."

The child smiled contentedly and said, "I'm glad I could help, Grant. I so like to help."

Grant chuckled. "I'm sure you do," he said.

They walked the rest of the way home in silence as Grant dwelt on their conversation. He was amazed at how the Lord had spoken to him through his sweet little sister. As they walked up the stairs into the house, Grant knew he had some contemplating and reevaluating to do.

12

CONVERSATION

Grant sat at his bedroom window, elbows on his knees, staring at the darkness that now surrounded the house. After his walk with Gabrielle, he joined the rest of his family for the evening meal. As usual the food was quite delicious. However, he did not consume it with the same gusto he normally did.

"Grant, honey," his mother inquired, "is something wrong?"

"Si," Margarita said, entering the room, frowning in his direction, "you not hungry? I work and work, and you not eat? Humph!"

Grant smiled at their concern, and said reassuringly, "Oh, everything's fine. Especially the food, Margarita. I just have a few things on my mind, that's all."

"Did something happen today?" his mother quizzed.

"Nothing you need be concerned about," Grant answered. "I guess I'm at the age where I'm still unsure of my future and that's not a real comfortable feeling."

"I know," Kate said sympathetically. "I remember well the feeling of not knowing what to do. But just know that we're here for you, and that most of all God has it all in control."

"Thanks, Mom," he answered. "I appreciate that. I just want to do the right thing."

Alexander reached over and patted his son's arm. "We have the utmost confidence in you, son," he said, "and we're very proud of you."

Grant smiled, then said, "You know, I think I'll turn in early tonight." He placed his napkin by his plate. "I guess this country air is getting to me. After the hustle and bustle of the city, Progress's quietness and slow pace is calming me down a bit."

"Which is just what you need!" his mother stated emphatically. "By all means, go ahead and turn in early. We won't be offended at all!"

"Well, that's a relief," Grant said, wiping his forehead dramatically. "Just knowing I've not offended the famous Kate Hayes will certainly help me sleep peacefully."

"Oh, you!" Kate swatted him playfully. "Here I'm trying to be agreeable for once and what do you do? You make fun of me."

"I'm not making fun!" he argued. "I'm just agreeing with the agreeable you, and praising God for it as well."

"Now, that's enough!" Kate said, endeavoring to hide a smile. "You may certainly be excused after that statement."

"Well, Dad," Grant said, rising from his chair. "It seems that my case has been dismissed."

His father laughed. "It certainly does, son," he said. "It certainly does."

"I bid you all good night," he said bowing, as he exited the room.

"Good night, Grant," Gabrielle said shyly. "I'll see you tomorrow."

Grant stuck his head back in the door and pointed at her, "You can bank on that, Little Bit," he said. "And, Mom, tomorrow I'll be in better form for some more verbal sparring."

"That I'll look forward to," his mom's voice echoed in his ears as he climbed the stairs to his room.

He sat watching the velvet blackness overtake the sky. His confident feelings for Tina had wavered some in the last few hours. When he left Boston, he felt certain that Tina was the love of his life. Why, all she had to do was walk into a room where he was and his heart rate accelerated, he experienced shortness of breath, and began to perspire. He smiled and thought, "Sounds like the symptoms of a heart attack." Then he chuckled out loud, "I've certainly been too consumed with the medical field. Look at me—examining my reaction to a girl as a doctor would diagnose consumption or something. I definitely need a break, a Progress, Texas, interlude."

Grant pulled his quilt aside and piled the pillows into a comfortable position. He leaned back and placed his hands behind his head. He stared out the window for a few moments and then sighed. "Well, Dr. Grant Hayes, I think it best you put these confusing thoughts aside and get a little shut-eye while you have the chance. Tomorrow is another day and you can deal with your thoughts then." He leaned over and turned out the lamp, plunging the room into darkness.

The morning light slowly penetrated Grant's consciousness and he quickly jumped out of bed, awake much earlier than his usual hour. He completed his morning ritual and descended the stairs two at a time. He heard Gabrielle's bright chatter before he reached the dining room, and peered around the door in a playful manner. "What's all that noise?" he exclaimed sternly.

"Oh, Grant!" Gabrielle exclaimed. "You're up already! You must be excited about the social tonight."

Grant peered out the windows and stated, "From the look of that sky, there may not be a social."

"Oh, but there will be," Gabrielle said. "It's just a little bit cloudy and the sky is only sprinkling. This kind of weather is perfect for a social!"

"Is that right?" Grant asked with a grin.

"Oh, yes," she said dramatically. "It creates the perfect atmosphere for a lovely evening."

Grant stared at her in amazement. "And how old are you?" he asked.

"Why, Grant, you know how old I am," she said, looking at him in confusion. "Nine years old."

Kate entered the room, smiling as she caught the last of their conversation.

Grant looked at his mom and winked. "I could have sworn you were at least twenty," he said jokingly.

"Mom," Gabrielle said in protest, "what is wrong with Grant? He's forgotten how old I am."

"Oh, sweetheart," Kate said, hugging her. "Your older brother is just teasing you. He knows exactly how old you are. I think he's just surprised at how precocious you are."

"Pree-co what?" Gabrielle asked. "What does that mean?"

Grant sank to his knees and took his sister's hand, "Gabrielle, I know how old you are. I was just surprised at how well you talk. I'm so proud of how grown up you sound. That's what Mom means by 'precocious.' It means you act and speak like someone older than nine. You would amaze some of my Boston colleagues, that's for sure."

"Really?" Gabrielle said, giggling behind her hand.

"Yes, really," Grant said. "Now, about this social. So, you think the gloomy weather will not affect anything planned for this evening?"

"Oh, no!" Gabrielle said. "It'll be all that much more fun. If the evening is cool, they'll light a fire and everyone will gather around it and just talk and talk."

"So I assume you've attended a social?" he asked innocently.

Dejectedly, Gabrielle answered, "No, I've just seen them happen." Then looking dreamily at the ceiling, she said, "I can't wait to be sixteen so I can go to socials."

"Well, just don't grow up too fast because since I haven't had breakfast yet, I certainly don't have the energy to ward off all the young men that'll be falling at your feet," Grant said.

"You're so silly, Grant," Gabrielle answered, giggling. "No one's going to fall at my socials. Everyone will be standing up. I'll make certain of that."

Grant threw back his head and laughed. "I tell you what, young lady. I believe you're the most positive little thing I've ever seen. Always looking for the good in everything."

Gabrielle joined in his laughter, although she looked a bit confused. "I'm not sure what that means, Grant, but if it makes you happy, it makes me happy."

Grant shook his head, still chuckling. "She's certainly taken after you, Mom," he said. "Just hearing her talk lets me know she's definitely the daughter of Kate Jenkins Hayes. And, she may not understand everything that's going on, but if someone is laughing, she's certainly going to get in on the fun."

"Why certainly," Kate said, smiling. "What better person to take after than me, hmmm?"

"Yes, ma'am," Grant agreed. "I can't think of anyone that would be better to take after than you."

Kate reached down and gave him a hug. "It's so good to have you home, son," she said. "And I hope you're as glad to be here as we are to have you here."

Grant reached up and patted her arms. "I'm glad to be home, Mom," he answered. "For the next few days, let's just enjoy catching up on things and not get out of sorts with each other, okay?"

Kate peered intently into his face and extended her hand. "Okay, Grant. We have a deal."

Grant reached out to return her handshake and added, "Yes, we have a deal!"

"Good," Kate said, "Now let's help Margarita clean up this mess."

"Aw . . . " Grant and Gabrielle groaned in unison. But they both started gathering up dishes.

13

The Social

The mirror reflected quite a nice image of Alexander Grant Hayes. However, it was amazing how unsure he felt at this precise moment. He shook his head, finding his thoughts somewhat amusing. He'd attended all types of formal and informal social events in Boston, but he could honestly say that he'd never felt as ill at ease about any of them as he felt about this country social. He smoothed his hair and straightened his tie one more time. "Well, that'll have to do," he stated.

He heard a tentative knock on the door. "Grant, can I come in?" his little sister asked.

"Sure, Gabby," he answered. "Come on in."

"Woo-hoo!" she exclaimed as she walked into the room. "Aren't you fine!"

Grant laughed. "And *you* Little Bit, are too big for your britches," he said.

Gabrielle looked down at her clothes. "But I'm not wearing britches," she said, then added, "and I never do!"

"Oh, well, never you mind, Gabby," Grant said. "It's just another way of saying you're precocious."

"Oh," she said. "I know what that means—grown up. Grant, you sure did learn a lot of new sayings back in Boston."

"Yeah, I guess I did," he agreed. "You speak so well that I sometimes forget how much younger you are than I am."

"Well, you better hurry up," Gabby said interrupting. "You don't want to be late, but you don't want to be too early either. You need to allow just enough time to make a grand entrance."

He laughed as he shook his head in amazement. "Instead, I'll be making a *Grant* entrance."

"But I said 'grand' entrance," she said scowling at him.

"I know what you said, Little Bit." He ruffled her hair. "I'm just giving you a hard time."

"Oh, you silly!" she said, pushing him out of the room. "Now hurry."

"Okay, okay," he said grabbing his hat. "I'm going." She followed him down the stairs where their parents were waiting.

"Did you finally get him ready, Gabrielle?" asked Kate.

"Oh, he was already ready, Mom," Gabrielle answered mischievously. "He was just taking too long admiring himself in the mirror." Then she dodged out of his reach as he swatted playfully at her.

"I don't know what I'm going to do with her," Grant said to his parents. "Perhaps Mom has had too much influence on her."

"As I said, I'm the best influence she could have," Kate argued.

"You be sure and wake me up when you come in, Grant, and tell me all about it," Gabby said as they walked out on the porch.

"I'll make certain you know every detail," Grant promised. He pulled himself up on his horse and said, "Wish me luck."

"You don't need luck," Gabrielle said. "You're already good 'lucking.' "

Grant laughed as he guided his horse down the lane. "I'll be back soon," he said waving farewell.

"Have a good time, son," Alexander said.

"And be careful!' Kate added.

"Will do," Grant yelled.

Grant rode out the gate at a leisurely pace. The June evening was still a bit cool, but that was not unusual for the Texas panhandle. Just as Gabrielle predicted, the damp air created a feeling of security and comfort. He sniffed appreciatively and knew he was going to enjoy his ride to the social. He wasn't certain he would enjoy the event itself, but at the present moment, he felt quite content.

There was a hint of fog in the atmosphere as he rode along, but it was so thin that it did not make his ride difficult. As he rode toward Progress, he noticed a glow in the distance. *Must be the bonfire Gabrielle mentioned,* he thought. Then he smiled at the thought of his little sister. She was quite a little lady. He had no idea she would be so bright, or that he would enjoy being around her so very much. *She's so much like Mom,* he thought. *And she's certainly helped to refocus some of Mom and Dad's attention away from me.*

Now that he had reached the outskirts of town, he saw the church in the distance and the blazing bonfire that glowed beside it. Laughter penetrated the night as he rode up to the hitching post. No one seemed to notice his arrival, and he had a chance to dust himself off and smooth his hair before entering the circle of activity. He stepped around his horse and made his way toward the group gathered around the fire.

Sharon Russell looked up about that time and a smile lit up her face. "Grant," she said graciously, extending her hand. "We're so happy you could join us tonight. Come along and I'll introduce you to everyone."

Grant took her proffered hand and followed her to the group of young people. "Hey, everyone, this is Grant Hayes. Some of you know him I'm sure, but others may not have had the pleasure of meeting him."

Grant nodded politely. As he perused the crowd, he caught the eye of Danielle Johnson, who waved cheerily. "Hello, Grant," she called, coming to stand beside him. "I'm so glad you could come tonight. And I'm so happy to see that you still know your way around this huge metropolis."

He smiled amiably and answered, "Oh, yes. It's been quite a challenge, but I've managed to conquer the unfamiliarity of my surroundings." He paused and then asked, "And how have things been with you, Miss Johnson, since your arrival home?"

"Oh, pretty good, Dr. Hayes," she answered politely. "I'm still trying to adjust to the laid-back atmosphere of Progress."

Sharon Russell then asked, "So ya'll remember each other?"

"Well, as a matter of fact," Danielle began, "we sat near each other on the train ride from St. Louis, so we renewed our acquaintance."

"I see," Sharon said. Then she said dreamily, "I so enjoy traveling, but my parents will hardly allow me out of their sight. They just can't seem to realize I'm grown up now."

Grant looked at her and commented, "I know what you mean. I've been away from home for seven years, but my mom still tries to tell me what to do."

A murmur of agreement was heard from the other young people. "Yes, it must be a parent thing," said a black-haired, slim young man. "I get frustrated with all the 'where are you going' and 'what are your plans.' By the way, I'm Todd Herrington. I don't believe we've met."

"Todd," Grant said, meeting his handshake. "It's nice to meet you. Have you lived here long?"

"Not really," Todd answered. "After Grandfather passed away, our family moved here from back east to be near my grandmother. My father purchased some land outside of town and has built quite a spread."

A tense silence followed his statement, and then Grant said, "I see. Well, that sounds great." He looked around, trying to understand the sideways glances and the undercurrent of emotion he felt running through the group.

Todd continued. "Oh, yes. We hope to change this Podunk place into an up-and-coming town. It definitely needs some updating."

Danielle interrupted, "Oh, Todd, why do you always have to bring up your beefs about Progress? Most of us have lived here all our lives and we like the town just the way it is."

"Well, that just shows how dumb you are!" Todd responded.

Even though he himself had chafed about the lack of growth in Progress, Todd's statement riled Grant, but Danielle quickly touched his arm.

"Dumb, *you* say," Danielle flashed back. "Hmmm, let's see, you attended college where?"

"Oh, college doesn't matter when you have money. Money talks," he said arrogantly. "Money can get you anything you need. So why should I waste my precious time on college when the only reason you go in the first place is to make money?"

Heads swiveled from Todd back to Danielle to see if the argument would escalate, but Danielle laughed and said softly, "Oh, Todd, you haven't changed a bit. But let's not let a trivial argument ruin all of Sharon's plans and preparations for this evening. Come on, everyone, let's hit the food table."

The group immediately began laughing and talking as they migrated toward the tables spread with wholesome food and iced tea. Sharon gave Danielle a grateful look as she followed the others to partake of the food.

Grant and Danielle stood silently alone. "So," Grant said, looking down at the blond young lady, "I take it Todd is a bit full of himself."

Danielle laughed pleasantly. "You could say that," she answered. "He and his father intimidate most everyone around here and everyone lets them get away with their condescending attitude."

"But why?" Grant asked.

"Well, I'm sure you remember Todd's grandparents. In fact, my mother told me his grandfather was the one who procured your mother's services as teacher for the school," she explained.

"Ah, I remember that. Mr. Herrington was school board chairman and also held positions on the church board and the town council," Grant said.

"That's the one. Not long after you left for university, Mr. Herrington died suddenly and so their only son decided to return to Progress," Danielle explained. "Now, I'm not one to gossip," she said cheekily, "but I heard Todd's dad had some financial difficulties back east, so the passing of his well-to-do father was the perfect solution to his financial problems. They moved back here and his dad has become the overseer of the

Herrington fortune. I think Todd's arrogance is a cover for some of the family's former difficulties."

"Well, you saved the day with your 'soft answer,'" Grant said. "I'm quite impressed."

"Well, if I've impressed the great Dr. Hayes, my evening has indeed been a complete success," she added mischievously.

Grant laughed, then offering her his arm, he added, "May I escort the woman who saved the day to partake of some fine food?"

She placed her hand lightly on the proffered arm. "You may indeed, sir. Let's go liven up this no-account town a bit."

Grant laughed again. "My! From your country language, one wouldn't know you were a college-educated city girl!"

"Well," she said haughtily. "That's my forte! I haven't been gone so long or had so much schooling that I can't slip back into Texas lingo when I've a mind to. If a newcomer hears me talking when I'm at home in Progress, I can fool them into thinking I've been here all along."

"Thanks for the warning," he responded. "I'll be on my guard so I won't be one of the foolish!"

"Oh, now, you've no need to worry, Dr. Hayes," she said cheekily. "There are exceptions to my rules for those I fool. And you, my dear sir, would definitely be one of those immune to my wiles."

Grant dramatically wiped his forehead. "Whew! That's a relief," he said. "Just knowing I'm not on your list will make our relationship much more pleasant."

"Oh, we have a relationship?" Danielle teased.

Grant looked at her uncertainly. Seeing his expression, Danielle laughed merrily. "It's so much fun to tease you," she exclaimed, giggling.

Grant joined in her laughter. "You're something else!" he said. "I can tell it's going to be a very interesting summer here in Progress. Especially if I am in your presence."

"I certainly hope so," Danielle said, lifting her chin. "I hope to make your stay here as enjoyable as possible."

"Thank you, ma'am," Grant said, bowing slightly. "I certainly appreciate your consideration." Laughing, they walked to join the others.

❧ ❧ ❧ ❧ ❧ ❧ ❧

Soft music from the gramophone continued to fill the air and the young people sat around in small groups, talking and enjoying the beautiful late spring evening.

"Okay, everyone," Sharon said, raising her voice. "Before we all go home, I thought we might enjoy a game of musical chairs. Everyone gather round!"

The group worked together among much chatter and laughter to move the chairs in the proper fashion, and quickly changed the record to a livelier tune. The young people formed an oblong circle outside the chairs and began the game. They continued walking until the music stopped and everyone scrambled for the nearest chair. Chair after chair was eliminated until there were only three chairs left. The final contenders were Danielle, Todd, Daniel Johnson (Danielle's brother), and Grant.

"Okay, men," Danielle breathed out a teasing threat. "Prepare to lose."

"Yeah, right!" Todd shot back, "I don't lose to *anyone*, much less a girl."

"Well, I don't lose either, so that makes three of us winners," Daniel Johnson added.

Grant looked at Danielle and rolled his eyes as the music started once again. They marched around the chairs, intensely anticipating the ending chord. Suddenly, the music ended and the four scrambled to claim a seat. Todd started shoving, and when the dust settled Todd was on the ground. Glaring at Daniel who had 'stolen' his chair, he pounced on the offender and knocked him to the ground. A fight broke out.

"Hey," Grant said, quickly trying to stop the fracas. Ignoring his efforts, Todd swung at Daniel, knocking him back against a nearby tree. The sound of his head hitting the base made Grant cringe in alarm.

14

Scuffling to Win

"Daniel!" Danielle screamed, kneeling by her brother. "Daniel! Can you hear me?"

Grant knelt beside her, taking in every detail of the unconscious form of the young man. Danielle turned to meet his gaze and moved swiftly out of the way to give Grant more room to check on her brother.

Grant gently lifted Daniel's head and grimaced when he felt the huge lump on the occipital bone. His hand came away slippery with blood.

"I warned everyone! He had it coming!" Todd Herrington said, swaggering among the group gathered around.

Danielle jumped to her feet and said in a steely voice. "He had nothing coming, Todd Herrington. It's always everyone else's fault, to hear you tell it. Well, I tell you right here and now, this was *your* fault. If something is seriously wrong with my brother, I'll make certain you're brought to justice."

Todd snickered. "Justice? What does a silly girl know about justice?"

"I know plenty, Mr. Know-it-all," she answered, shaking a finger in his face. "I know you can be charged with assault if we press charges."

"Oh, now, we were just having a fun scuffle," Todd's braggadocio had suddenly switched to a conciliatory whine.

"I certainly don't call it 'scuffling,'" Danielle said. "I call it going in for the kill, and whether you realize it or not, killing is against the law in what you call this Podunk town."

In spite of his concern, Grant had to smile at Danielle's spunk. Then he said, "If we could, perhaps some of you could clear one of those tables to make room for Daniel so I can better examine him."

Quickly the young people did his bidding and stacked the dishes and other items on another table. Then Grant and two others carefully carried the unconscious man to the table. "Could someone hold the lantern close?"

Danielle grabbed the lantern and held it up so Grant could see. He assured her, "It's worse than it looks, Danielle. You know how profusely head wounds bleed. Now while I try to stop the bleeding why don't you go see if you can find a needle so we can close the wound?" She nodded and went to do his bidding. "And, Sharon, perhaps you could locate some water and boil it over the fire." Sharon hurried away to find the water.

Grant checked the young man's pulse and breathed a sigh of relief to find it was strong and steady. His respiration seemed steady as well. Grant grunted in satisfaction.

"What?" Danielle asked, suddenly appearing at his side with a needle, some thread, and a tiny pair of sewing scissors one of the girls had in her purse for torn hems or split seams.

"His pulse is steady and his breathing seems stable. That lets me know the injury isn't as severe as it could have been," he explained.

"See," Todd Herrington said, "I told you he was putting on."

Grant looked at him sternly over his shoulder. "No, Mr. Herrington, that's not what I meant. He's definitely not 'putting on.' He's sustained a serious head injury, which was caused by your impulsiveness, and which could potentially lead to a concussion. Now, if you don't mind, perhaps I could get on with taking care of this wound."

Todd slunk into the background at the authoritative tone of Grant's voice. One or two others followed him and they sat away from the rest of the group.

Grant looked kindly down at Danielle, "Well, Nurse Johnson, it looks as if we have our first patient. Can you help me with this?"

His soothing tone relaxed the tenseness of Danielle's face and she immediately responded. "Yes, doctor, I believe I can. Just tell me what you need."

For the next hour Grant and Danielle worked together suturing her brother's wound. The gash was approximately two inches long and Grant often had to discontinue his work to staunch the flow of blood. Danielle seemed to know exactly what Grant needed whether it was cutting lengths of thread or helping with sutures. He was very impressed with his assistant's thoroughness. *She's going to make a fine nurse*, he thought.

Just as they finished the final stitches, Daniel started stirring. "Daniel," Grant said softly, "please remain very still. You've been injured."

Daniel looked up at Grant with glazed eyes and tried to get up.

"Daniel!' Danielle said, gently grasping his arm. "I'm right here. Now please do as Grant says."

At her words, Daniel lay back down. "Can you see me?" Grant asked him. Daniel hesitated, blinking to adjust his vision.

"Yes," he answered, slurring his words, "but not very well."

"There's nothing to be alarmed about," Grant assured him. "That's perfectly normal after a bad head injury like you suffered." Grant held up two fingers. "How many fingers do you see?"

Daniel squinted and said, "I think four."

"Well, that's not exactly right, but at least you can see my fingers," Grant answered.

Then catching Danielle's concerned gaze, he said, "Your brother's going to be fine. The stitches will be uncomfortable, he'll have a colossal headache, and I'm fairly sure he has a concussion, so you'll have to watch him for a while and keep him quiet. Besides the double vision and headache he may develop nausea or lack of motor communication."

"I'll watch him," Danielle answered.

"We need to get him home," Grant said. "Why don't I tie my horse to your wagon and I'll ride with you out to your place? That way I can keep an eye on him for a while longer."

"I don't want to trouble you, Grant . . . " Danielle began.

"It'll be no trouble," Grant insisted and was rewarded by a dazzling smile from Danielle.

"Several of the others have already hitched the horses to the wagon and tethered your horse behind it," Sharon said, coming up to them.

"Good job, Sharon," Grant said. "That'll save some time."

Several young men carefully helped Grant load Daniel into the wagon as Danielle took the driver's seat. Grant looked at her uncertainly.

"I'll drive so you can sit in the back with Daniel," she said.

"The city girl nurse can drive the wagon?" Grant asked.

Danielle smiled, some of her feistiness returning. "Do you question my capability, Dr. Grant?"

"Oh, not at all," Grant quickly said. "Pardon me for doubting." After Grant settled in beside Daniel, Danielle flicked the reins and yelled, "Hyah!" Immediately the horses responded. Grant smiled slightly and shook his head at her spunk. In no time at all, they saw the town's lights receding into the distance.

Daniel moaned several times during the ride home. Grant reassured him and apologized for the discomfort. Finally, Grant recognized the entrance to the Johnson ranch. Danielle pulled the horses to a stop at the hitching rail by the front porch.

Grant quickly jumped down and commented, "Some driving."

"Thank you, kind sir," Danielle answered, dimpling. "Not all good drivers are men."

"Touché," he answered.

Just then the front door opened and Susie Johnson came out onto the porch. "My goodness!" she exclaimed. "Whatever is the matter? You came roaring in here, driving like Jehu. And why is a man riding in the back of the wagon?"

"Sorry, Mom," Danielle apologized. "Daniel got in a scuffle with Todd Herrington and got hurt. But he's going to be fine thanks to Dr. Grant."

Mrs. Johnson ran to the wagon wringing her hands. "Oh, dear Lord. Daniel, my poor boy!"

Danielle came to put her arm around her mother. "It's all right, Mom. You remember Grant Hayes, don't you? He's Alexander and Kate's son, the one I rode home with on the train."

"Oh," said Mrs. Johnson in a daze, "of course. Dr. Hayes, thank you so much for looking after my boy."

"It's Grant, ma'am," Grant quickly answered. "And your daughter did as much for Daniel as I did. She's quite an efficient nurse."

Mrs. Johnson smiled, glancing at Danielle. "Thank you, doctor . . . I mean, Grant. We're quite proud of her."

"As you should be," Grant agreed. "Now let's get Daniel inside so we can put him to bed."

A shadowy figure came from the side of the house and yelled, "What in tarnation's going on? And who in the world has the gall to trespass on Johnson land?"

15

Taking Daniel Home

Nervously, Mrs. Johnson answered, "It's all right, dear. It's just the children."

Butch Johnson reeled over to the wagon and bellowed, "I don't see 'just the children.' I see a third varmint I don't know, and I don't like that at'all." Grant grimaced when he caught a whiff of alcohol fumes.

Danielle went toward her father and took him by the arm. "Father," she said. "This is Grant Hayes and he's helping us with Daniel."

"Grant Hayes?" Mr. Johnson asked. "As in the Hayeses from next door?"

"Yes, sir," Danielle answered.

"Well, you can just get your carcass off my land," he yelled, raising a threatening fist.

"Father, please!" Danielle cajoled. "Daniel got hurt in a scuffle and Grant sewed him up and helped me get him home."

"Don't make no never mind to me!" Mr. Johnson continued. "Knowing *that* family I'd say he probably knocked my boy out himself."

Mrs. Johnson put her hand to her mouth, embarrassed by her husband's outburst. "Please, dear," she said softly, "calm down so you don't upset Daniel."

"Sir," Grant interjected, "I only want to help get Daniel into bed and I'll be on my way. Would you at least allow me to do that?"

Butch Johnson peered into the wagon and seeing the state of his son, sobered a bit. "Well, looks like the boy done it this time. I guess it's okay if you help. But just hurry it up."

Grant nodded and gently lifted Daniel from the wagon.

"Grant!" Danielle exclaimed. "You can't carry him all the way in there by yourself." She looked to her father, but Mr. Johnson made no move to help. His wife stayed with him, a gentle restraining hand on his arm. Grant thought, *He seems more concerned about my being on his land than he does about the welfare of his son.*

Grant continued up the porch steps as the anxious girl followed. "Just show me his room. I'm fine."

Danielle hurried ahead to lead Grant into the house. Grant glanced at the neatly arranged living room and followed Danielle down a hallway into what he assumed was Daniel's room. She folded back the bedcovers and he gently tried to lay the unconscious man in a comfortable position.

Grant checked his pulse again and noted it still beat steadily. He turned to Danielle. "Someone will need to stay close by him for at least twenty-four hours, Danielle. Perhaps you and your mom can take turns. I just want to make certain there's nothing going on with him besides the concussion. You'll need to wake him up every little bit and check his pulse and his breathing."

When Danielle didn't respond, he turned to see why. She stood just inside the door, her eyes filled with tears. "I'm so sorry about my dad," she said in a trembling voice.

"Hey, don't worry about it," Grant said waving his hand as if brushing it off. "Believe me, I know how dads can be sometime."

"No, I don't think you do," she responded, with tears still in her voice. "Here you are trying to help us and he acts like you're some kind of criminal or something." Then she paused. "You know, he's not the easiest person to get along with anyway, but when he drinks, he's unbearable. I don't know how my mom can stand it." Grant went to stand beside her.

"It's okay, Danielle, really it is." He patted her arm. "I know you and your mom appreciate the help, and most of all, I don't want you all to feel embarrassed by the way he reacted. Whiskey can poison a man and his relationship with his family and neighbors."

"I appreciate your understanding, but I just wish he didn't have such a chip on his shoulder all the time," she said. "My mom has always been the sweetest, most wonderful woman, and I get so mad sometimes at the way he takes advantage of that." She paused. "And now I worry that Daniel seems to be emulating his disposition. I was so hoping that he'd take after mom in my absence, but it seems Dad has become the stronger influence."

"Perhaps with you home, all that will change," Grant suggested.

"I doubt it!" she responded. "The Johnson men have a reputation for being difficult. I sometimes wish I was in another family just for that very reason. It seems everyone in Progress expects me to act like them, and I vowed when I was a little girl to not be 'roped' in with that lot."

"Well, then, just believe you can change them to your side. After all, from what I've seen the last few days, you have a stubbornness about you . . . "

"Hey, I resent that!" Danielle interrupted at his observation.

"Whoa! Let me finish. I was going to say you have a stubbornness about you, but in a good way."

"Okay then," she said smiling slightly. "You redeemed yourself somewhat."

"Whew! What a relief!" Grant said, wiping his forehead in mock relief. "Seriously, Danielle, I don't judge people by their family. And you seem like a fine young lady."

"I do?" she asked cheekily.

Grant flushed slightly. "Yes, you do. Tell you what. My mom has always said that prayer can do anything, so although I haven't quite been the Christian I should have these last few months, I'll pray that you can have an impact on your menfolk to promote change."

Soberly, Danielle looked into Grant's eyes. "I really appreciate that, Grant. That means a lot to me."

They looked at each other for several seconds and then Grant dragged his gaze away and cleared his throat. "Uh, well, I better get out of here before your dad comes and bodily drags me out the door."

"Yes, perhaps you're right," Danielle agreed. "Let me walk you out."

As they walked out onto the porch, they could both feel the tension between Danielle's parents. "Ma'am, sir," Grant said nodding in their direction. "Daniel is settled in now and if it's okay, I'll come back tomorrow to check on him."

"That won't be necessary," Butch Johnson said ungratefully.

Mrs. Johnson reached out and grasped his arm. "That would be fine, Grant. We'd really appreciate it."

"Okay, then, I'll see you tomorrow," he said walking down the steps.

"Thanks again, Grant," Danielle said as she followed him, reluctant to have him leave. "I don't know how we'll ever repay you for your kindness."

Grant looked up at the night sky and then mischievously said, "I'll think of something." Then mounting his horse, he rode off into the night

16

A Remarkable Narration

"Well, it's about time!" Kate exclaimed as Grant entered the front door. She stood in the doorway of the parlor, her arms folded. "I was about to call the Pinkerton men to go out looking for you."

Alexander Hayes appeared behind her, trying to hide a smile. "Yes, son, it's a good thing you're back. She was becoming quite agitated."

"Mom, there's no need to worry about me. And as I've said so many times before, I'm a grown man now," Grant said in exasperation.

"Grown man or not, you still should arrive home at a decent hour, or let us know beforehand if you intend to be late," Kate said stubbornly. "I mean, it's the least you can do."

Grant crossed to his mom and pulled her to him in a playful hug. "There now, Mother, I'm sorry. I didn't intend to cause you concern. Come on into the parlor and I'll fill you and Dad in on what happened." Still pursing her lips and looking sternly at him, she allowed Grant to lead the way into the parlor.

Grant flopped down on the settee and rubbed his forehead with one hand, hoping to ease the tension.

"See there," Kate said, noticing the action, "you must have a headache from keeping such late hours."

Grant sighed. "No, Mom, I don't have a headache. I'm just a bit weary is all."

"Well," Kate said impatiently. "We're waiting for an explanation."

"Kate, could you at least give the man a chance to catch his breath? I'm sure there's a plausible explanation," Alexander said, gently taking her hand.

Realizing her unkindness, a soft smile finally appeared on her face. "I'm sorry, ya'll," she said apologetically. "I was just so worried, Grant."

"It's okay, Mom," Grant said. "I really didn't mean to cause such an upheaval in the Hayes household." He paused for a moment before continuing. "The evening began very well. Sharon had prepared quite a spread for us all. And the bonfire was nice. The whole event was totally different from the Boston affairs I normally attend, but it was quite nice."

"My, my!" Kate interjected. "You sound a bit snobbish."

Grant laughed. "Yeah, I guess I do. Sorry, Mom. I know how you feel about all that snobbery stuff. To be honest, I guess I was surprised at how much I actually enjoyed myself." Grant leaned forward, elbows on his knees, hands folded. "The evening was going well and everyone seemed to be having a good time. Sharon Russell and Danielle Johnson introduced me around and I remembered several others there." He paused. "I'm sure you all know the Herringtons."

Alexander paused and glanced at Kate. "Yes, son, we do know the Herringtons. You know the elder Herrington was the one who initially hired your mom to teach school in Progress."

"Yes, I remember you all talking about that. Well, Danielle explained to me about the Herringtons moving back here to take care of elder Mrs. Herrington. I met their son, Todd, at the social tonight."

"And?" Kate questioned.

Grant stood, walked to the mantle, and continued the story. "The last thing on the agenda was an innocent game of musical chairs. Finally the number of contenders narrowed to the final four: Todd Herrington, Danielle and Daniel, and me. When the music stopped there was a tussle and Todd landed in the dirt, which he didn't like at all. So he lunged at Daniel Johnson and they went at it. Todd shoved Daniel, and he fell back and rammed his head into a tree trunk."

"Oh, no!" Kate exclaimed. "I thought this was supposed to be a *church* function."

"It was," Grant said, "but just because it's 'church,' Mom, doesn't mean everyone who attended the social was an angel." He continued, "So, with Danielle's help, I got the bleeding stopped and sewed up the wound, then I helped Danielle get him home."

"You mean you went to the Johnson ranch?" Kate questioned.

"Yes, ma'am, I did," Grant said.

Kate looked unbelievingly at Alexander. "Oh, Grant. Why did you have to take him home?"

"Perhaps because I was the doctor, Mom," he retorted.

"Surely there was someone else who could've helped," Kate said, wringing her hands.

"What's the problem?" Grant asked in frustration.

"They're such . . . such . . . unpredictable people, Grant. They've caused havoc in our community and they don't hesitate to hurt others if it means they come out ahead," Kate explained.

"Mom!" Grant said sternly. "Danielle's not like that at all. And her mother certainly didn't seem unkind. She was very gracious and thankful that I'd helped Daniel."

"And the father?" Kate asked.

Grant was silent.

"Oh, I see you don't have much to say about the father," Kate said emphatically.

"He was a . . . a . . . bit drunk," Grant said hesitantly.

"See there!" Kate shouted. "I knew it! Did he hurt you?"

"Of course not, Mom!" Grant responded forcefully. "I can take care of myself. I simply helped Daniel to his room and got him settled in."

"Well, I want you to leave those people alone. The more distance between you and them the better," Kate folded her arms stubbornly.

Grant frowned and looked at his father, who raised his eyebrows and shrugged as if to say, "Don't ask me." Grant continued. "Mom, why do you think all the Johnsons are like Butch Johnson? I know for a fact that Danielle is a very sweet-natured young lady."

"I would just prefer that you stay away from all of them," Kate insisted.

"But isn't that being prejudiced and not giving people the benefit of the doubt?" Grant asked quietly. "I'd think of all people, Mom, you'd not want me to cast judgment unnecessarily."

The room became very quiet as mother and son stared at each other. Then Kate slowly smiled, and asked innocently. "You're a doctor and not a lawyer, right?"

"I may not be a lawyer, Mom, but I do have my dad's genes," he answered.

Alexander's laughter resounded around the room. "You two do beat all!" he said, still chuckling. "This is going to be quite a summer, and I'm not referring to q-u-i-e-t. It's going to be interesting to see who has the final word!" Mother and son joined in his laughter.

Kate walked toward Grant and put her hand on his arm. "Grant, dear, I know I worry too much, but I just want the very best for you and perhaps I overstep my bounds by trying to make certain you do get the best."

"Yes, ma'am, but . . . " he started.

Kate held up her hand. "Let me finish," she said. "I have reservations about you socializing with anyone in the Johnson family because of our past, how shall I say, encounters. I wouldn't want to see something happening to you because of their jealousy."

Grant reached out to take his mother's hand. "Mom, I appreciate your concern, believe me. But you have Danielle pegged all wrong. I know I haven't spent that much time with her, but in the time I have spent with her she's shown me nothing but kindness and mannerly consideration. And you know what? She's a smart young woman and handles herself very well." He paused, forgetting his parents were in the room. "And, she has the most intense green eyes. When she's happy, they sparkle. When she's sad, they seem to pool. And when she's upset, they seem to send fiery darts right into your soul." He laughed softly. "Yes, those green eyes are really something."

The profound silence that engulfed the room brought Grant back from his reverie. He found his parents staring at him in surprise.

"What?" Grant asked. "What's wrong? Why are you looking at me like that?"

"Well," his father huffed, "you've just given us quite a description of the eyes of one Danielle Johnson," his father said.

Grant looked as surprised as they did. "I did?" he asked.

"Yes, you did," Alexander answered, smiling. "Your mom and I didn't know eyes could have such an impact on a person."

Grant shook his head as if to clear his thoughts. "Well, I never intended to share so much information, that's for sure," he answered uncomfortably.

"What are Tina's eyes like?" his father asked mischievously.

"Pardon me?" Grant asked in confusion.

"I was just wondering what Tina's eyes were like," his father said again.

Grant paused and then dropped to the settee as if he'd been struck by lightning. "Wow!" he exclaimed. "What's wrong with me? How can I be thinking about another young lady's eyes, when I'm in love with Tina? I'm going to have to get my focus back, that's for sure."

Kate looked as bewildered as her son. "Grant, are you okay?' she asked.

He looked up at her uncertainly. "Yeah, Mom, I'm fine," he answered. "I think the events of the night have addled my brain." He stood up and stretched. "I think I'll go up to bed now if you don't mind." Grant walked toward the door, and then turned back to his parents, "By the way, one day I'd really like to sit down and talk to you about Tina." With that, he left the room.

17

Unforeseen Circumstances

Kate and Alexander watched Grant's rapid exit with astonishment.

"Hmmm," mused Alexander. "That was interesting, wasn't it, my dear?"

"Interesting is a good word, I guess," Kate agreed, "but I might tend to call it shocking."

"Now, dear, I don't think it's quite that bad," Alexander soothed.

"I do," Kate argued. "I mean, just think about it, Alexander. Just think how long we've prayed for the time when Grant would find the kind of love you and I have shared for so many years. I mean, next to our relationship with the Savior, finding a mate is the next important aspect of life." She began pacing. "And look what choices we have so far. A snooty Boston lass or the offspring of the ingrates of Progress. We are doing well, aren't we?"

"Kate!" Alexander softly admonished. "There you go just like our son said, judging someone on their background." She glared at him, and he chuckled. "I know it makes you mad that I agree with him, but just think, sweetheart. Have you even met either of these young ladies?"

"I've seen Danielle, but not Tina. Clarissa has written me about that Tina girl, and I certainly don't like what I've read. Oh, yes, she's beautiful, according to Clarissa, but she likes herself more than anyone else and expects others to treat her as if she's royalty. Grant will be miserable if he marries someone like that."

"Now, dear," Alexander started.

"Don't you 'now dear' me, Alexander Hayes. I have a mother's intuition and you know I'm right," she said adamantly.

"I have to admit I do have reservations about Tina Hamilton," Alexander said, rubbing his chin. "I find it hard to believe our son would be interested in someone like her in the first place. But I know that sometimes beauty can overwhelm a young man to the extent that he can't see any faults." He paused thoughtfully, then continued. "Although I hate to admit it, I'm sure the boy was pleased when he won the redheaded beauty away from all the other gentleman vying for her attention. Perhaps that's one reason why he's so enamored of the young lady."

"Probably so," Kate agreed. "That would boost a man's ego, I guess."

Alexander grinned. "Are you talking about me personally, ma'am?"

"Of course not, Mr. Hayes," then turning and charging toward him, she stood on tiptoe and looked him straight in the eye, "Or I better not be."

He roared with laughter and reached out to hug her. "How could I possibly be interested in anyone else with you around? My beautiful, incomparable Kate."

"Oh, you certainly know how to get my attention off the subject at hand. We were discussing our son, not me," she smiled, then teased, "although I don't mind you interjecting comments on my beauty."

"Well, you can bank on it, my fair maiden, that I'll never cease to sing your praises," Alexander promised, smiling lovingly at his wife.

"Now that that's settled," Kate said with finality, "let's get back to Grant. We agree that Tina wouldn't be good for him, but I don't want him to be interested in Danielle Johnson either, and I certainly don't have to explain why. Why couldn't he like that nice Sharon Russell?"

"Let's not form a final opinion on anyone until we've had the chance to meet them, okay? Now, you'll probably never think anyone deserves our son, but we must remember he'll marry someone and we'll need to learn to care for whomever he chooses," Alexander patiently reminded her. "So why don't we just let things happen as they will and trust God? You know, my love, the Bible reminds us to be anxious for nothing."

"Yes, I know," Kate agreed, "but it's so hard for me to let God take care of something as crucial as this."

Alexander chuckled. "But if anyone's going into competition with God, I'm not in the least surprised it's you."

Kate paused at his comment, then realizing what she had said, laughed at herself as well. "Now, I didn't mean it that way, Alexander Hayes, and you know it. I know God will take care of things, and thanks for reminding me, my dear husband. I promise you I'll try to remember . . . "

"Now that that's settled, can we perhaps get some rest?" he asked.

"That we can, dear sir," she answered, taking his arm.

Alexander laughed softly as he escorted her up the stairs.

Unaware of his parents' conversation, Grant stared sleeplessly at the ceiling. He had returned to Progress knowing what he wanted concerning his future. Most of all, he wanted to marry the beautiful Tina and make her happy. He knew her expectations for his career and life in general would be hard to achieve, but he loved her.

He stood up and walked to the window to look out at the night sky, still deep in thought. Although he was in love with Tina, something bothered him that he had pushed to the back of his mind. When he would mention church or making the Lord a part of their life, she would skirt the issue by saying church was really just a way to make social contacts.

Her comments always concerned him, but he thought once they were married, he could change her and help her see the importance of serving the Lord. She was bound to change once she learned how important religion was to him and his family.

In the midst of his thoughts, a pair of startling green eyes floated through his mind.

"My goodness, Grant Hayes," he muttered, "whatever's the matter with you? Another woman shouldn't come to mind when you're thinking about Tina." He sat down on the bed and dropped his head into his hands. "You've got to get control of things here." He paused and then slowly lay back on the pillows. "I came home to rest my mind from so much intense studying. Now this!" he thought. For the first time in several months, he felt a need to talk to God.

18

A Family's Interaction

Grant awoke early Saturday morning and hurriedly dressed. As he jogged lightly down the stairs, he heard the normal light chatter and clink of dishes as he headed to the dining room.

"Good morning," he said upon entering the room.

Alexander and Kate both looked up at his entrance.

"Morning, son," Alexander said.

"Good morning, dear," Kate said, eyeing him speculatively.

Grant sat down and noticed his mother's perusal. He looked back at her and questioningly said, "Is something wrong, Mother?"

"Oh, no, dear," she said, looking quickly away. "Just had my mind on other things. I didn't mean to give you the 'once over.'"

"Okay, then," he said, picking up his napkin and placing it in his lap. "Where's Gabrielle?"

"She's a late sleeper, that one is. Kind of a nice contrast to you, since you never knew what sleep was," Kate answered.

"Buenas dias," Margarita said, placing a plate of food in front of him. "Eat up, hijoito."

Grant chuckled. "In case you haven't noticed, my dear Margarita, I'm no longer your 'hijoito.'"

Huffily she stated, "I no forget. You always be 'hijoito' to me." Then she turned and marched out of the room to refill the coffeepot.

Alexander smiled. "Seems as if she's taken on some of your mother's characteristics, doesn't it?"

Grant returned his smile. "Yes, sir, I definitely notice the similarity."

Kate smiled, "Okay, okay. We're both feisty, but we have to do something to counteract your male arrogance."

"Whoa!" Grant answered, holding up his hand. "You're talking about *our* arrogance? Now, Dad, help me out here. Have we ever shown arrogance around Mom?" Before his dad could answer, he continued. "I don't think so. Even if we did, I think she'd quickly nip it in the bud with her cutting words."

"Now, I'm not that bad," Kate protested. "Well, not unless I know I'm right about an issue, then I'll take a stand on it."

"Oh, I see," Grant said. "Then I take it you're right about everything?"

"Son," Alexander quietly admonished.

Grant looked up at his father's unexpected tone and noticed his mother's fallen countenance. He quickly said, "Oh, Mom, I'm sorry. I was only teasing you."

"It's okay," Kate said. "My feelings are a bit on edge this morning."

"Que ha ocurido?" Margarita said, coming back with the coffee. "The food gets cold while you talk."

"Okay, okay!" Grant laughingly responded. "We'll eat. By the way," he continued. "I'm going to run over to the Johnsons' this morning and check on Daniel."

Alexander quickly reached for Kate's hand. "Do you think that's necessary, son?"

"Look, Dad, I'll be fine," Grant reiterated. "I told Danielle and her mom I'd come over today and check on Daniel. So I'm going to do what I said I'd do."

Kate swallowed and asked, "So how long will you be gone?"

"I hope not long," Grant said. "Don't worry, Mom. I promise that they won't kill me."

"Well, that's comforting," Kate said sarcastically. Then she added softly, "Please be careful, Grant, okay?"

"I will, Mom. Really, everything will be fine." Grant stood and laid his napkin by the plate. "Tell Margarita I enjoyed breakfast. Now I'd better get out of here before she comes in with another plate. See ya!"

Alexander looked at his wife as she stared down at her plate. "Kate, you're going to have to let Grant be his own man. Remember we promised each other we would let God resolve the problem."

Kate reached for her husband's hand. "I know, Alexander. It's just hard to let him go. I mean, I let him go when he moved to Boston, but I didn't have to compete with all these other women either." Then she laughed. "I don't mind the other woman if it's a woman *I'd* choose."

Alexander chuckled as well. "Yes, it would really be nice if we could go back in time to the era of arranged marriages, wouldn't it?"

"Yes, it would," Kate agreed. "I mean, we should have the right to choose our lifetime partners, but we should definitely get to choose our children's mates. Is there anything in those law books of yours that gives us that right?"

"Sorry, ma'am," Alexander drawled. "I don't think so."

"Well, I guess we'll just have to pray then, huh?" Kate said.

"I guess so," Alexander agreed. "We'll just have to let the Master Planner take care of things."

"You're right again, Mr. Hayes. And I so hate it when you're right." Kate teased.

"You should be used to it by now, Mrs. Hayes," he retorted. Kate's laughter resounded, indicating her good humor was restored.

Grant sighed contentedly as he rode toward the Johnsons' ranch. It was a fine morning. Instead of the usual gusty wind of that part of the Panhandle, a light breeze stirred the leaves. Although it was June there was still a slight chill in the morning air. But the chill brought exuberance to the atmosphere.

I had forgotten how flat it is here, Grant thought as he looked across the prairie. Although the land was flat, the spring rains had given the usual dry vegetation a beautiful green hue. *This land has a beauty of its own, but it certainly takes awhile to get used to the bald prairie after being around Boston's parks and lush landscaping. At least my view here isn't hampered by grimy factories and jostling crowds of people and traffic. At this moment my only companions are my horse and a solitary prairie dog, which is quite nice!*

He had not slept well following last night's conversation with his parents. And when he did sleep, his dreams were chaotic. However, he'd spent a few minutes in prayer before he slept, something he hadn't done in a long time. Perhaps that's why he was not overwhelmed by the confusion that swirled around in his life.

Grant thought back over the conversation with his parents. He cringed when he thought of the look on his mother's face at his caustic remark. He never intended to hurt his mother. At least he had finally told his parents how important Tina was to him. *That's one hurdle behind me*, he thought. *And how many more to go? Well, I won't think of that now. I just want to enjoy the morning right now.*

He glanced up in surprise at the entrance to the Johnsons' land. The ride had passed much more quickly than he realized. *I've got way too much on my mind*, he thought.

"Hold it right there!" a man growled. "Don't take one step further or I'll shoot."

19

Rudeness Personified

Grant reined in his horse as someone shoved a rifle into his back. He slowly and carefully raised his hands and caught a backward glimpse of Butch Johnson, Danielle's father.

Slowly he said, "Good morning, sir. It's nice to see you again."

The older man scowled, "Whaddaya mean, 'it's nice to see me *again*'? I've never seen you in my life."

Still raising his hands, Grant kindly said, "Oh, yes, sir. I met you last night when your daughter, Danielle, and I brought Daniel home."

Butch shook his head as if trying to clear it. "You stuck-up whippersnapper! Don't try your fancy city talk on me. I know your kind."

"Sir, I'm not certain what you're referring to, but I really did meet you last night. In fact, I came over this morning to check on Daniel," Grant explained.

Butch shoved Grant again with the rifle. "I've no idea what you're talking about. My son, Daniel, isn't sick and has never been sick. I raised him tough."

"I'm sure you did, sir," Grant began, "but . . . "

"Dad!" Danielle screamed, galloping up on a frisky palomino. "What are you doing?"

"I found this here scoundrel trying to trespass on our land," he glared, answering her with his own raised voice.

"Dad, please!" Danielle begged, her voice quieting. "Put the rifle away. This is my friend, Dr. Grant Hayes, and he's being kind enough to drop by to check on Daniel."

"What in tarnation is wrong with everyone?" Butch roared. "Daniel's not sick."

Danielle had slowly been sidling her horse toward her father. She laid a gentle hand on his arm and said, "You're right, Dad. Daniel isn't sick, but he does have an injury from a scuffle last night at the social."

Butch's cackling laughter pierced the morning stillness. "Now, that's my boy!" he proclaimed. "I learned him right; he better *not* step down from a fight."

Grant watched as Danielle's expression changed from one of fear to one of anger. "That's enough, Dad!" she stated sternly. "Put that gun down immediately and let Mr. Hayes alone."

Butch Johnson again shook his head as if trying to clear away the cobwebs and very slowly began to lower the weapon. "I'm still not sure what's going on here," he said in slurred tones, "but if you're up to something, young lady, I'll take care of you later!"

Danielle flushed, "I'm not up to anything, Dad. Now, if you'll just go on about your business, I'll show Mr. Hayes to the house."

Finally, Mr. Johnson lowered the rifle and after glaring at them both, stumbled back across the yard toward the barn. He stopped for a moment and seemed to look for something. Then he bent over and picked up his brown keg. A groan escaped Danielle and Grant looked her way. Her face said it all. Emotions of consternation, embarrassment, anger, and unhappiness marred her countenance. She glanced back at him and asked shakily, "Grant, are you all right?"

"As you see, I'm quite well, madam," he assured her.

Danielle nervously adjusted the reins. "I'm so sorry, Grant," she said apologetically. "To think that he could have hurt you . . . "

"But he didn't!" Grant interrupted. "Don't worry about it, Danielle. Everything's fine."

"Ohhhhh," she exclaimed between clenched teeth. "I get so mad at him! My dad is so headstrong and thinks he knows everything. And, on top of that, his drinking makes him even worse."

"That does present a dilemma, doesn't it?" Grant opined.

"You can't talk to him; you can't reason with him," Danielle continued, gesturing agitatedly. "If only he'd stop drinking and think of his family for once."

"Danielle," Grant said soothingly. "Really, it's fine."

Coming to her senses, she blushed at her unguarded outburst. "I'm sorry, Grant, for the treatment you received from my father. I want you to know my mother and I appreciate your kindness so very much. So, if you could just overlook my father's . . . "

Grant interrupted by raising his hand. "Really, Danielle, it's just fine. How about showing me to the house?"

"All right." But before they started off, she turned and looked at him. "Thanks for being so understanding, Grant."

"Certainly," he answered. "Anything to aid a lady in distress."

"Well, I'm certainly distressed," she said, her good humor gradually being restored. She nudged her horse forward and they started toward the house. "Oh, my word!" she suddenly exclaimed. "I couldn't believe my eyes when I rode up and saw Dad holding that rifle in your back. I could've died right there, not to mention you could've too."

"Well, I for one, am glad neither of us did," Grant stated. "It would've been a lot more difficult to convince your father I had permission to be here if you'd died. And I may have died if you hadn't ridden up."

"So we're helping each other again, it seems," Danielle stated.

"Yes, I guess we are," Grant agreed. "Now let me do my part and check on that ornery brother of yours."

"Certainly, doctor," she said. "Come this way."

"Well, how are you today?" Grant asked as he entered Daniel's room.

The young man gave him a surly look and answered, "Who wants to know?"

"Daniel!" scolded his sister. "You could at least show some politeness since Grant has been so kind to see to you."

"If he hadn't gotten in the way last night, I would've creamed that creep!" Daniel said vehemently.

"Grant was not in the way, Daniel, and you know it!" Danielle argued. "This was between you and Todd, not you and Grant."

"Well, he could've stepped aside and given me *his* chair," Daniel pouted.

"Oh, yeah, right!" Danielle said sarcastically. "And that would've been totally fair, right?"

"It doesn't matter," Grant said, interrupting. "I just want to make certain your head injury is doing okay. I really didn't come to argue with you or bother you, Daniel. Just wanted to check on you."

"That's right!" Danielle agreed. "Now don't be a baby and let Grant take a look at you."

Begrudgingly, Daniel submitted to Grant's examination and grimaced at his touch.

"Looks like you're going to have quite a sizeable headache for a few days, Daniel, and I'm sorry about that," Grant explained. "But you're very fortunate because the place where you hit your head was only a minute distance from the point where the blow could have been fatal or caused severe paralysis."

"Oh, my goodness!" Danielle exclaimed. "It looks like God was looking out for you, Daniel."

"Yeah, right!" Daniel answered sarcastically. "God doesn't even know who I am."

"Well, I wonder why!" Danielle responded. "You better be glad I'm not God because I would've written you off a long time ago, believe me."

Daniel's only answer was to glare at his sister. "Why don't you two get out and leave me alone?"

"That we will, dear brother," Danielle answered, "But not before you properly thank Grant for his help."

"Oh, all right," Daniel answered sullenly, then added mockingly, "Thank you, thank you, thank you." Then he paused with a glare and said, "Is that good enough for ya?"

"How can you be so rude, Daniel?" Danielle asked, tears of humiliation pooling in her eyes.

"Look, it doesn't matter, Danielle," Grant said. "I need to go anyway." Then turning to Daniel, he said casually, "Take care, man." Then he turned and walked out of the room.

"You're a jerk!' Danielle hissed at Daniel before following Grant out.

"Look, I'm sorry about that," she began as she reached his side.

Grant shook his head, "Don't worry about it, Danielle. I only came here to check on him for you and your mom. If he chooses to be rude, it doesn't cast any reflection on you or your mom."

"I'm glad you understand, Grant," Danielle said with relief. "He's been around my dad too much. Neither of them have much use for Hayses."

"Perhaps with you home, you can change all of that," Grant said consolingly.

"I don't have much faith, right now, that either one of them will change," Danielle confessed.

"Now, what happened to the 'faith' girl?" Grant asked. "Aren't you always Miss Positive?"

A grin appeared unexpectedly. "Yes, yes, I am, Grant. Thank you for reminding me. Just pray I can remain Miss Positive around the two of the biggest negatives I know. In this case, these two negatives certainly don't make a positive!"

Grant laughed as they stepped out onto the porch, "I've a feeling no matter how much negativity surrounds you, you'll always find the positive."

Just then Danielle caught her boot on an uneven porch plank and stumbled into Grant's side. He instinctively reached out to steady her and found himself looking into her beautiful face. For a few seconds their eyes locked and Grant was astounded at the bolt of emotion that surged through his body.

20

Needing Advice

Danielle gasped in surprise and quickly gained her footing. "Sorry," she said shakily, and then, "It seems you've just knocked me off my feet." Grant let go of her reluctantly. He cleared his throat in an attempt to cover his unexpected feeling. "Well, I don't know whether to take that as a compliment or as an indication of my clumsiness," he stated louder than he intended. Then added, "Are you all right?"

"Yes, yes, I'm fine," Danielle said, brushing off her dress as if to brush the situation aside. "I just wasn't paying attention. It wasn't your fault at all."

Silence followed her statement and they both stood gazing off into the distance. Then Grant cleared his throat again, and said awkwardly, "I best be going. I know you have a lot of things you need to do, and so do I, so I'd better be going because I know you have a lot of things to do."

Danielle, not noticing his flustered repetition simply said, "Yes, I guess you better be going because you probably have a lot of things to do." Then looking intently at him, she said sincerely, "Thank you again, Grant, for coming by to check on Daniel. We really appreciate it."

Again silence, then Grant looked at her hair, trying to avoid making eye contact. "Yes, well, if you need me for anything, please let me know. Daniel should be fine if he rests for a few days."

"I'll make sure he does, Grant," Danielle said, still regarding him intently.

"Okay, then, see you soon," Grant said, mounting his horse. Then he looked straight into her gaze and said softly, "Good day, Miss Danielle Johnson. It's been really . . . nice seeing you again." With that he lifted his hat in farewell and rode away.

For several minutes, Grant simply rode in stunned silence. Then gradually, he started chuckling. *Well,* he mused, *there's nothing like starting the day off with a good shock to your system.* Instead of galloping he allowed his horse to walk with a slow gait. Thoughts bombarded his mind as he relived the last few minutes with Danielle. He wasn't quite certain what happened, but he knew he was stunned at the intense feelings he experienced when he reached out to break her fall and came face-to-face with those intense green eyes. There was something about her expressive eyes that made him want to fix things for her or at least make things better.

"Whoa, man, what are you thinking?" Grant said aloud. "You already have a girl!" Then he shook his head as if to clear those unwanted thoughts. *It seems this Panhandle is casting some kind of spell on me. I'm just not myself,* he thought. *I'm not myself at all.* He continued riding, trying to decipher his emotions. An owl hooted in the distance and he looked up as an eagle soared across the plains. *It would be so nice to be able to soar above the earth and just forget things for a while,* he thought. *But I can't. Here I am, in Progress, Texas, with things happening that I definitely had not planned on. I need to get things straight in my mind and the sooner the better.*

Instead of riding home as he intended, he found himself entering the city limits of Progress. *Oh, well!* he thought. *I'm not the least surprised at my meanderings after the way the first part of the day has gone. Well, since I'm already here, I might as well see if Dad's in his office.*

Grant rode by the church and surprisingly felt a wave of emotion grip him at the memories of that little white building. *I'm becoming worse than a girl, the way my emotions are today,* he thought, then smiled. *But there's nothing wrong with being emotional about church. At least that's what Mom would say, so I'm safe there!* He rode by Smith's Mercantile and wondered who had taken over since Ezra had passed. Danielle's great grandfather had been a wonderful man. *Well, I never!* he thought *There I go! Thinking about her again. I definitely need help!* He was still deep in thought when he rode up to his dad's office, and was happy to see the window open indicating his father's presence.

"Hey, Dad," he called. "Are you here?"

"Well, my goodness," Alexander said as he came down the hall. "To what do I owe this great honor?"

"Honor? Right!" Grant said, "I don't feel very honorable this morning."

"Uh, oh!" Alexander said, patting his son on the shoulder. "What's going on in my favorite son's life that would evoke such a statement?"

"I'm glad I'm somebody's favorite!" Grant stated.

"Oh, my! Things must be bad. Perhaps you need to come have a seat in my office and let me give you some counsel," Alexander said teasingly, leading his son into his office.

Grant looked around at the decor and noticed the changes. The white paint had been altered to a light tan color and a vibrant red painting of a landscape dominated the wall behind his father's desk. The mahogany furniture accentuated the rich warmth of the room.

"Nice, Dad," Grant said, nodding his head in approval.

"Glad you like it," Alexander said. "You know your mom is always changing things and although I fuss about the cost, I really appreciate her efforts once it's finished."

"Just walking into this room makes me feel like I'm in Boston instead of Progress, Texas," Grant responded.

"Well, that comment does make all Mom's effort worthwhile," Alexander said grandly.

Grant looked at his father sheepishly. "Sorry, Dad," he said contritely. "I guess I did sound a bit snobbish. I'm really going to have to watch myself. It seems I've let the high-handed Boston ways infiltrate my thinking without realizing it."

"Oh, it's fine, son. I'm just giving you a hard time."

"Don't you go and tell Mom what I said or I'll never hear the end of it!" Grant pleaded.

"Your secret is safe with me, son," Alexander said reassuringly. "I find it's best to keep some things from your mother, if you know what I mean."

"I know what you mean!" Grant chuckled.

"Now, what seems to be the problem, Grant?" Alexander asked, sitting down in his reddish-burgundy leather office chair.

"As you know, I went to the Johnsons' to check on Daniel," Grant explained.

"Yes, your mother was very anxious about that," Alexander said.

"Well, first off, Mr. Johnson held me at gunpoint . . . " Grant began.

"What!" his father exploded.

"Yes, Dad, Mr. Butch Johnson himself threatened me with his shotgun and told me to leave his property," Grant continued.

"Well, I never!" Alexander said.

"But Danielle came to the rescue and angrily told her dad I was there because she and Mrs. Johnson had invited me to check on Daniel." Grant paused.

"That's a relief. That's certainly something we'd better not tell your mother," his father smiled conspiratorially.

"You're right about that!" Grant agreed.

"What else happened?" Alexander asked.

"I'm not sure," Grant said thoughtfully. "Dad, did you ever feel uncertain about your feelings toward a woman?"

"Oh, yes," Alexander said. "Your mother caused me such turmoil that it drove me out of town."

"Really?" Grant asked.

"That's right! I'd always dealt with a different type of woman than your mother, something like your Boston-type women who thought quite a bit of themselves," Alexander explained. "So when she came on the scene with her genuineness, I didn't know quite what to do."

"Well, I had an encounter with Danielle and something happened I can't explain." Grant paused and then continued. "She tripped, and when I reached out to help her, something happened when we made contact."

"Such as?" Alexander asked.

"It felt almost like I'd been hit by a lightning bolt," Grant said. "Now, here I am, in love with Tina and another woman shouldn't affect me like that, right?" He looked at his father, hoping for reassurance.

"That's interesting, Grant," Alexander said slowly. "Perhaps the change of scenery and the change of people caused a ripple in your plans." He stopped, tapping his fountain pen on the desk. "I regret that you're so confused right now, and I wish I had the right answer for you. Unfortunately, all I can tell you is to pray about it and ask God to lead you in the right way." He looked across the desk at his son. "You do still pray, don't you, son?"

"Yes, sir," Grant said. "Although I've fallen far short of the prayer life I should have. However, I really was hoping for a definite answer from you, but I guess God is going to have to help me on this one."

"I'm afraid so," Alexander said. "Your mom and I are very concerned about your choice of companion, and we've been praying about it earnestly. All I can tell you, son, is that it's best to try to find a companion who has similar family values as your own and believes God should be a part of your life. God should be the utmost priority."

"Yes, sir," Grant agreed.

"Let me add here, son, that although a girl's family may not be at all like ours, we can work with that. But if you choose someone who disregards the importance of God, it will break our hearts." Alexander leaned back in his chair. "I hate to bring up something like that on your first few days here, but I want you to know how important it is to us.

"Yes, Dad, I know. I'm just trying to find my way for my future and know I need God's wisdom on this."

"That's what we want to hear, son." Alexander said, coming around the desk and giving his son a bear hug. "We believe in you, my boy, and know you're going to do the right thing."

"Thanks, Dad," Grant said, returning the hug.

"Hello?" said a shrill female voice, interrupting the father-son scene. "Is anyone here?"

21

Uninvited Guests

Grant froze at the sound of the all-familiar voice. "Oh, my goodness," he exclaimed quietly to his father.

Alexander leaned down and whispered back, "What is it, son?"

"Dad, I think Tina just walked into your office," he answered.

"Really?" Alexander said in disbelief.

"Oh, I can't believe this," Grant said in exasperation. "What in the world is *she* doing here?"

"Well, I think you better greet her properly and find out," Alexander answered resignedly.

Grant took a deep breath, and said, "You're right, Dad." He took one more deep breath. "I better get out there."

"Hello? Is anyone here?" Tina demanded again.

Grant gave his father a look of consternation and walked toward the waiting room. When he saw her, Tina was looking impatiently around the waiting room and peering down the hall.

"Tina!" he exclaimed coming into the room

"Well, what took you so long? Didn't you hear me calling?" she asked coming toward him.

"I'm sorry. Father and I were having an in-depth conversation," Grant answered.

"Well, I hope it was about me," Tina preened her ego. "How are you, darling? I had to come because I missed you so," she said giving him a quick kiss. "Surprised to see me?"

Grant looked back and met his father's raised eyebrow. "Yes," he answered, "yes, I'm quite surprised to see you. I just can't believe you'd come all this way."

"Well!" she pouted. "You don't act very happy to see me."

"I'm sorry, Tina. You took me completely by surprise," Grant explained.

"That was my whole purpose, darling! The station master told us where to find Mr. Hayes's office." Tina laughed gleefully.

"Well, well, old chap," Fred Thomas chuckled, walking into the room. "We did find our destination after all."

"My word!" The pleasure Grant felt at seeing his friend was evident. "What're you doing here?"

Tina piped up, "Well, I never! You seem happier to see Fred than you do me."

"Well, can you blame him?" Fred teased.

"I'm totally shocked!" Grant said, hugging his pal. "It's good to see you. It's good to see you both." Then turning, he motioned to his father. "Hey, Dad, come meet my friends."

Alexander walked toward the three young people.

"This is Tina Hamilton, Dad," he said, "And, Tina, this is my father, Alexander Hayes."

"Oh, hello, sir," Tina gushed. "I've so wanted to meet Grant's family. And now I see where Grant gets his good looks."

Alexander flushed, "Uh, well, thank you. Nice to meet you, Miss Hamilton."

"Oh, come now, call me Tina," she said, patting his arm. "After all, we're going to be family."

Grant quickly pulled Fred to his side. "And, Dad, this is my good friend, Fred Thomas. He befriended me from the time of our first college encounter and we've remained fast friends."

"Hello, sir," Fred said politely, extending his hand. "It's a pleasure to meet you. Grant has spoken of you so often that I feel I already know you."

Alexander smiled at the young man's easy conversation. "It's nice to meet you, Fred. Grant wrote often about you as well." Then he extended both hands as if to indicate "what you see is what you get" and said, "Welcome to Progress, Texas. Not quite up to Boston standards, but a wonderful town to live in."

"Oh, yes," exclaimed Tina. "It's a rather odd little town, but it's quite . . . quaint."

"Well, I for one love it!" Fred exclaimed. "I'm more than ready for a slower pace after Boston's rat race."

Alexander laughed. "Oh, you can definitely plan on a slow pace here. But at least the name of the town brings somewhat of a feeling of activity."

"I just couldn't wait any longer to see you, Grant," Tina said clinging to his arm. "So I bribed poor Fred to come along with me to protect me from all the varmints in the Wild West until I reached your side."

"Yeah," Fred interjected, "poor Fred." Then conspiratorially, he whispered loudly to Alexander. "I don't know why Tina refers to me as 'poor.' After all, I do have a few pounds to my name. Sadly, I think she's probably referring to my personality. But I'm trying to improve that as well so I may be counted worthy to be in her company."

Alexander chuckled in spite of his efforts to maintain his composure.

"Fred!" Tina scolded. "Why do you insist on making me look bad? Especially to Grant's father. He'll get the wrong impression of me."

"Sorry," Fred said winking at Alexander. "Tell you what. I'll let you prove yourself to Grant's parents. They'll find out how you really are in no time."

"Okay, you two," Grant interrupted. "So, do you have accommodations already?"

"Why, no, darling!" Tina responded as if offended. "We thought you'd want us to stay at your country estate. In fact, I've looked forward to it."

Grant caught his father's eye, and Alexander gave him a reassuring nod. "Okay, then," Grant said, "but I know Mother's not expecting company and it may put her at a disadvantage."

"Oh, pish-posh!" Tina said, slapping him playfully. "Just tell the servants to fix up some rooms for Fred and me."

Grant looked down to hide his embarrassment and answered. "Tina, we don't have servants, as I've already explained. We have a cook and housekeeper, but Mom runs the house."

"We won't be a bother at all, darling," Tina said cuddling up to him. "Just think what a wonderful time we'll have together being so close every day. This is so exciting!"

"Tell you what, son," Alexander said. "I'll run out to the house and get one of our wagons. I'm sure your guests have luggage and that way I can let your mom know what's going on."

Grant gave his father a grateful look. "Thanks, Dad," he said. "If you could meet us at the station, I'll head back that way with Fred and Tina to retrieve their luggage."

Alexander patted his son on the shoulder reassuringly. "Sounds like a plan. I'll be on my way then."

Alexander mounted his horse with astonished thoughts swirling in his head. He could well imagine what Kate would say when she found out they were to have unexpected guests. And what type of guests! He was astounded that a young lady of supposedly good breeding would show up unannounced and expect everyone to accommodate her specific needs.

It looks like this is going to be a more interesting summer than I thought. He gently kicked his horse and sped up. Fifteen minutes later he crossed the entrance to the estate. He thought, *Brace yourself for the reaction you know you're going to get from Kate.* "Here goes," he said aloud and opened the front door.

"Kate!" he called. "Hey, sweetheart, where are you?"

"Goodness gracious!" Kate said, coming quickly into the entrance foyer. "Why so impatient today, my dear husband? That's not like you."

"No, no, it's not," he agreed. "I have a surprise for you, but I don't think you'll like it. Please promise you'll remain calm while I deliver the news."

"What is it?" Kate asked warily.

"It seems . . . " he hesitated, "that some unexpected visitors arrived on the train today."

"Oh?" Kate said, wondering what that had to do with her.

"Yes," he said. "A young lady by the name of Tina Hamilton arrived in Progress along with a young man named Fred."

"Tina?" Kate asked. "You mean the Tina Hamilton Grant seems to think himself in love with?"

"Yes, my love, the exact Tina Hamilton," Alexander answered.

"Oh dear!" Kate whispered.

"My feelings exactly," Alexander agreed. "I think no one was more surprised than Grant, though. He had no idea she was coming."

"Hmmm," Kate mused. "And where are they staying?"

"Well, that's the crux of the matter," Alexander continued. "Tina says she plans on staying here."

"What!" Kate exclaimed.

'Yes," Alexander said. "In fact, let me see if I can remember her exact words. I believe she said, 'Just tell the servants to fix up some rooms for Fred and me.' "

"Well, I never!" Kate declared in shock. "For someone who's supposed to be from Boston's upper crust, she perhaps needs some further instruction on proper etiquette and manners."

"My thoughts exactly," Alexander said. "But, dear, let me assure you that Grant seemed quite put out with her arrival."

"Really?" Kate asked. "And why would you surmise that?"

"Well, Grant and I were having a conversation about some of the things he's been feeling when Tina showed up and yelled out a greeting. I could tell by the look on Grant's face he was more shocked and annoyed than he was happy to see her. Then when she made the statement about our servants, he quickly informed her we didn't have servants. And from the tone of his voice he didn't like her assuming things and taking charge."

"Well!" Kate said thoughtfully and then said something that surprised Alexander. "Although I'm put out about having to make arrangements for them to stay here, it might be an answer to our prayers, Mr. Hayes."

"What do you mean by that?" Alexander asked.

"I assume Grant has been around Tina only when she's at social settings, which is where she excels. Perhaps if he sees her in *his* element, he might decide she doesn't fit in," Kate explained.

"Hmmm," Alexander mused, rubbing his chin. "Perhaps you're right, my dear. Although it's imposing on your time and effort, it would give us more control of the situation if she's in our home."

"Exactly!" Kate declared. "You know, my dear husband, we've prayed for God to work this out, and this just might be His way of answering our prayer."

Alexander laughed. "Kate, you never fail to surprise me! Here I thought you were going to be all out of sorts and instead you find something good about the situation."

"Now wait a minute, Mr. Hayes," she said, shaking her finger at him. "I never said I was okay with all of this. I am 'out of sorts' at this unexpected turn. But, I'll do whatever it takes to make certain our son is okay. And if it means putting up with a rather snooty young lady, I'll do my dead level best to help with her accommodations."

Alexander reached out and took Kate in his arms. "I'm so glad you've decided to rally, sweetheart. And I want you to know that I'll do anything I can to help while they're here."

Kate hugged him back. "Thanks, honey. We're in this together!"

"That we are, sweetheart, that we are," Alexander replied. "Now I better get back to town so I can bring back our guests and their luggage. And Grant's probably anxiously awaiting my arrival at the train station."

"Okay, I'll get our servants whipped into shape and start preparing rooms for our guests," Kate said with a laugh. "Don't worry, dear, I'll get Gabrielle and Margarita to lend a hand. We'll be fine."

"I know you will," Alexander said, overwhelmed with love for Kate. Then shaking his head he added, "Living with you is never dull, darling! In spite of the various flares of temper, you eventually come around and work with whatever situation we face. I knew there was a reason I married you!"

She hit him on the arm. "You'd better remember you married me because I was the most beautiful, most adorable, most accomplished young lady you ever encountered."

"Well . . . " he hesitated purposefully. "That too!"

"Oh, get out of here!" Kate laughed in return. "I know how you feel about me."

Alexander leaned down for a quick kiss. "You'd better know how I feel and you'd better never forget it." With a wave of his hand, he opened the door and headed toward the stable to hitch up the wagon.

22

A Disgruntled Tina

After giving his friends a tour along Progress's main street, with Tina peppering the tour with disingenuous comments such as "charming" and "how quaint," her only sincere one was, "well, it's certainly not Boston." When she began to complain that her feet were hurting, Grant turned in the direction of the train station.

When they arrived, Fred said, "Our luggage is over here," and led the way across the plank platform toward a suitcase mountain. "You may notice that unlike Tina I have only two bags. She packed as if she's staying for quite some time." The young men surveyed the luggage. *It's a good thing Dad went to get the wagon*, thought Grant. *I hope all of this will fit.*

"A lady needs many more things than a man, Fred," Tina flounced her ruffled skirts. "I did the best I could, but I wanted to make a good impression on my future in-laws." Then she sidled up to Grant, taking his arm possessively. "Oh, my darling, I'm so happy to see you," she declared. "It seems like forever since you left me destitute in Boston."

Grant cleared his throat in discomfort. "Tina, we discussed this before I left. I needed to spend some time with my parents and try to prepare them for the plans we've made."

"And why should it take that much time?" Tina pouted. "I mean, I'm quite an accomplished young lady and am considered the catch of Boston society."

Grant paused, surprised at the annoyance he felt at Tina's statements. "Yes, Tina," he agreed, "you're the belle of Boston society, but this isn't Boston. Here in Progress folks enjoy a much simpler lifestyle and don't place much emphasis on pomp and circumstance. Although there are wealthy people around here, they don't flaunt their money or their status."

"I don't flaunt!" Tina declared emphatically.

"My, my!' Fred teased. "We're a bit testy today, aren't we, Tina?"

She turned her fury toward Fred. "What's your problem?" she roared. "You've done nothing the whole way here except criticize and find fault with whatever I do."

Grant, noticing the attention they were getting, said, "Tina, please calm down. We don't want to create a scene on your first day here."

Embarrassed, she contritely answered, "I'm sorry, Grant. It's just that Fred has been absolutely boorish during this entire trip. I had a right to be upset."

Grant glanced at Fred, who quietly said, "Sorry, old chum. I really didn't mean to annoy Tina. You know me. I enjoy teasing and probably went too far. Sorry, Tina."

Tina haughtily lifted her chin. "Well, it's about time you acknowledged your ungentlemanly ways."

"Tina!" Grant said in disbelief. "Fred just said he was sorry and the proper response should be to accept his apology graciously."

Tina stared in disbelief at Grant, then realizing he was serious, she turned to Fred, "Only because Grant wishes me to, I accept your apology. But after this try not to be so irritating—although I know that would require great effort on your part."

Fred smiled and shook his head. "Right, Tina. Perhaps it might be best if I stay here in town then, Grant."

"Now I won't hear of that!" Grant argued. "You were good enough to accompany Tina here and I wouldn't want you to be out any expense on my account. You're welcome to stay with us." He gently disengaged Tina's arm and started toward their luggage. "Look! Here comes Dad, and just in time." He turned to Tina and continued quietly, "By the way, Tina, I want to caution you not to say anything about us getting married. I haven't told my parents of our plans as yet."

"What!" Tina exclaimed. "Why, I thought you were going to speak to them right away. And you've been here how long?"

Trying to hide his irritation, he answered quietly, "The right opportunity never seemed to present itself. So if you'd just kindly let me handle this, I'd appreciate it."

In a huff she folded her arms, and declared. "Well, I never!"

Trying to ignore her attitude, Grant raised his arm and shouted, "Hey, Dad, over here!"

Alexander brought the wagon to a stop where Grant indicated and set the brake. "Well, here I am!" He jumped down, then noticing Tina's scowl explained, "I know this mode of transportation isn't fancy, but since I thought you all might have quite a bit of luggage, I brought our supply wagon so we'd have to make only one trip."

"This will be fine, Mr. Hayes," Fred said respectfully. "The three of you can ride up front and I'll ride in the back with the other baggage. Seems like a good place for me right now anyway," he aimed a pointed look at Tina.

Alexander looked quizzically at Fred's answer and then decided it best not to inquire. "Okay, boys, let's get this loaded and we'll head on out to the hacienda." The men talked and laughed as they loaded everything, and then Grant turned to Tina.

"Here, let me help you up on the buckboard bench," he said. Barely hiding her revulsion, she did as he bid. Once she was settled, Grant jumped up on the one side and his Dad climbed up on the other side. That left Tina sandwiched in the middle. "Ready, Fred?" Alexander called, glancing to the back of the wagon.

"Yes, I'm quite comfy," Fred said good-naturedly, sprawled among the trunks, boxes, and bags. "This will be a fine ride."

Grant laughed. "That's good old Fred," he declared, "always handling things in a gentleman-like manner."

Alexander, getting into the spirit, with maybe a pinch of mischief to irritate Tina, shouted, "Forward ho to the Hayes estate!" He flicked the reins and the loaded wagon groaned and began to roll toward home.

"So how was the trip from Boston?" Alexander asked Tina.

"Bumpy, dusty, uncomfortable, and tiresome, but what should one expect from such a desolate land?"

Silence followed her comment, and then Fred said, "I rather enjoyed the trip. It was quite interesting to see how the landscape changed along the way. And in the American West everything is expansive and much dryer than in England where I'm from. I'll enjoy telling everyone back home that I actually got to come to Texas. They won't believe it!"

"So I take it Brits actually have heard of Texas?" Alexander asked.

"Definitely. They're quite enamored of stories of the Wild West," he explained.

Alexander laughed. "Well, you might be disappointed once you see we're a bit past those wild and wooly days. But Texas still has an old-west aura about it. That's why I like it here."

"I can see that," Fred acknowledged.

"What in the world do you find to do around here?" Tina interrupted. In her eyes the land looked ugly and barren.

"We have a rather quiet life," Alexander explained. "But we attend church and once in a while either the town or the church hosts a social."

"There are no theaters?" Tina asked disbelievingly. "No museums or opera houses? No specialty shops?

Alexander chuckled. "No, we don't have any of that. But we have plays and things sometimes at the church, for special holidays and such. And we order many things we need from Sears and Roebuck."

"I see," Tina said, indicating her disappointment. "And this is how you were raised?" she asked Grant.

"Yes," Grant responded.

"No wonder you couldn't wait to leave here. I totally understand now."

Grant tensed at her statement. "I never said I couldn't wait to leave here, Tina. I just said I enjoyed what Boston had to offer."

"Same thing," she said. "And I certainly don't like this constant breeze," she said, making sure her hatpin was still firmly in place. "It makes it impossible to keep one's hair tidy."

"I rather like the breeze rustling through my hair," Fred contradicted. "Especially when it doesn't seem to matter to anyone how your hair looks."

Grant and Alexander both laughed. "You're right there!" Alexander answered. "When my wife first came here, she had a few things to say about the wind as well. But now that she's used to it, she loves it."

"I don't think I would ever get used to it," Tina insisted.

"Hey, look," Fred said, changing the subject. "Is that your home place just ahead?"

"Yes," Alexander said. "We're almost there."

"Well, it's about time!" Tina declared. "This has been a most uncomfortable ride. My teeth rattled so that I think they're loose."

Again silence followed her statement. Alexander looked over her head at Grant and frowned slightly. Grant looked down and said, "Sorry about that, Tina. But remember we were surprised at your arrival so we weren't quite as prepared as we would have been if we'd known you were coming."

Realizing she had perhaps complained too much, she gushed, "Oh, I'm sorry. I don't mean to be difficult. I'm just tired and weary from the journey." Then she tucked her hand in the crook of Grant's arm. "I promise my disposition will be much better after I've had a chance to get cleaned up."

Grant smiled slightly. "That's fine, Tina. Perhaps you'd also benefit from a rest." When the wagon rolled to a stop, Grant jumped down and turned to assist Tina. She fell into his arms and he quickly righted her. Then turning to Fred he stated, "Welcome to our home."

Just then the front door opened and Kate and Gabrielle walked out onto the front veranda. "Hello," Kate said graciously, quickly noting Tina's unpleasant expression.

"Welcome to our home." Gabrielle said nothing as she simply stood and surveyed the scene.

Kate walked down the stairs and extended her hand to Tina, "I'm Kate Hayes, Grant's mother," she said. Being carefully not to stare, Kate found to her dismay that the young lady was indeed strikingly beautiful. Her red hair was a bright frame for perfect features and complexion. *I can see why this young woman caught Grant's attention*, she thought. *However, the sullen expression certainly detracts from her beauty.*

Tina, trying to rally herself, took Kate's hand and gave a slight curtsy. "Hello, Mrs. Hayes," she gushed. "I've looked forward to meeting you. Grant does nothing but talk about the attributes of his mother." Then she added saucily, "So much so that I sometimes feel I'll never match his expectations of me because of you."

23

The Relief of Fred's Banter

A familiar silence followed her comment, and Fred quickly came to the rescue. "Hello, ma'am," he said, taking her hand and bringing it to his lips. "I'm Fred Thomas. I'm the chap who rescued Grant when he first arrived at Boston U. And may I say, I can see where Grant gets his good looks." Then he jokingly added, "I would say 'beauty,' but it might offend my old chum."

Kate laughed, grateful for the insight of the young man. "Well, thank you kindly, young sir. I adore your manners," she said. "It's not often one receives a proper greeting around here. And I love your sophisticated British accent. It's quite a contrast to our West Texas drawl."

Fred chuckled. "Thank you, my dear madam," he responded, "but I was thinking how charming *your* accent is." Then turning to Gabrielle, he said, "And who is this beauty?"

Gabrielle grinned and walked towards him. "My name is Gabrielle and I'm Grant's baby sister," she explained.

"Well, you certainly don't look like a baby to me, miss," Fred said, taking her hand just as daintily as he had taken her mother's hand and, bringing it to his lips, he kissed it. "If you were a few years older, I would consider never going back to Boston." Gabrielle blushed with pleasure and giggled.

Grant breathed a sigh of relief as the tension eased. He was so thankful for Fred's troubleshooting. He had not realized until this moment what a good friend Fred was to him and decided to make certain he thanked him later. He caught Fred's eye above Gabrielle's head and shot him a grateful look.

"Come on in, everyone," Kate said, ushering them into the foyer. "Margarita is preparing a light meal for us, and while she's doing so, I'll show you all to your rooms."

"Can I show Fred to his room?" Gabrielle asked, slipping her hand into the hand of her new friend.

Grant ruffled his sister's hair, and observed, "And I thought you had difficulty making conquests, Fred."

"As you can see, it's usually the younger set that seems taken with me," he commented.

"You boys want to help me with the luggage?" Alexander asked. "As we seem a bit short on servants, it's up to us!"

Fred turned to Gabrielle and said, "Don't go away. Let me get my share of the bags and I'll follow you to my domain."

Tina sighed impatiently, and Kate quickly said, "Why don't you come along with me and I'll show you to your room?"

Tina inclined her head and followed Kate up the stairs.

"I put you in Clarissa's old room. Do you know Clarissa?" Kate asked.

"Oh, yes," Tina answered. "You're referring to Mrs. Clarissa Grant? She's quite a lady."

"Yes, Clarissa's very special," Kate said, opening the door to the room. "She loved this room because it had a great view of the garden. She used to open the windows during the spring and, as she called it, 'drink in the beauty.'" Kate paused, realizing that Tina was not listening. Instead she was wandering around the room, running her finger along the furniture as if checking for dust. She inspected the chest of drawers and sat briefly on the mattress. It was almost as if she was inspecting the state of Kate's housekeeping. Kate watched for a few moments, and then asked. "Is everything to your satisfaction?"

Tina, quickly turning to face her, said, "Oh, of course. This should be fine. Thank you, Mrs. Hayes. If I need anything, I'll certainly let you know."

Kate caught her breath and quietly said, "I'm sure you will." Then with her hand on the doorknob, she said, "I'll give you a chance to freshen up. The washroom is right down the hall and when you get ready, come on down and we'll have a bite of lunch."

"Thank you," Tina responded without turning to face the hostess. Kate softly shut the door, paused, and then slowly started down the stairs. She met Grant and Fred as they came up carrying the luggage.

"Goodness!" Kate exclaimed. "I didn't realize you were moving in."

"Believe me, ma'am," Fred stated breathlessly. "All of this isn't mine. This belongs to well, you know who. I was informed that it takes much more paraphernalia for ladies to be properly dressed and accessorized than men require."

Kate laughed. "That it does, Fred. And sad to say, the gentlemen are responsible for carrying our baggage around for us. Remember that before you marry!"

"I think that's why I haven't found anyone," Fred retorted. "Just the thought of being burdened down from now on has put a damper on my ardor."

Kate involuntarily laughed again. "I tell you one thing, my dear Fred. I think I'm going to enjoy your visit very much if you continue to keep us in stitches."

The men continued up the stairs with the luggage while Kate, smiling at their antics and giving them a wide berth, descended the staircase. Turning she called after them, "Don't wait too long to come back down. Margarita has a good lunch prepared for us."

"And after this momentous feat, I'll require some substantial nourishment to regain my strength," Fred called as he knocked on the door of Tina's room.

Kate's spontaneous laughter echoed back up the stairs as she went to assist Margarita.

The family, along with their visitors, finally settled at the table. Grant and Fred continued with their banter and Gabrielle looked on with awe. Tina still appeared disgruntled but was endeavoring to hide her irritation. Kate entered the room and sat down.

"Well, then," she said. "We're just about ready. Alexander, would you return thanks?"

"Certainly," he said, taking her hand. Kate took Gabrielle's hand and Gabrielle took Fred's. Tina looked uncomfortable as Grant took her hand and bowed his head. "Heavenly Father," Alexander began, "thank you for this wonderful food of which we are about to partake. Bless it to the nourishment of our bodies and help us to do Your will. And, Father, thank you for the guests who've come to us today. I ask that you would bless Fred and Tina as they visit with us and that we enjoy a great time together. In your name we pray. Amen."

"There now!" Kate responded. "Margarita, we're ready."

Margarita made a grand entrance. "Ola!" she greeted them. "All is ready."

Grant looked at the table fare and covered a smile. His mother and Margarita had gone all out. The china was his mother's best, and crystal glasses and the best silverware sparkled on the white lace tablecloth. The table was set in a grand style. He hoped Tina appreciated the effort.

He sensed Tina had been uncomfortable during the prayer and that bothered him. Ironically, her blasé treatment of all things spiritual had never yet bothered him, but now he was baffled by it. He glanced at her pouty expression that he once thought was so endearing but now seemed so unattractive. She caught his perusal and, taking it for admiration, possessively took his hand. "It's so very nice to be in your home, Grant," she smiled coyly at him. "It makes me feel so much more a part of your life."

Margarita rolled her eyes as she leaned across Grant to place a delectable dish of fruit on the table. Kate quickly covered a smile. Alexander, always the gentleman and ignoring the undercurrents, said graciously, "We want you to feel welcome in our home, Tina. We want you and Fred to have a great time here."

"Oh, I intend to," Fred interjected. "Perhaps Gabrielle can show me the lay of the land."

"How would I do that?" Gabrielle asked.

Grant laughed along with the others and explained, "You'll have to get used to the way Fred talks, Little Bit. You know he's from a foreign country."

"Really?" Gabrielle asked in fascination.

"Now wait a minute, man," Fred objected. "You Americans originated in my country, so how can I be considered foreign when we all came from the same place?"

Alexander laughed. "You have a point there, Fred. What d'you say, Grant?"

Grant paused and said dramatically. "May I say, dear Fred, that we won the war that separated our country from yours. Further, you were the one who broached the idea of you being from a foreign country when we first made our acquaintance."

Fred smiled. "Touché!" he acknowledged, raising his glass in a mock salute. "You'd think with your argumentation that you were the lawyer instead of me."

Kate interjected. "I've often said that as well, Fred. But you must remember he has his dad's lawyer genes somewhere inside that head of his. I've encountered that on many occasions."

"Now remember, Mr. Hayes," Fred said, leaning forward conspiratorially. "We must stick together in the midst of the greatest medical mind anywhere. On several occasions, Grant here has put me in my place, and I feel it only respectable to defend my honor. Would you perhaps vow to stand as my second should the occasion ever arise? After all, fellow attorneys should stick together."

Alexander raised his glass toward Fred. "That I will, Fred. After all, I also feel woefully outnumbered when my beautiful wife and stalwart son join forces against me. If you'll reciprocate, we can stand strong against these forces of adversity."

"You have my word, my good man," Fred acknowledged. "I'll be by your side, holding the ammo."

Gabrielle clapped her hands gleefully. "I really don't understand what's going on, but this is fun!"

Laughter resonated around the table, but Tina suddenly interrupted their mirth: "So," she said, "what are we planning on doing while we're here?"

Grant paused and looked questioningly at her. "What do you mean, Tina?" he asked.

"I mean what social events will we attend?" she continued.

"Unfortunately, Tina," Kate began, "there aren't many social events in Progress. We do have some special dramas and things at the church, but there are no special events at this time."

"Oh," Tina responded in disappointment. "So what do you do here?"

"Well," Alexander said. "Tomorrow we have church services. We always look forward to that."

"*Church?*" sarcasm dripped from her voice. "Well, I must admit that in Boston church attendance is a way to advance oneself socially. But I can't see what social benefit it would be to attend a dull country church. Surely there's something more stimulating to do here besides that." Then turning to Grant, she added, "Grant, darling. I'd really rather not go to church. It's certainly not in my list of favorite things to do."

24

An Unplanned Announcement

Alexander, noticing Kate's heightened color, reached out to take her hand to calm her response. She glanced at him and he slightly shook his head.

Grant, sensing his parents' disapproval, began, "Tina, we . . . "

Gabrielle interrupted, asking innocently, "Tina, why don't you want to go to church? Don't you want to go to Heaven?"

Tina looked at her in disbelief. "Heaven? Of course, I want to go to Heaven, but that doesn't mean I have to go to church every Sunday. I've gotten along quite well without attending church regularly, and Grant knows I'm a good girl."

Gabrielle insisted. "But you have to go to church to go to Heaven, Tina. That's what the Bible says."

"Oh, the Bible!' Tina declared. "I don't have time to read such a dull old book. I have too many other things to do."

Noticing Gabrielle's confused expression, Grant interrupted, "Yes, Little Bit, we do have to go to church to go to Heaven." Then looking pointedly at Tina he added, "And that is specifically why we're all going to church in the morning." Then looking at Fred, he stated. "And, I might add, my dear fellow, we have some rather attractive young ladies you might be interested in becoming acquainted with."

Grant glanced across the table at his mother and sent her an apologetic look. He saw her breathe a sigh of relief as the tension seemed to ease. She gave him a slight smile.

"Well, Grant, I certainly hope you haven't been surveying any young ladies in my absence," Tina interjected.

Fred quickly said. "I'll look forward to making their acquaintance, old chap. I always thought the women of the Wild West would appeal to my tastes more than society ladies. I'm rather looking forward to going to church."

Gabrielle smiled at Fred, and said, "I always like going to church. Do you think I might sit by you, Fred?"

Fred leaned down and smiled at her. "Of course, you can sit by me, Gabrielle." Then looking at Grant he asked, "How could I possibly look at the other young ladies when I have such a beauty sitting right next to me?"

Gabrielle giggled and the conversation flowed normally once again. Grant caught Fred's eye as if to say thanks, as Fred continued teasing with Gabrielle during the remainder of the meal.

Kate endeavored to finish the meal in a hospitable manner, but heaviness descended upon her. She was very apprehensive about Tina and her designs on her beloved son. In Grant's long sojourn in Boston, he seemed to have changed his values and priorities. She decided it was time to petition God further.

"Are you ready, my English friend?" Grant asked, peering around Fred's bedroom door.

"Just about, Dr. Grant," Fred answered. "I'm taking a bit more pains with my appearance this morning, you know. Since I keep company with such a handsome fellow, I tend to fade into the background when he's around."

"Right!" Grant said sarcastically. "And who might this fellow be?"

"Well, he's one outstanding and stupendous character; one who has stooped to befriend this lowly Englishman," Fred stated dramatically.

Grant chuckled. "You never change, do you Fred? Man, one of the best things I did at university was finding you as my friend."

"And I've been of great benefit to you ever since, haven't I?" Fred mused, tying his tie.

"Yes, as a matter of fact, you have, Fred," Grant answered. "In all seriousness, I don't know what I would've done if you hadn't come along on this trip with Tina." Then shaking his head, he continued, "I don't know what's happened to Tina, Fred. I didn't notice her being so disagreeable back in Boston."

Fred glanced at Grant's image in the mirror and answered with a raised eyebrow. "As they say, 'Love is blind.'"

Grant looked startled at Fred's statement. "What d'you mean?"

Fred grimaced. "I don't wish to cast aspersions on your lady love, my friend," he said slowly, "but you must've seen she's disagreeable most of the time." At Grant's jerk, he continued, "Now, don't get me wrong, she's a beauty. And she's agreeable as long as she gets her way and everything runs according to her plan."

"I think you're being unfair, Fred," Grant said. "And I'm surprised that you think such of her."

"Well, I hope I'm wrong, Grant, old chum, because I want nothing but your happiness. But I hope you'll really consider things before you make a final decision on your feelings for Tina. Suffice it to say, she'd make a lovely wife for a doctor. You know, she does very well working the social scene. But what will she be like to live with for the rest of your life?" He finished his tie and turned to Grant. "Believe me, old chap. I hope she'll change, perhaps while she's here in Progress. And please don't be upset with me as I only have your best interests at heart. But will you promise to really think about this?"

Grant, still reeling from Fred's perspective, slowly smiled. "I'm not upset at you. Friends are supposed to tell each other what they think. And, I can assure you I'll think long and hard about what you said, but I believe in my heart that Tina will come around while she's here. I think she's just weary from the trip." Then he slapped the door frame, "Are you ready now? We've got to go. After all, you can't keep the ladies waiting!"

Fred laughed. "I'm coming. My appearance is about as good as it's going to get. Let's go!"

They ran down the stairs joking back and forth. His mother, father, and Gabrielle were waiting for them in the foyer.

"Is everyone ready?" Kate asked. "We need to hurry or we'll be late."

"Fred and I are here and accounted for," Grant answered, then looked around and asked, "Tina hasn't come down yet?"

Just as he asked the question, they heard Tina's heels clicking on the stairs. Automatically, they looked up and watched as she continued slowly down, apparently in no hurry whatsoever. Tina was dressed in an expensive lime green suit, complete with all the accessories—hat, gloves, purse, and parasol. The effect was quite stunning.

"So sorry to keep you all waiting," she said graciously. Then taking possession of Grant's arm she smiled demurely. "I trust your wait was worth it."

Kate was the first to speak. "You look very nice, Tina. Now, if we don't hurry, we'll be late."

Tina looked impatiently at Kate. "But that's the point, Mrs. Hayes. It's quite the rage to be fashionably late and make a grand entrance."

Kate endeavoring to hold her temper said, "That's probably the rage in Boston, but it's not here in Progress."

Alexander quickly interrupted, "Shall we go?" He directed everyone out the front door to the waiting buggies. He had hooked up the four-passenger as well as the two. Before anyone could say anything, Gabrielle asked, "Could Fred and I please ride in the buggy for two?"

"Well, that's up to Fred, Gabrielle. He may not want to haul you around," Kate answered.

"I'd be more than honored to escort Miss Gabrielle Hayes to Sunday service," he said politely. Gabrielle giggled in response.

The remaining four walked to the other buggy. Kate noticed the look of displeasure on Tina's countenance at the proposed arrangements. Grant, however, was oblivious to her displeasure. When he turned to assist her into the buggy, she gave him a brilliant smile as if nothing was wrong.

"Everyone ready?" Alexander asked loudly. Then with a flick of the reins shouted, "Let's go!"

"What a beautiful morning!" Kate breathed. "I love the mornings in springtime."

"You love everything about the warm weather, dear heart," Alexander said, leaning toward Kate. "As for me, the colder weather gives me much more energy than the warm."

Kate glanced quizzically at Alexander. "Now, correct me if I'm wrong, but I don't think I've ever seen you low on energy in either warm or cold weather."

Alexander shrugged, "What can I say? I like to keep busy."

"Yes," Kate agreed, "and never dally."

Grant laughed. "You two never change. Always sparring with each other, trying to best the other."

"My mother is quite different," Tina spoke up. "She always has a quiet dignity. And when she's around my father and their peers, she carries herself with grace and elegance and doesn't speak unless addressed directly." Silence filled the carriage and then she added, "I think that's the way I'll be when we marry, Grant darling."

25

ATTENDING CHURCH

Grant caught his breath, and Kate grabbed Alexander's arm in a death grip.

Tina, knowing she had said too much, asked innocently, "Oh, I'm sorry. Did I say something wrong?"

Grant glared at her and then glanced quickly at his mother. Her crestfallen countenance spoke volumes.

Tina, noticing Grant's expression, said pointedly, "I said I was sorry."

Grant looked grimly at her and said quietly, "I asked you not to say anything until I had a chance to speak with my folks."

Tina dramatically covered her mouth, "Oh, my word! I totally forgot, my love," she said, patting Grant's arm. "But surely they want your happiness and that includes me, so there shouldn't be a problem, right?"

"We'll talk later," he whispered firmly. Then leaning up to his parents, he said, "Look, I'm sorry. I intended to speak with you about this earlier, but the time just never seemed right."

They both continued to sit in silence. Grant continued, "Look, I know this is not a good time to talk about this, so why don't we talk later?"

Kate, regaining some of her composure, answered, "You're right, Grant. This is not the time to discuss such a matter, especially since we'll be arriving shortly at the church, and I certainly don't want anyone sensing there's something wrong in our family." Adjusting her hat and continuing to hold her husband's arm, she stated softly. "I'll try to assume a manner of quiet dignity this morning, which seems to be the proper thing."

Grant's heart constricted when he heard her statement. "Mom," he said, placing his hand on her shoulder, "I want you to know that I totally adore your demeanor and wouldn't change it for anything in the world. You know that, don't you?"

Kate turned and met his gaze. "I hope I haven't been an embarrassment to you, son."

Grant looked imploringly at her. "I can assure you, mother, that you've never been an embarrassment to me. I've been nothing but proud of you my entire life. And that will never change." He then grasped his father's shoulder as well. "I'm proud of my heritage. I count myself very fortunate to have you both as my parents."

Alexander cleared his throat and said, "Thank you, son."

Grant leaned back and slowly disengaged Tina's hold on his arm. When she shot him a questioning look, she was met with a stern side view of his profile. The remainder of the trip was made in tense silence.

As they pulled up into the churchyard, several other families were arriving as well. They quickly exited the buggy and found Gabrielle and Fred nearby.

"We had such fun!" Gabrielle exclaimed excitedly. "Grant, I'm so glad you invited Fred here."

Grant smiled slightly and was thankful that his little sister brought some sort of relief to the atmosphere.

"I say, my dear chap," Fred said, laughingly. "Your little sister is quite the conversationalist. I found out a lot on our journey this morning."

"I'm sure you did," Grant answered soberly.

Fred, looking intently at Grant and asked, "Is everything all right, old man?"

Grant slightly shook his head. "Not really, but I'll explain later," he said for Fred's ears only.

"Okay then," Fred said, trying to cover for the uncomfortable atmosphere. "Shall we go in so I can see this bevy of beauties?"

"Hey," Gabrielle exclaimed, slapping him playfully. "What about me?"

"Oh, my goodness gracious!" Fred declared. "Believe me, small one, I haven't forgotten about you. I could never do that! How about you lead the way so you can show me about the place?"

"Okay," Gabrielle agreed.

Alexander and Kate were already heading in, so Grant turned to Tina and said, "Are you ready?"

"Of course," she said, still eyeing him uncertainly. She noticed that he didn't offer her his arm as was his usual practice, so she reached over and took possession of it. Although he allowed her to take his arm, he remained tense and stiff. As they entered the church and walked to their usual pew, he unexpectedly caught Danielle's eye on their way down the aisle. He was puzzled by the sadness he detected in that quick glance. He would have thought at least her smile would have given him some encouragement, but there was no evidence of it. Grant sighed. This morning had turned into quite a disappointment on several accounts, to say the least.

The service started with an exuberant worship chorus. The congregation joined in as they sang praises to God. After the worship concluded, Pastor Russell stepped up to the podium.

"What a great morning it is to serve the Lord!" he exclaimed. "Welcome to everyone. We're thrilled beyond measure to have you here today. It seems we have a few visitors among us, so why don't we make them feel welcome. Let's take a moment and welcome them properly."

The congregation began to meander about, greeting the guests as Pastor Russell instructed.

Grant turned and found Sharon Russell standing by them. "Hello," she said graciously.

"Sharon!" Grant said, "Allow me to introduce you to some Boston friends of mine. Fred, this is our pastor's daughter, Sharon Russell. And this is Fred Thomas and Tina Hamilton."

"How do you do?" Sharon said politely.

Grant noticed Fred's interest right away. "Fine, thank you," Fred said, bending over her hand. "I trust you're doing well."

Sharon, not used to such a greeting, blushed slightly. "Yes," she said, "yes, I'm well, thank you. It's very nice to meet you both."

Tina's only greeting was to look her up and down and nod slightly. Grant endeavored to hide his disappointment over her action and turned to greet someone else.

"Grant," someone said. He turned and met the gaze of Danielle Johnson. The usual smile that accompanied her greeting was still not in evidence. "Danielle," he acknowledged. "I trust you're well today." She nodded slightly. He continued, "Allow me to introduce some Boston friends of mine." He performed the introductions.

Danielle reached out for a handshake and again, dear old Fred instead kissed her hand. Her dimpled smile bloomed. "Now this is a beauty," Fred declared. "It is indeed a pleasure to meet you, Miss Johnson.'

"Likewise," Danielle answered, her mischievous smile sparkling at his unexpected greeting. "Nice to meet you as well, Miss Hamilton."

Again Tina's only response was a rather haughty nod. Grant looked at her unbelievingly before turning back to Danielle. "So how's Daniel today?" he asked.

"Oh, you know Daniel," she said tolerantly. "He's still disagreeable. But, he's much improved physically, thanks to you, Dr. Hayes."

"Well, that's good news," Grant said. "Let me know if you need me to check on him again."

"I will, thank you," Danielle answered, and then with a slight wave, she returned to her seat.

"You're right, old chap," Fred whispered. "There are indeed some beauties to be found in Progress."

Grant laughed quietly, thankful for his friend's humor.

The congregation slowly settled back down and Pastor Russell began his message. He preached an inspiring message on seeking God, using the verse of Scripture found in Isaiah 55:6: "Seek ye the LORD while he may be found, call ye upon Him while he is near." As he listened to the sermon, Grant sat mesmerized. He had forgotten what a great orator Reverend Russell was. It seemed he spoke directly to Grant's heart and made him realize how far he had strayed from the presence of the Lord. During his exhortation, Grant sadly recognized that he had made education and professional growth his priority and had let these things crowd out his commitment to the Creator. When Pastor Russell made the appeal to pray, Grant was the first one to make an altar. While seeking the Lord, Grant suddenly became aware of someone praying earnestly next to him. Raising his eyes to see who so entreated the Lord, he was met with quite a surprise.

26

SUNDAY, A DAY OF REST

Grant could not believe his eyes. His good friend, Fred Thomas, was kneeling by him sobbing quietly. The friend who usually disregarded God was now in the process of seeking Him. Grant was thrilled beyond belief. Never in his imagination would he have believed Fred would be touched so profoundly by the power of the Savior's love. He reached out and grasped his shoulder and for several minutes the two friends prayed together.

Finally finding peace, the two looked up simultaneously and slow grins filled their features. "I say, my man," Fred exclaimed, clasping Grant's hand. "I've never felt quite like this!"

Grant laughed and leaned in for a quick hug. "Wow!" was all he could say.

"Why didn't you tell me more about this religion of yours?" Fred asked. "I had no idea it would make me feel such . . . tranquility. You were holding out on me, man."

"No," Grant responded. "I wasn't what I should have been. And thus, I couldn't minister to anyone else in my lukewarm state."

"Well, whatever the case," Fred continued. "I'm so glad I came to Progress!"

"So am I!" Grant said, helping Fred to his feet. "Wow, I feel good, too!"

As they turned to start back to the pew, Grant was enveloped in his mother's arms. "Now I can really say welcome home, son," she said tearfully. Alexander took Fred's hand, and said, "And you, son, welcome to the kingdom."

"Thank you, sir," Fred said returning the handshake. "I'm speechless right now."

Alexander laughed. "I totally understand. Meeting the Savior is an exhilarating yet humbling experience."

As they walked down the aisle Grant stopped at their original pew and extended his hand toward Tina. She stared straight ahead for several moments and then stood up slowly before turning to face him. The look of haughty irritation she gave him smote Grant. Then she brushed past him into the aisle without taking his proffered hand. He knew beyond a shadow of doubt she was put out with everything. Before he could think through the ramifications of this development, Danielle intercepted their family as they made their way out of the sanctuary door.

"Grant," she said, extending her hand. "It was good to see you here today."

"Thank you, Danielle," he responded. Then feeling Fred's nudge, he turned to his friend. "I think you met Danielle Johnson, during service, didn't you?"

"Yes, we did make an acquaintance," Danielle said, inclining her head graciously. "It's a pleasure to greet you again, Mr. Thomas."

"And it's my delight to see you as well, Miss Johnson. However, I would prefer we forget the formality. Just call me Fred," he said.

"Okay, then, Fred," Danielle answered with a giggle.

"And, may I remind you, I'm Tina Hamilton," interrupted Tina, "Grant's soon-to-be fiancée."

A short, startled silence followed her statement, and Danielle quickly recovered. "Yes, Miss Hamilton, it was nice to meet you as well." Grant shot her a grateful look and in the process noticed the anxiety in her glance.

Tina inclined her elegantly coifed head. "Yes, and you too, Miss Whoever You Are," she responded. "Now can we just forgo all these dreary introductions and get out of here, Grant. I've had about all the church I can stand for now." With that, she swooped down the stairs in a huff.

Grant cleared his throat uncomfortably and said, "Sorry about that, Danielle."

Danielle swallowed and answered softly. "Don't worry about it, Grant. See you all later." Grant watched as she made her way across the churchyard.

"Well, our dear Tina is still up to her old tricks," Fred said, standing at his shoulder. "Never thinking of anyone but herself and not bothering to disguise her rudeness."

"Hey, Grant," Sharon Russell said, coming up to them. "I just wanted to let you all know we're getting together for a small social tonight. It's nothing big, just a few of us friends. I hope you all can come."

"Well, Fred?" Grant said, looking at his friend.

"Sounds good to me," Fred said. "I'd be honored to attend."

Sharon blushed becomingly. "Great!" she stated, "we'll see you then."

"You can count on it," Fred responded, climbing into the buggy with his faithful little companion, Gabrielle. "Are you ready, my beauty?"

Gabrielle squealed with delight. "Yes, I'm ready. Let's go fast."

Fred laughed at her response. "So you want to hurry and get ahead of the rest of our party, eh?" He continued to tease her as they pulled out of the churchyard.

The return trip home started out in silence in the other Hayes buggy. Alexander and Kate seemed lost in thought, and since Grant was still pondering the service, Fred's breakthrough, and Tina's reaction to his friends, he too sat in silence. The persistent wind was the only sound for the moment. Grant looked out upon the flat plains and felt the comfort and serenity of being home. Boston's bustle and excitement had almost made him forget what home really felt like, but it was with a great sense of satisfaction that he once again remembered.

Grant thought back to the times he and his father experienced the exhilaration of galloping their horses over the plains. He reminisced about the walks he took with his mother through the garden she so painstakingly developed. He smiled as he remembered smelling all the beautiful flowers and the reward of picking some and placing them in a vase for her. The tears that came to her eyes when he presented them to her still made his heart catch.

He knew his parents loved him beyond measure and knew it was most likely because they had longed for a child for several years before he arrived. And then the manner in which he arrived caused much concern as well. They therefore went out of their way to make certain he was safe, happy, and secure. Grant knew he was fortunate indeed to be raised by such wonderful parents. But in pursuing his medical education, he let the importance of his roots get away from him. He was thankful the Lord did not forget him, although he had almost forgotten about God. A peaceful smile crossed his countenance when he remembered the cleansing he had experienced just minutes ago.

"So what are we smiling about?" Tina asked, cuddling up to his side. "I hope thoughts of me have brought about your happiness."

Grant looked blankly at her. Lost in thought he had almost forgotten about Tina being there. He did not answer and directed his gaze back to the passing landscape.

"Well?" she insisted.

"Sorry," he answered. "I was thinking about something else."

The coy smile quickly disappeared. "What's wrong with you?" she whispered agitatedly. "You're acting so odd. Perhaps I shouldn't have bothered to leave Boston and come all this way."

Trying to cover his confused feelings, Grant responded, "As I said, I'm sorry. I just have a lot on my mind."

Kate sensing the tension looked back and said, "We're almost home. I know Margarita will have a wonderful meal prepared and I for one can hardly wait. My stomach protested quite profusely in church this morning."

Alexander looked teasingly down at her. "Yes, I know," he said. "I thought the great beast had come to church."

"Oh you!" Kate said, playfully hitting him. "No pity at all. Oh, what is a girl to do?"

Grant smiled at their playful exchange and glanced at Tina. She looked bored and impatient, tapping her fingers on the side of the wagon. She acted as if their immature banter was far beyond her level of tolerance. Grant frowned and then caught his mother's eye. He smiled reassuringly.

"Yes, I agree with Mom," Grant responded. "Although my stomach didn't growl like the great beast, it still feels like my stomach is touching my backbone."

"Then we must obtain some nourishment quickly!" Kate said, jumping down once the buggy came to a halt.

Alexander shook his head and smiled. "You're always in such a hurry. You don't even give me time to be a gentleman," he said, scolding her gently.

Looking contrite, Kate said, "I'm sorry. You're right! I'm always in a hurry and I really should slow down and 'smell the roses' as they say. After all, Sunday should be a day of rest."

"Yes, it should be, Mrs. Hayes," Alexander agreed. "But I wonder sometimes if you know the meaning of the word 'rest.'"

"One mustn't dally," she responded quickly. "Now, enough of this. I need to get inside and see if Margarita needs any help."

"See what I mean?" Alexander said, shrugging his shoulders and smiling at Grant and Tina.

Grant, turning to help Tina, caught her look of disbelief. "Is it necessary that she always serves your servant?" she asked.

Trying to cover up her comment, he answered, "Oh, my mother thinks everyone needs help. It's a thing of hers."

Gabrielle came running up and shouted, "Come on, everyone. I'm starving." Grant sighed in relief, thankful for his little sister's innocence as she cheerfully led everyone into the dining room.

27

Going Out for the Evening

"Are you two about ready?" Grant heard Fred shout from downstairs. "Come on, it shouldn't take you two nearly as long to get ready as it takes me."

Grant smiled and took one final glance in the mirror. He had chosen a red cotton shirt and blue denim pants. He put his belt through the last loop and then left his room. Coming down the stairs, he said, "You're a bit antsy, aren't you?"

"Yes, I guess I am," Fred agreed. "But I feel the bevy of beauties calling me and I mustn't keep them waiting."

"Oh, I see," Grant responded.

"I see we're waiting for the beautiful Tina, as usual," Fred commented.

Grant responded with a grimace. "Sorry, pal. I'm certain she's about ready."

Fred paced back and forth impatiently.

"What are you doing?" Grant asked.

"I'm trying to walk off that delectable dinner we had earlier today," Fred quickly answered.

"Right!" Grant said chuckling. "So you aren't just being impatient?"

"Whatever gave you that idea?" Fred said innocently. He stopped pacing for a moment and looked intently at Grant. "Are you okay, old chum?"

Grant returned his look, and said, "Why do you ask that?"

"There seemed to be a bit of tension at the table earlier today, as if something wasn't quite right," he answered. "And you mentioned at church that you'd tell me later."

"Oh, I'm just surprised at some of Tina's actions," Grant said, "and I don't quite know how to deal with it." He paused. "On the way to church today, she blurted out to my parents that we were planning to marry, and of course, they were totally taken by surprise. I just couldn't believe it! I'd told Tina to give me some time but she just burst out the news."

"I'm sorry, my friend, that she's being difficult," Fred consoled. "Perhaps it's because she's uncomfortable when she's out of her element."

"Well, whatever the reason, I wasn't at all happy that she took so much upon herself," he answered.

"But," Fred said, raising his hand, "one good thing that happened today was that I've felt wonderful since we attended your church service. Man, I've never felt anything quite like that in my whole life. And here I thought God was just a distant Being who could care less about us earthlings."

Grant laughed. "No, that's not the case at all, and I think you found that out today."

"I certainly did," Fred agreed. "And I'm looking forward to finding out more about this God of yours." He paused. "I mean, this God of *ours*."

"The more you find out the more you'll want to find out," Grant said slapping him on the shoulder. "I'm very glad I found you as my friend when I did."

"Likewise," Fred answered.

They were so focused on their conversation that Tina was halfway down the stairs before they noticed. She cleared her throat.

"What are you two talking about so intently that you didn't even notice me?" she asked, exaggerating the sway of her hips in her favorite slim skirt with the deep ruffle at the hem.

Fred looked up the stairs, bowed mockingly and said, "Forgive us our rudeness, my lady. One should never fail to notice one so grand!"

"Goodness, Fred," Tina sounded annoyed. "When will you ever grow up?"

"I could ask you the same thing, Miss Tina," Fred retorted.

"Okay, you two," Grant quickly said. "Let's get going or we'll miss the social altogether." Then glancing at Tina, he asked. "Are you going to be all right at a country social attired so elegantly?"

Tina reveled in what she took as a compliment. Her eye-catching outfit was made of delicate blue gauze with exquisite silver threads interspersed throughout the fabric. "Surely this attire is suitable for any social occasion. Mother purchased it at an exclusive shop in Boston."

"Well, there's no doubt that it's very beautiful, but I was just concerned it might not be appropriate for our get together," Grant mused. "You know, it really isn't a formal affair; it's a casual, last-minute gathering."

"Let me tell you something, Grant Hayes," Tina said sternly, pausing on the last step so she was nose to nose with Grant. "I'm not countrified and have no intention of ever being countrified. You should already know that I'm used to attending formal affairs. So," she adamantly said, "these country bumpkins will just have to look and learn from someone who belongs to a higher social class."

"Okay, then," Fred said, breaking the tension. "Shall we go?" Grant still staring in disbelief at Tina, finally recovered enough to say, "Yes, I think we're ready."

Kate came out of the parlor, smiling at the young people. "Well, I see you're all ready. I hope you have a wonderful time tonight."

Grant walked over and gave her a quick kiss on the check. "Thanks, Mother," he said. "We won't be late."

Kate patted his check, sensing something awry. "Is everything okay, son?" she asked.

Grant smiled reassuringly. "Sure, Mom," he answered. "Everything's just fine."

"If you say so," Kate said walking them to the door. "Be careful and don't get chilled."

"Oh, Mom," Grant laughed. "It's the last of June. I don't think we'll have a problem with being chilled."

"Yes, I know," Kate answered good-naturedly. "But a mom must always give some kind of instruction and that's all I could think of at the moment."

Grant and Fred chuckled as they pulled away into the twilight. Tina sat in silence, so Fred began chatting.

"This is a wonderful land you have here, Grant," he said. "I'd always visualized it as being barren and desolate, but it certainly grows on a person."

"Yes," Grant responded.

Fred looked intently at the stoic back of his friend and continued, "I like this flatness. You would never feel claustrophobic out here, and it feels as if you can see forever."

"Yes," Grant responded again.

Fred tried again, "And the sky is so clear and beautiful at night. You can look up and see all kinds of stars and alien spaceships zooming between them."

"Yes," Grant said again.

Fred burst out laughing. "I knew you weren't listening to me. I might as well have been talking to the air."

"What?" Grant asked. "What did I say?"

"In the course of polite conversation I mentioned all the alien spaceships I could see in the sky and you agreed with me," Fred snorted. "Listen, old chap, you better get with it before we arrive at the social or everyone will think you're bonkers."

Grant's demeanor relaxed immediately. "Sorry, my friend. You're absolutely right; I need to get my act together." Then he turned to Tina and said, "I'm sorry, Tina. I didn't mean to be rude about your outfit. I was just worried that you might damage it in some way at the social and I'd feel very bad about that."

Tina looked at him and immediately cuddled up to his side. "Oh, that's all right, my darling," she said condescendingly. "It's lovely of you to admit you were wrong. All is forgiven." She paused then continued, "Your parents seem to have put a damper on your feelings for me, but I want to assure you that as soon as we get back to Boston everything will return to normal. And the sooner the better."

Grant flashed back to his years in Boston. It seemed now that he hadn't been his "normal self" the entire time there. He had had to come home to find "normal." He glanced back at Fred over Tina's head and gave him a quizzical look of disbelief.

Fred quickly stifled his laughter and started humming tunelessly.

"My, my!" he commented. "This land also makes one become a singing cowboy."

Grant laughed. "Hold on there, friend. Please don't give this country credit for everything. A singing cowboy, you say? I think you'd have problems with both of those areas—singing and being a cowboy."

"Now wait a minute," he exclaimed. "You've got to give a guy a chance to adjust to his environment. It's not an immediate changeover, you know."

"All right," Grant agreed. "Perhaps you're correct. Just give you a little time and you'll be a singing cowboy. But have you considered that to be a cowboy you'd have to learn to ride horses and rope cattle?"

"Righto!" Fred declared. Then he added, "Looky there my fair-weathered friends, it seems I see a glow on the horizon. It looks like we're approaching the campsite."

"Indeed we are," Grant said. "Now, how about we make a vow to have a good time tonight. No disagreements, no tension, no unkindness. Just lots of fun." Grant halted the horses and helped Tina out of the buggy.

"I do so vow!" Fred said, raising his hand as if being sworn in.

Tina sighed. "I'll try to tolerate this, Grant, darling," she said. "Just for you." She squeezed his hand.

"I do appreciate it," Grant said. "Now, let's go join the party!"

The three walked to join the others gathered about the campfire. Sharon Russell came forward to greet them. "Welcome, ya'll," she said graciously. "We're so happy you came. Come join the others."

Fred nudged Grant and whispered, "Quite a beauty, that one!"

Grant smiled. "Yes, she is."

"What did you say?" Tina asked, not being able to hear their conversation.

"Nothing, Tina," Grant answered. "Fred was just commenting on the beauty of things in Progress."

"Oh," she responded. "I really don't see any beauty here."

"Well, *I* do, believe me!" Fred said, elbowing Grant again.

Tina looked quizzically at them. "Sometimes I don't understand you two. It seems as if you have a secret code and you totally leave me out of things."

"Sorry," Grant apologized. "You know Fred. He's a witty individual. And we communicate so efficiently because I've become quite accustomed to his wit. You know, that's what having a friend is all about, Tina. You understand each other without actually saying anything."

Tina frowned. "I don't think I have a friend like that," she said. "All my friends don't seem to understand much of anything."

"Well, you finally got something right," Fred declared, smiling.

Before Tina could open her mouth to retort, Grant said quickly, "That's enough Fred."

Todd Herrington disengaged himself from the others and came toward them. Bypassing Grant and Fred, he took Tina's hand and bowed formally.

"Hello, there," Todd said. "It's about time a real lady arrived in Podunk. You introduce elegance and charm into our midst."

Tina laughed merrily. "Why thank you, kind sir. It's about time I heard a compliment. They've been rare these last few days."

"I certainly don't know why," Todd said graciously. "I'm almost speechless at your beauty." Fred smirked. Then Todd turned to Grant. "May I steal this lady for a few moments and offer her some refreshment?"

Before Grant could agree, Tina took Todd's proffered arm and the two walked away chatting and laughing together. Fred slapped Grant on the shoulder. "Quite a charmer, isn't he?"

"Quite," Grant agreed.

"Hello, Dr. Hayes," Danielle said, appearing at his side.

'Now, who in the world is already calling you 'doctor'? Fred asked. Then bending toward Danielle, he whispered conspiratorially, "You must be careful about calling this man 'Dr. Hayes.' You know he has a real ego problem and we shouldn't do anything that would make him more sure of himself than he already is."

"Really?" Danielle responded. "I hadn't noticed. But thanks for the warning."

"Okay, you two. I'm standing right here," Grant interjected, laughing good-naturedly.

"You must remember, Mr. Thomas . . . " Danielle began.

"Fred," Fred interrupted.

"Oh, yes, I forgot," Danielle continued. "You must remember, Fred, that I've known the good doctor a long, long time. I knew him even before he decided to become a doctor. In fact, I know many interesting things about the doctor."

"And what might those things be?" Fred asked, enjoying the easy banter with the young lady.

"I'd rather not go into detail right now if you don't mind," she answered, inclining her head in Grant's direction. "You do understand, don't you?"

Fred laughed, "Oh, yes. I most certainly understand. Perhaps we could have a more private conversation about it later when the guilty party isn't present."

"Certainly," Danielle said. "I'll look forward to sharing many things about him with you."

"Okay!" Grant said again. "May I be included here?"

They laughed as they ambled toward the group. "Quite a young lady," Fred whispered to Grant as they walked. "In fact, she looks to be the most attractive lady here. And she has intelligence to boot. What more can a man ask for?"

"Yes," Grant agreed. "She's a very nice young lady." They had stopped a few feet back from the others.

"Oh, what is a man to do?" Fred said in mock consternation. "I find myself torn between two beauties here."

"Really?" Grant asked. "And would you like to share with me who the two beauties are that have roped in your affections?"

"Well, that would be the lovely Danielle and the parson's daughter, Miss Sharon Russell," he confided.

"Oh, I see," Grant said. "And which do you prefer?"

"It's a difficult decision indeed," Fred answered, rubbing his chin thoughtfully. "I find Danielle to be the favorite in the beauty category, but I'm not certain I could compete with her brain power, not to mention her spunk, both of which are, I might add, not often found in the female species. On the other hand, Sharon Russell has such a sweet disposition. And, with her I could have a direct link to the throne of God through her father." He stopped rubbing his chin as if in deep thought. "Perhaps I'll pursue the parson's daughter." Then turning to Grant, he dramatically said, "Thank you for listening to my innermost thoughts and helping me to sort them out."

Grant chuckled, "That's what I'm here for, my friend," then added, "although I couldn't get a word in edgewise." He paused a moment wondering why he felt relieved when Fred decided to pursue Sharon. Fred noticed his quietness.

"You okay, old chap?" Fred asked.

"Sure," Grant assured him, mentally shaking off the unsettled feeling. "Everything's fine. Let's get the party started."

28

A Shocking Revelation

They joined the others around the refreshment table and heaped their plates with delicious country fare. Grant looked around and found Tina and Todd talking in a huddle at the end of the table. Fred had made overtures to Sharon and they were sitting and conversing as well.

"So, doctor," Danielle said appearing at his side. "Do you have a dinner companion?"

"No," he answered. "Are you offering your companionship?"

"Yes, I think I am," she said.

"Okay, then," He said. "Shall we?"

They located two places near Todd and Tina.

"Are you having a good time, Tina?" Grant asked. "Did you find everything okay?"

Tina glanced up. "Oh, yes, darling, everything's wonderful. Todd here is meeting my every need. He's such a gentleman."

"I'm sure he is," said Grant, slightly embarrassed. "You remember Danielle, don't you? She was introduced to you this morning at church."

"Oh, I think I do," Tina said, looking her up and down as she had done earlier. "It's very nice to see you again . . . oh dear, would you mind repeating your name?"

"Danielle."

"Oh, yes, I must remember—Daynelle." She turned back to Todd, ignoring them both.

Grant looked apologetically at Danielle and she said softly, "It's okay, Grant. Don't worry about it." They settled in and began eating pork and beans, slaw, potato salad, and cracklin' cornbread.

Grant and Danielle were immersed in their own conversation until Danielle's delighted laughter caught Tina's attention. She scowled and looked over at them.

"What's so amusing?" she asked snootily.

"Oh, Danielle's always tried to draw attention to herself in some way or other," Todd said maliciously.

Danielle blushed and lowered her head. Grant said, "Now, see here . . . " Danielle touched his arm to stop his interference.

"I'm sorry," Danielle said kindly. "I didn't realize we were bothering anyone."

"Well, it's quite rude to snub people," Tina said unkindly.

"I'm sorry," Danielle said again. "Grant and I certainly would never have snubbed you on purpose. We were talking about the things of God and the service this morning."

"Really?" she said unbelievingly. "Well, I for one was not at all impressed with that country service we endured this morning."

Shocked silence followed her statement until Todd broke in: "Oh, Tina, *you* went to church this morning?" Todd asked with mockery in his voice. "I didn't peg you as a churchgoer."

Tina's face turned red and she retorted loudly, "I went, not because I wanted to, but to please Grant's Bible-toting parents." It seemed time stood still as Grant became aware that everyone heard her comment. Sharon Russell's face paled and Fred reached out his hand to offer comfort.

"Tina," Grant's voice held a steel quality. "That comment was totally unnecessary."

"Oh, why are *you* being so high and mighty?" Tina said rudely. "You never went to church when you were in Boston so why are you trying to act all holy now?"

Grant stood, endeavoring to hold his temper. "Tina," he said in warning. "Perhaps we ought to have this conversation in a more private setting."

"Why should that be necessary?" she asked. "After all, in country towns, doesn't everyone know everyone else's business?"

Todd roared with laughter. "Oh, this is great! Someone is finally here who thinks the way I do." He turned to Tina and explained, "I hate living here and dealing with all these lower class people who think they're something special. It's just about more than I can take. You, my beauty, are a breath of fresh air."

"I so despise people who try to put on airs, don't you, Todd?" Tina asked.

"I certainly do," Todd agreed. "And sitting at this table are plenty of them. They don't even realize they're absolute nobodies."

By this time, Fred and Grant, along with several other young men were standing. "I think your commentary is quite over, Mr. Herrington," Grant stated strongly.

"Oh, what are you going do?" Todd asked, mocking fear. "Challenge me to a duel?"

"You don't deserve to even be recognized," Danielle interrupted, rising to stand by Grant. "In my opinion, characters like you are a disgrace to society."

"Society," sneered Todd. "Here? This town doesn't even know the meaning of the word 'society.'" He skewered Danielle with an arrogant look. "And may I add for all to hear, I know that in your heart of hearts you want to be my girl. You may put on a front, but you so want to be with me. After all, who can blame you? I'm quite a catch."

Danielle paled and began to tremble. "That is absolutely not true, Todd Herrington."

"Oh, yes it is," he argued. "Your dad and my dad have talked of our marrying and forging an alliance for a long time. In fact, just the other day, your father said you were quite attracted to me and that you'd be thrilled to be a part of our family. Listen, sweet thing, together we can own the whole town." Then leering at Danielle, he added, "Having you as my little wife would definitely help me get over my hatred of this place. Of course, I haven't come to a decision on you as yet."

Tears flooded Danielle's eyes. Calmly and quietly, she looked at Grant and then around the table. "If you all will excuse me," she said quietly, "I think I'd best be going." She quickly turned and literally ran from the group.

Grant reached out as she raced by, "Danielle, wait . . . "

Tina's disdainful laughter pierced the profound silence. "Well, well," she exclaimed. "This is certainly a switch from Boston socials. I didn't know country socials could be so entertaining—with everyone airing each others' dirty laundry." Then she turned to Todd and said, "We have a lot in common Mr. Herrington. Both of our beloveds are harboring secrets. Your Daynelle hasn't told anyone of her love for you, and my beloved is putting up a front of Christianity so he can pacify his parents until we get back to Boston. This dull party has taken an interesting turn, hasn't it?"

Grant looked sternly at her and said, "Perhaps we should be going, Tina."

"But why?" she pouted. "Things are just starting to sizzle." Grant was appalled that Tina seemed to be enjoying herself. Instead of the utopia he had imagined, would living with her be a constant parade of insults, slights, and pettiness?

Grant felt a hand on his arm and turned to find Fred and Sharon standing nearby. Sharon was as pale as Danielle had been, but she kindly said, "Grant, did you get enough to eat?" Then she turned, ever the gracious hostess. "Hey, everyone, come back for seconds. There's plenty of food, yours just for the taking."

The tension gradually eased and everyone began hesitantly talking and making their way back to the refreshment table. "You okay, old chap?" Fred asked, concern showing on his face. Grant paused, and then looked back at his friend. "I'm fine, Fred," he said quietly. Then he added softly, "Kind of at a loss for words right now, but other than that . . . "

"Are you ready to go then?" Fred asked.

"Well, I was," Grant said. "More than ready. But after thinking about it, it would probably be better if we stick around a few more minutes and at least help Sharon revive whatever we can of the social, not to mention protect Danielle's character from the mouths of the lions."

Fred smiled at his friend. "Always the same, Grant," he said. "Thinking of others before your own well-being. Let me just say here, that Tina's nasty remark was uncalled for. I for one am a witness of what the power of a Savior can do. You may have gotten sidetracked from things for a while, but there's no doubt that God can completely change someone's life. I felt that this morning, and I know you did too. So, don't worry about what others may think. I'm new at all of this religion stuff, but I say it doesn't matter what others may think anyway. What matters is what God thinks."

Grant looked unbelievingly at his friend and then his countenance broke into a brilliant smile. "My, my," he exclaimed. "If I didn't know any better, I'd think instead of a new convert, you were the preacher."

"Hmmm," Fred mused. "That might not be a bad idea."

Grant laughed, and Fred stated sincerely, "Now, that's much better. Shall we join the party and try to assist my new lady friend, Miss Russell, to salvage this social disaster?"

"Sounds like a good idea," Grant said. Then paused, "Do you think Danielle is okay?" he asked.

Fred paused as well. "I certainly hope so," he answered. "She seems to be a very strong young woman and I think she'll survive the unkindness just displayed by that rogue, Todd Herrington and the high-and-mighty Miss Hamilton."

"You never change, do you, Fred?" Grant chuckled. "You can express yourself with just the precise words."

"That's the lawyer in me, my man," he answered. "You should know that from experiences with your father."

"You're right there," Grant said, "and I know something else: I intend to use a few choice words when I talk to Tina about tonight."

29

Time for a Confrontation

A headache woke Grant early the next morning. He slowly massaged his temples and sat up on the side of the bed. Events from the previous night flooded his memory and he held his head and groaned. He sat motionless for a few moments and then walked carefully toward the window. He sat down on the window seat and peered out into the pale dawn. An abundant cloud cover hinted at possible rain, so the sun might not make its usual bright appearance.

Grant remembered sitting here as a child when he was sick; he would look out the window at everything below him. It seemed to give him hope that soon he would be better and could again run and play in the yard below. He smiled at the memory. *Oh, how simple things seem when one is a child,* he thought. On this gloomy morning, he longed for the simple days of childhood. Ironically, he had wanted to grow up so badly back then, but now for a moment he fantasized about being a little boy once again. He could well remember when Mom or Dad would wrap their loving arms around him and chase away the hurt or obstacles in his young life. *There are definitely some obstacles in my life right now,* he thought. Last night's Tina-and-Todd fiasco had been very unsettling. First of all, Tina's display of temper, especially her criticism of him and his parents in front of the others, was very difficult to understand or endure. After all, she was the one making overtures to Todd right under his nose and in view of the others at the social. Then, she openly insulted Danielle and accused him of "putting on a show" of Christianity in order to appease his parents.

Grant sighed involuntarily. He had never noticed her arrogance before she came to Progress. In Boston she was the most beautiful, desirable thing he had ever seen and he wanted so badly to make her the most important person in his life. But since she had come to Progress, he had seen a side of her he had never seen before. He had fully intended to speak to her about her actions when they got home last night, but Tina had feigned tiredness and escaped to her room. During the ride home, the static between the two of them would have been unbearable had it not been for Fred's unflappable cheer and conversation.

Thankfully, with Fred's help, they had managed to revive the church social somewhat. Fred and Sharon walked around and brought a feeble semblance of a party mode to the atmosphere. Grant smiled at the antics of his friend's endeavor to bring laughter to the group. Grant shook his head thinking of the times Fred had come to his rescue since their first meeting in Boston. There was no doubt about it; Fred Thomas was his best friend.

His head still pounding, Grant walked to the chest of drawers to see if he had any headache powders. Thankfully he found the small package and quickly downed a dose with the water on his nightstand. He gently lay back down on the bed and closed his eyes. He finally dozed off, and when he awoke about an hour later, his headache had eased somewhat. He chose his clothes and dressed for the day. Then straightening the last few items in his room, he descended the stairs. Walking slowly, he entered the breakfast room.

"Why, good morning, Grant, dear," his mother greeted him.

His father glanced up from the newspaper and said, "Good morning, son."

"Good morning." Grant walked toward the sideboard and stated, "I could sure use a cup of coffee."

"Coffee, coffee," Margarita said. "Bah. You need food. No coffee."

Smiling at the older lady, Grant said, "Are you hiding the coffee from me this morning, Margarita? Why, you're the one that got me started on the ghastly stuff."

In spite of her intention, Margarita smiled at Grant. "Ah, okay. You beat. I get your coffee."

Grant sauntered back to the table, smiling slightly. "Margarita hasn't changed, has she? She still likes to give me a hard time."

Kate looked up and smiled. "She loves you dearly, son. You know that."

"I know, Mom," he said distractedly.

Noticing his somber expression, she asked, "Something wrong, Grant?"

"Uh, no, I'm fine, Mom," he answered.

"You don't seem fine," his mother insisted. "Did you all have a good time last night?"

"Uh, yes, we had a nice time," Grant said hesitantly. Margarita came in bearing his cup of coffee proudly.

"Here go, hombre pequeno," she said.

Grant laughed. "When are you going to learn, my dear Rita, that I'm no longer your little man?"

Margarita scowled, "You always be a little man to me, Mr. Grant."

"Okay, okay," Grant said in mock surrender. "Thanks for the coffee, Margarita."

"De nada," she said, as she walked back into the kitchen.

"Now back to last night," Kate insisted.

"Mom, really, everything's fine," Grant assured her.

"I don't think so, son," Kate still probed. "Something's bothering you."

Alexander looked up from the paper and said slowly, "You might as well tell all, son. She won't be satisfied until you do."

Kate countered, "Now be serious, Alexander Hayes. Something's wrong with our son and we need to find out what it is."

"Mother, really. There was only a small incident, but we handled everything just fine," Grant explained.

"Incident?" his mother questioned. "What kind of incident?"

"Well," Grant began, realizing his dad was right, "Tina and Todd Herrington created an unfortunate scene last night at the social." He paused.

"Really?" Kate said. "And?"

"And it created some difficulty for me and several others there."

"What kind of difficulty?" Kate asked.

"Good morning, everyone," Fred said, entering the room.

All responded distractedly and Fred asked, "Am I interrupting something?"

Grant turned to greet him. "I'm sorry, Fred," he said. "Come on in and have some breakfast."

Fred walked to the buffet and filled a plate. "I take it you're discussing last evening," he said.

"Well, my dear mother's trying to pry out of me what happened." He turned back to Kate. "Well, Mom, Tina said some unkind things, but I intend to talk with her today about it," Grant explained.

At that precise moment, Tina entered the room in her elegant dressing gown, her skin glowing, and sang out, "Good morning, everyone. I know I'm up earlier than normal, but for some reason, I'm ravenous today." She stooped over Grant's shoulder and kissed his cheek. "Good morning, my love."

Grant involuntarily turned his head away, trying to avoid her show of affection, but Tina did not notice as she was already spooning food onto a plate at the sideboard. Kate looked intently at Grant and then Tina, but did not say anything. Tina walked back to the table and sat down.

"Sleep well, darling?" Tina asked coyly, looking up as she took a bite of melon.

"I wish you'd quit calling me that, Tina."

"Why?" she asked innocently. "You didn't seem to mind in Boston."

"As I recall," Grant said quietly to her, endeavoring to hold his temper, "you didn't call me that in Boston. However, I don't think this is either the time or the place to have this discussion." Then turning to his mom, he changed the subject. "Lunch was great yesterday, wasn't it, Mom?"

"I'm sorry?" Kate asked.

Alexander laughed, "Well, my dear, one of the rare occasions when you're at a loss for words."

Grant smiled and continued, "I said that one of our best meals during the week is on Sunday. When I was a kid, we used to have roast, roast, roast. I got to where I didn't like roast very well. Then, Margarita came up with the idea to fix Mexican food on Sunday. I mean, she fixes the works, doesn't she? Enchiladas, tortillas, tamales, chile rellenos. It was absolutely awesome."

"Yes, she has a natural-born knack of fixing authentic Mexican cuisine," Kate agreed, still puzzled by his line of conversation.

Margarita came in about that time to remove the used dishes. "Are you going to fix us your Mexican delicacies next Sunday as well, Margarita?" Grant asked.

She patted his shoulder playfully. "I have no decided yet. I wait to see how you treat me this week."

Tina gasped at her response. "How dare you allow her to address you in that manner!"

"Tina, please!" Grant implored.

"Well, I for one would never allow the help to address me is such a casual way," she declared haughtily.

Grant, reaching the limit of his patience, said sternly. "Tina, that will be enough. You are in our home and you don't have any right to instruct us on how we're to act. Now, if my parents will kindly excuse us, I'd like to speak to you alone. In the garden. Now, please."

Tina looked shocked at his reaction and her face flushed to a fiery red. Then with tears filling her eyes, she stood up and ran from the room.

30

Not an Easy Task

Grant looked apologetically at his parents. "Sorry," he said, before leaving the room. Walking toward the garden, he wasn't quite certain what to say to Tina. All he knew was he was shocked that she considered it her due to treat others so rudely and expected to have everything done her way. *Why didn't I notice this before?* he thought.

When he walked into the garden, he found Tina sitting on his mom's favorite bench with her back toward him. He paused and walked toward her.

"Tina," he began.

To his surprise, she stood up, turned toward him and coldly said, "How dare you."

Grant looked in disbelief at her. "How dare I?" he asked. "How dare *I*, you say? Let me turn the question around. How dare *you*!"

Tina looked taken aback at his response. Not used to him challenging her, she looked uncertainly at him. "Grant Hayes, I don't know what's happened to you since you came home, but you're certainly different than when we were in Boston. And I don't care for the way you're treating me."

Grant said in frustration, "Don't try to turn the tables on me, Tina. I'm appalled, to say the least, at *your* behavior." Tina opened her mouth to protest, but he held his hand up and continued. "You've made fun of my home, been rude to my parents, abused my friends, and most of all been caustic about God. And, Tina, I've had enough."

When she saw he was genuinely angry, she suddenly took another tactic and said pitifully, "But people have been so unkind to me and I abhor this town." Then sidling up to him and looking imploringly into his eyes, she added, "This stinky little town is no place for you, darling."

"Don't call me that," Grant said with raised voice. "Listen, Tina, I never in my wildest imagination ever thought I would say this, but from what I've seen of you and your mannerisms the last few days, this is not going to work."

"What's not going to work?" she asked, placing her hand over her heart.

"Us," Grant simply said.

"Oh, no, darl . . . I mean, wait, Grant. We can work this out. I'll do whatever you want me to do. I'll be whatever you want me to be. Please, Grant, don't do this," she implored, this time genuine tears welling from her eyes.

Grant sadly shook his head. "Tina, this can't be fixed. You've gone too far. Believe me, I've tried to make excuses for you and your behavior from the minute you arrived here. I really thought I loved you and could tolerate anything if only we could be together. But I just don't think I can anymore."

"You aren't yourself, Grant," Tina said, clawing at his arm.

"Oh, yes, I'm quite myself," Grant said. "In fact, I'm more myself than I've ever been. I've made peace with God and that accounts for everything."

"Please, Grant," she begged. "I know you do love me. Look, I'm sorry I've been acting spoiled and bratty, but I'm just having trouble adjusting to the ways of this place."

Grant sighed. "I appreciate your efforts at apologizing, Tina. But it's too late for me. I could perhaps go along with your haughtiness to my long-time friends. I could even go along with your being unkind to me. But when it comes to comments and insinuations made about my parents, that's just too much. And," he said, stopping her interruption, "when it comes to discounting

God and His house, well that goes beyond the pale, and I won't tolerate it." He paused again and shook his head in disbelief. "Wow. It just dawned on me that our whole time together has been about catering to your needs and wants, not my own, not those of others. And if I'm going to be a doctor, that's not going to work for me."

Grant looked sadly at the girl he once thought he loved. "I didn't mean to hurt you, Tina, but I'm so disappointed at what I've seen from you. They say that 'love is blind,' and it's definitely true when it comes to us. I thought I loved you so much that I didn't see what you were really like." She bowed her head and cried silently. "Now," he continued kindly. "Why don't you get your things together? I can take you into town and you can still make the train back home without delay."

Without looking at him or saying a word, Tina simply turned and walked away.

Returning home from taking Tina to the train station, Grant walked into the parlor and his mother immediately ran to his side. "Are you all right, Grant dear?" she asked anxiously.

With tiredness evident on his features, he answered, "Yes, Mom, I'm all right." He plopped down into a chair and laid his head back. "I do have to say, though, that this task was definitely one of the hardest but most liberating things I've ever done."

"I'm sure it must have been uncomfortable, son," Alexander said, leaning toward his son's chair.

"It was, Dad. I stood on the platform after Tina got on the train wondering how I could've been so blind to what she was." Grant shook his head slowly, emphasizing his consternation. Then he continued, "But to be perfectly honest, once I located a married couple to watch out for her on the return journey and I saw the train pull out, I feel as if a huge burden has been lifted from my shoulders." He sighed deeply. "My goodness! What was I thinking to want to be saddled with her for life?"

"Now don't beat yourself up, Grant," Kate said. "Just be thankful you came to yourself."

Grant smiled. "Sort of like the prodigal son, huh?"

"Now wait a minute. You're definitely not like the prodigal. He was much worse than you," Kate said emphatically.

Grant chuckled. "Thanks, Mom. That's a comfort."

"Oh, my," she said. "I didn't mean it like that."

Grant waved his hand at her. "I know, Mom. I'm just teasing you." He sighed again. "I did want to say, though, that I appreciate you both praying about this. To think I could have married her. Can you imagine?"

"Let's not think about that. Let's just thank the Lord for caring enough to watch out for us," Kate said.

"Oh, I'm very thankful," Grant reiterated. "And I'm so glad the Savior guided me back home, in spite of the fact I had strayed so far from Him. I can't imagine what my life would've been without Him. And I was headed in the wrong direction while I was with Tina."

Fred peered around the door frame. "Am I interrupting?" he asked.

Grant perked up. "Well, I can't believe my friend would actually ask if he was interrupting. He usually just walks right in."

"Okay, now," Fred protested.

"Come on in here," Grant said, extending his hand.

"Well, did we get the young lady sent off?" Fred asked.

"Yes, I think so," Grant answered. "So I suppose you sensed all along how Tina really was. I mean, I remember your few comments and the arguments you used to have."

"Well, old chum, I admit that I thought our Tina was a gorgeous woman, but after being around her some, I found her attitude made her much less desirable. She just thought too much of herself and never about anyone else," Fred explained. "I think the old adage goes 'pretty is as pretty does.' And, I don't think Tina knew how to 'do pretty.'"

Grant smiled in spite of the seriousness of the situation. "But why didn't you say something?" Grant asked.

"Well, I hinted at it, but I saw how much you cared for her, and I thought there was a chance she might change," Fred responded. "Of course, my faith got a bit weak after I had that grueling train trip with her."

They all laughed at Fred's expression. Then soberly, Fred said, "I hate to be unkind, but I'm really glad she's gone."

"Life must go on," Grant said. "I hate to say so, but right now I'm at a loss at exactly what I plan to do."

"Why don't you just clear your mind for a few days, Grant dear," Kate said, patting his shoulder as she stood behind his chair. "You have the rest of the summer to make decisions anyway."

"Yes, you're right, Mom," he agreed.

"Well, I'll be here for you, old chum," Fred stated, "and I totally intend to visit a few of the ladies in the area before we return to school." Then with a devilish lift of one eyebrow, he added. "I could probably find you someone as well, if you'd like."

Grant laughed. "That's mighty kind of you, my friend, but I think I'll take a few days off from the female species."

Their laughter was interrupted by the sound of someone beating on the front door. Grant, followed by the rest of the family, rushed across the foyer and pulled the door open. To their surprise, Danielle stood there with tears streaming down her face.

31

Danielle's Dilemma

"Oh, Grant, thank God you're still here," she said frantically, gripping his arm. "I thought you might have already left town."

"Danielle, what's the matter?" he asked.

Trying to wipe the tears from her face, she explained, "My dad was just thrown from a horse after it broke into a wild gallop. It looks like his leg is broken, and he's unconscious. I did everything I could to stop the bleeding, but he's in bad shape. Is there any way you could come see about him?"

Without hesitation, Grant answered. "Certainly. Just give me a minute to grab my bag and I'll be ready."

Alexander ran to the barn to saddle Grant's horse while Fred reached out to still Danielle's wringing hands. "It's going to be okay, Danielle."

"Oh, I hope so," she said in agitation. "My dad is such a mean-spirited person and if something happens to him before he can get right with God . . . " Her voice faded and she looked at Kate appealingly. "Do you think God can forgive someone on their deathbed?" she asked.

In spite of the girl's distraught appearance, Kate had to admit she was indeed a beauty. Trying to cover her uncertainty about the girl, she answered kindly, "All I know, Danielle, is that we serve a merciful God."

Danielle's countenance brightened at Kate's comment and she said gratefully, "Thank you so much, ma'am, for your reassurance. That means a lot to me."

Grant charged down the stairs carrying his bag, "Ready?" he asked, all business now.

"Yes," Danielle declared, running out the front door and jumping on the back of her horse. She charged down the lane and suddenly remembered that Grant was supposed to be coming as well. She looked around behind her and to her relief found him close at hand.

"I'm coming," Grant assured her, thankful that his dad had responded so quickly in saddling his horse. As they galloped toward the Johnson ranch, his thoughts kept pace with their racing horses. It seemed like eons ago that he chanced to meet Danielle on the train on his way back home. He remembered how much he enjoyed their lively conversation and the teasing they shared back and forth. He should have noticed then the difference between Danielle's attitude and Tina's attitude. Danielle was easy to get along with and didn't require his constant, undivided attention. She was simply there, a comfortable presence. Of course at that time, he hadn't made things right with God so perhaps that was why he hadn't noticed what a fine girl she really was. At that precise moment, she looked across at him, and said, "We're almost there." He nodded.

They rode for several more minutes and finally arrived to find Susie Johnson anxiously holding her unconscious husband's hand. "Oh, thank God!" she exclaimed, running toward Danielle and hugging her close. "You're finally here."

"Has he responded in any way?" Danielle asked.

"No, he's still just layin' there." Mrs. Johnson turned to Grant. "Thank you for coming."

"Certainly, Mrs. Johnson," Grant said.

One glance at Butch Johnson told Grant that Danielle had not exaggerated. His leg lay at an odd angle and there was a huge gash on his forehead. Grant noted his ashen pallor. He laid his bag on the bed, reached for a small light, lifted each eyelid, and peered into Mr. Johnson's eyes. Grant became even more concerned when he saw that the pupils were dilated and unresponsive.

"What do you think?" Danielle asked anxiously.

He paused and then explained, "Well, I really can't say for certain until I've had more time to examine him. He's suffering the consequences of trauma to the head." Grant picked up his arm. "Lots of scrapes and bruises are evident." He then raised the bloody shirt and unconsciously grimaced. "His injuries are severe and widespread."

Grant looked into the frightened eyes of the Johnson women and said reassuringly. "I promise I'll do all I can to help him." Turning to Mrs. Johnson, he requested, "If you could gather some clean strips of cloths, boil some water, and bring it in two basins, that would be a tremendous help." Susie Johnson looked relieved at having something to do and left the room. Danielle came to stand by Grant's side and asked, "So what do you really think?"

Grant sighed, "I'm very concerned, Danielle. His eyes not responding to light could be an indication that his brain may not be functioning."

Danielle gasped, "Oh, no!"

Grant reached out and grasped her hand, "I'm being honest with you, Danielle, because you have a grasp of medical knowledge."

Danielle gripped his hand in return, "I know and I appreciate your honesty, Grant. It's just that the truth is hard to face when it concerns a family member."

He gently let go of her hand and turned back to Mr. Johnson. "Let's get him cleaned up; that is, if you're up to helping me." At Danielle's nod he continued, "We need to set his leg and he'll require plenty of stitches. Then we'll go from there."

Danielle quickly wiped away her tears and said matter-of-factly, "Certainly, Grant. Anything I can do to help." As she turned Grant said, "Please get Daniel to find two straight, sturdy sticks; I don't care what he finds, but they have to be straight and very sturdy. We'll use them to keep his leg stable."

Danielle hurried from the room. He was amazed at her tenacity and strength. He knew Mr. Johnson had often been unkind to Danielle, but he was still her father. He prayed that he would be able to help him. He shook his head as he listened to the man's stertorous breathing. To be so mean and cantankerous, he certainly seemed vulnerable now.

In no time at all, Danielle and her mother came back into the room carrying the cloths and basins. She quickly added carbolic acid from Grant's doctor's bag to the water to wash their hands and instruments, and to clean Mr. Johnson's wounds. After everything was clean, she began setting up what they would need, and he noted that he did not have to instruct her on the proper procedure. As they worked, Daniel entered with two narrow boards sawed off in equal lengths. He didn't look too happy about being told what to do.

"Well, I see the good doctor has returned to our ranch once again," he said arrogantly. "I'm certain Father would be displeased to find himself at your mercy."

"That's enough, Daniel," his mother said sternly. "You apologize immediately. Dr. Grant came to help your father and you have a fine way of showing appreciation. We certainly don't need your insolence now, son. Especially at this point."

Grant could tell from the brother and sister's shocked reaction that they were not used to this type of firm outburst from their mother. She continued, "Yes, I can tell you're surprised that I've finally spoke up. I should've done it years ago instead of letting your father run roughshod over us for so many years." She sighed, and went to stand by Mr. Johnson's bedside. "But in spite of his unkind ways, I still love him," she said softly.

Danielle went to her mother and hugged her close. "I know you do, Mom, and Dr. Hayes is going to do everything he can to bring Dad back to us."

With a firm resolve, Mrs. Johnson stood tall and looked back at Daniel who looked surprisingly contrite. "I'm still waiting for you to apologize to Dr. Hayes."

"Uh, okay," Daniel said. "Sorry, doc. Didn't mean any offense."

"That's okay, Daniel," Grant said, with a slight smile. "Then perhaps you could do something else for me."

Daniel nodded.

"Would you ride over to my house and tell my folks I'll be staying here tonight to look after your father?" Grant asked. "I just don't want them to worry."

"Sure, I'll ride over there now," Daniel said.

Grant sighed and looked at Danielle. "Now let's get down to business," he said.

Grant and Danielle worked together diligently for some time. He stitched the gash in Butch Johnson's head and several other wounds as well. The instruments he needed were available before he even had to ask. He smiled at Danielle, letting her know she was doing an excellent job. Mr. Johnson was thankfully unresponsive as they worked together to pull and set the broken leg. Grant firmly wrapped the cloth strips around the leg and splints. They washed their hands and instruments again and began to put everything away.

Grant tested the patient's feet with a pin and still couldn't detect any reflexive movement. Danielle could not hide the anxiety she felt as she watched his ministrations, well aware of the consequences they faced.

Finally, Grant folded his arms and leaned against the wall, deep in thought. Danielle asked softly, "So can you tell if he'll recover?"

"Well, Danielle, as you know, these types of injuries are so unpredictable," he answered. "Why don't we all go to the living room for a few minutes where we can sit comfortably and talk?"

He motioned toward the door and Mrs. Johnson and Danielle preceded him to the living room. The two women settled on the settee and Mrs. Johnson indicated that Grant should sit across from them. Grant did her bidding and leaned forward to address the ladies.

"I don't have to tell you that Mr. Johnson's condition is critical," he began. Both ladies nodded. He continued, "When he was thrown from the wagon, Mr. Johnson must have landed headfirst, and then the heavy wagon ran over his leg. His head and body sustained massive trauma. I believe we were successful in setting the leg properly in spite of a severe break. That's at least some good news." He paused and rubbed the back of his neck. "With this type of accident, there are usually spinal injuries involved, along with trauma to the head. I'm concerned that Mr. Johnson may have suffered some paralysis."

Both women gasped. "What do you mean exactly?" Danielle urged.

Grant answered, "When I tested his reflexes by pricking his feet, there was no reflexive movement, which indicates your father may not have felt the prickle. However, I don't believe his back is broken because while stitching his arms and a few abdominal areas he would flinch, which indicates he felt the pain of the stitches. If he had broken his back, he most likely would have been paralyzed from the neck down and wouldn't have been able to feel anything."

Danielle squeezed her mother's hand. "Well, Mom, at least there's *some* good news." Then looking back at Grant, she asked, "What else did you find?"

"We can also be thankful that he didn't suffer any brain stem injury because that can also be fatal. However, the blow to the brain is probably what caused his coma. I'm not certain if you remember or not, but my mother suffered such an injury just before I was born."

Mrs. Johnson brightened, "Oh, yes, Dr. Hayes. I remember that. It was when that fearsome tornado wrecked the town. Your mother was hurt trying to get in a cellar right before the tornado hit." She paused. "I remember everyone was concerned and didn't know how serious she was hurt."

"That's right, Mrs. Johnson," Grant answered. "In fact, she was in a coma for several days before she ever responded. I was born during the time she was in the coma as my brother-in-law,

Stephan Grant, performed a Cesarean section on my mother. What I'm trying to say here is that I just have to guess at the extent of your husband's injury as we don't have access to hospital facilities. Our only option is to wait and see."

"Is there anything we can do?" Danielle persisted.

"Not really, I'm afraid," Grant said. "I'm going to spend the night by his bed, just to keep a close watch on his every movement."

"We so appreciate it, Dr. Hayes," Mrs. Johnson breathed. Then she stood. "How about I fix some supper? I think a bite of food would make us all feel better." She patted Danielle on the shoulder as she left the room.

Grant looked at Danielle's downcast face. "Your mother is a strong woman," he commented.

Danielle looked up with tear-filled eyes and answered. "Yes, she is. She has always shown her strength in a quiet way, but she's always been my rock while growing up." Grant remained silent as she continued. "This hasn't been the easiest home to grow up in. You know, Grant, I don't know how she put up with all she did." She stood and walked across the room to look out the window. "I'm really not certain how she and dad got together. I do know that she believed she could pray enough to change him and still believes he will change. Isn't that amazing?" She shook her head. "I would've given up long ago seeing the way Dad is, but every time I get frustrated, she'll simply say, 'God still works miracles, Danielle, and I love your Dad enough to stick with him until he does change.'"

Danielle gave a half-hearted laugh. "Can you believe it? That's really loving someone, isn't it? I used to get so mad at the way he treated her and she would just softly pray for him while he hurled insults, swear words, and degrading names at her."

Grant came to stand by her side and laid a comforting hand on her shoulder. She turned, surprised to find him so close. Danielle tried to wipe the tears so he wouldn't notice. "I'm sorry, Grant. You didn't ask to hear all of this," she said with embarrassment. Then her teasing manner returned for just a moment. "I do realize that you are a medical doctor, not a psychiatric counselor."

"Really, it's fine, Danielle. I'm glad you trust me enough to feel comfortable talking to me about such private things. And, whether you realize it or not, I'm interested in finding out more about you and your family," Grant assured her.

"Oh, yes, we're the perfect family, aren't we?" she said with sarcasm. "I can still remember Grandpa Smith telling the story of how upset he was when Mom married Dad. He just couldn't believe she'd settle for 'such a scoundrel,' he'd say, lifting his fist in the air. I can still see the set of his stubborn jaw when she'd take us to Grandpa's house to get a bit of relief from Dad's mean ways." She paused and then continued softly. "Yet Mom always told Grandpa that God was going to change Dad and that she loved him. Isn't that something, Grant? I don't think I could ever do that."

Grant looked intently into her face. "You have the strength of your mother deep inside of you. And you've taken that strength and added your humor and positive outlook. And, in my opinion, you've grown up to be a fine and beautiful young lady. So to contradict your opinion about doing what your mother has done, I think you *could* because love is the most powerful force in the world."

Quietness settled over the room as they looked at each other. They were so absorbed in each other they didn't notice Daniel standing in the doorway shuffling his feet until he said, "Uh, 'scuse me," he began. "Am I interrupting something?"

32

SHARING THOUGHTS

Danielle dragged her eyes away from Grant's. "We were just talking about Dad."

"Can you tell yet if he's going to be all right?" Daniel asked.

Danielle went to him and gently took his hands. "It's still too soon to tell, Daniel," she answered. "Dr. Grant is doing everything he can without the benefit of a nearby hospital."

Daniel looked at Grant. "I gave your parents the message and they said if you needed anything to let them know," he explained. Then he added sheepishly, "They also said they'd be praying for us."

"Well, that's very nice indeed," Danielle said. "We certainly could use as much prayer as possible."

"I think I'll go back and be with your dad, Danielle," Grant said, still affected by their previous encounter.

"Certainly, and I'll go check to see if Mom needs any help," she responded.

"Can I see Dad?" Daniel asked hesitantly.

"Sure," Grant responded. "Your being here is very important to your dad right now. Come along."

Grant led Daniel back into the sickroom and saw that his patient's condition had not changed since they'd left the room. He touched his forehead, which thankfully was cool.

"He looks so battered," Daniel whispered, close by his side.

"Yes," Grant answered in hushed tones. "He's in a bad way, Daniel. But the best thing we can do for him is to just be here.

Talk to him and tell him how much you love him. Talk about the ranch and any other interests he has." Grant positioned a chair close to the bed and said, "Why don't you just sit here a few minutes?"

Daniel did as Grant suggested and while Grant checked to see that everything was replaced properly in his doctor's bag, he listened to the guttural tones of the young man as he talked to his father. It was evident this was a whole new realm to Daniel and he felt uncomfortable talking to his dad, but he was at least making an effort.

Danielle came quietly into the room and went to Grant's side. "My mom has some food prepared if you'd like something."

"Thanks, that sounds good," Grant answered.

"Daniel, are you ready to eat?" Danielle asked, laying a hand on her brother's shoulder. The young man looked up at her sadly and answered. "Not right now, Danielle. If you don't mind, I'll just sit here a little longer with Dad."

Surprised at the change in her brother, she simply said, "That's fine. Just come get us if you need us." Daniel's only answer was to nod.

Grant followed Danielle to the dining room where Mrs. Johnson had prepared a fine meal of fried chicken, corn on the cob, black-eyed peas, green beans, and yeast rolls. Grant found it hard to believe she'd been able to prepare such a meal with all the circumstances surrounding them, but he was eager to partake.

Mrs. Johnson smiled sweetly and invited, "Do sit down, Dr. Hayes."

Grant returned the smile and said, "Thank you, Mrs. Johnson, and please call me Grant. I don't abide by protocol that much. After all, I'm just a country boy."

Danielle's merry laughter was a welcome sound. "Yeah, right!" she said, with joking sarcasm. "The Boston U-educated doctor has now admitted the roots of his upbringing."

Grant responded, "And I suppose the St. Louis-educated nurse already had a grasp of her country roots."

"Oh, you're so right!" Danielle agreed, and began dramatically with an exaggerated southern drawl, "I knew all along where I come from. Even though the city life tried to pull me down, I still clung to th' old ways."

Grant laughed and looked at Mrs. Johnson, "I just can't seem to win with her."

Mrs. Johnson's face relaxed at the banter of the two young people. "Oh, to be young again," she said. "You know, I had a good time when I was young."

"I'm sure you did, Mom," Danielle said. "You were probably the belle of the ball."

"No, I hardly think so. That was always Clarissa Hayes. She was several years older than me, but she was always the life of the party, which she learned from your mother, Dr. Hayes . . . I mean, Grant," Mrs. Johnson said, taking a bite of food. "Kate Hayes was such a great teacher and made learning so much fun."

"So, is school where you met Mr. Johnson?" Grant asked.

"Well, in a way," Susie said. "Butch ran with the older crowd and was always in some kind of trouble. He'd often come in Grandpa's store and although he was mean-spirited to most everyone, he was always kind to me. I guess I was flattered that someone so much older would notice me. And, he'd call me Suzanne instead of Susie, which made me feel special." She sighed. "So when he came courtin', I accepted. I guess I've always believed that somewhere deep inside of him there had to be some goodness."

Daniel entered the dining room, "Is there anything left to eat?" he asked.

"Of course, there is, Daniel. Have a seat and I'll fix you a plate," Mrs. Johnson said.

Grant rose and graciously said, "Thank you for the good meal, Mrs. Johnson. Now, if you'll excuse me, I best get back to my patient." He rose politely and left the room. As he entered the master bedroom, he noted that Mr. Johnson's position had not changed. He hoped he would not develop any infection; that was the last thing Mr. Johnson needed at this time.

Grant sat down in the chair and thought back to the conversation at the dinner table. Mrs. Johnson seemed like such a pleasant lady and had a positive outlook in spite of her circumstances. He shook his head in amazement at her faith. Grant had been blessed with such a good life, and yet in spite of all that, he'd still lost his way for a time. Yet, Suzanne Johnson had never lost her confidence and had built faith in Danielle as well. It was quite evident, though, that Mr. Johnson had influenced his son to be as disagreeable as he was. But Danielle . . . the more he was around her, the more fascinating she became. And the more he came to love her.

Grant sat bolt upright. *Wait a minute!* he thought. *Love her? Did I just think that?* He was stunned by this unexpected revelation. After all, he had thought he loved Tina and found out it wasn't love after all. Did he even know what love was?

"Hey, there," Danielle said softly, entering the room. "Any change?"

Still reeling from his recent introspection, he looked in confusion at the object of his thoughts. "Uh . . . uh . . . "

"Did you find something worse about Dad?" Danielle asked fearfully.

Trying to bring his emotions under his control, Grant looked down into her anxious face and said reassuringly. "No, Dani, there's been no change. Sorry, I was just trying to work something out in my mind."

"Whew!" she exclaimed, noting that he called her by the nickname only her family used. "You scared me there for a minute."

"Sorry," Grant said.

"Are you sure you're all right?" Danielle said with concern.

"Yes, yes," Grant smiled reassuringly. "I'm fine. Now, let's talk about your dad. He hasn't moved or responded in any manner whatsoever so I'm quite concerned. The next few hours are going to be crucial. We must keep a close watch for any change. All that I can tell you, Dani, is that we really need to pray because that's our only hope."

Danielle looked down sadly at the still form of her father. "Not the best news I've heard by any means, but I believe God can change things. I mean, if Mom can have such faith for all these years, surely I can join her in believing God will take care of Dad."

"Would you like to sit with your father?" Grant asked, pulling up another chair.

"Thanks," she accepted, sitting down into the cushiony softness of her mom's favorite chair. She sighed. "It feels so good to take a load off!"

"Yeah, right!" Grant said with smile. "You've such a load to carry."

Danielle giggled. "Well, a girl will do what she can to fish for a compliment."

"I doubt you've had to fish for any compliments," Grant commented. "Those young doctors in St. Louie probably fell all over themselves trying to get you to be their nurse."

"What can a girl say when she's got what it takes?" Danielle answered, pretending to fan herself, and peering at him beneath her eyelashes. Then she smiled and whispered, "I so wish that was the truth."

Grant smiled back. "That's what makes you so appealing," he said. "You're unaware of your own charm and beauty." His attention on Mr. Johnson, Grant didn't notice Danielle's quick intake of breath until her silence caused him to refocus on her. Still unaware of what he had said, he asked in confusion, "Is something wrong?"

"No," Danielle quickly answered, looking away. "Nothing's wrong."

They sat quietly for a few minutes, and Danielle continued, "Grant, I'm sorry I burst in on you and your family earlier today. I was so desperate I wasn't quite myself."

"Don't even worry about it," he assured her.

"I bet Tina *really* hates me now. And I did so try to be her friend."

Grant quickly said, "I don't think we have to worry about Tina anymore."

Looking intently at him, she asked, "What d'you mean?"

He sighed and leaned his head back against the chair. "I put her on the train to Boston today."

"Oh, I know you'll miss her . . . So she returned to start preparing for your wedding?"

Grant shook his head, "There's not going to be a wedding."

Danielle was shocked. "I'm sorry? What did you say?"

"That's right," Grant reiterated. "There's not going to be a wedding."

"Oh, goodness!" Danielle uttered.

In spite of the seriousness of the conversation, Grant smiled at her shock. Then her chatter began, "Well, you don't have to talk about it if you don't want to. It's nobody's business but yours anyway. You don't have to be embarrassed or explain anything to anybody if you don't want to . . . "

Grant gently touched her arm, "It's okay, Dani. I'm going to be fine."

"Sorry," she said, shrugging her shoulders, nervously. "I sometimes talk too much when I don't know exactly what to say."

Grant chuckled. "Sounds like my mother." He paused, then continued. "I thought I was so in love with Tina. When I first met her in Boston, I thought she was the most beautiful creature I'd ever seen. Of course, all the guys wanted to date her, so when she looked my way, I thought I was one lucky fellow."

He rubbed the back of his neck and stood up. "I had no doubts at all that I wanted to marry her. She seemed just perfect." He rose and started pacing. "Then when she showed up here in town, I might add with no advance notice, everything seemed to change. I became aware of things about her I'd never noticed before. Oh, yes, her clothes were the finest. Her hair was flawless. She was the perfect lady. But as I came to find out, not the perfect girl in demeanor."

Grant stopped pacing and sat back down. "I was offended at the way she treated my parents. She corrected my mom about treating Margarita too familiarly, she admonished my father several times, and treated Gabrielle as if she was nonexistent. I thought it was just because she was trying to adjust to a different environment. So, I pushed my qualms aside and decided to give her time. But, her behavior didn't improve. In fact, she got worse!"

He glanced at Danielle before continuing. "Sorry, this might be more information than you want to know."

Danielle leaned forward and said, "I don't mind at all. Sometimes it does a body good to talk things out."

He gave her a sideways smile. "You sure you're not just being nice?"

"Listen to you," she said. "You of all people ought to know just how nice I really am."

"Oh, yes, I'm aware of how nice you are!" Grant agreed. "Perhaps that's why I noticed Tina wasn't very nice." Then he quickly began again, "That morning in church when I was trying to introduce her to you and several others, she treated everyone with such disdain. It was so embarrassing! And then, when the good Lord started working on me about making things right with Him, she was flat-out rude. She talked disparagingly about God and how church was just for social climbers. I knew then, or perhaps God helped me figure out, that it was just not going to work."

He shook his head in disbelief. "She did so many offensive things that she boggled my mind. As my mother would say, 'things unbecoming to a lady.' So to get down to the last straw, at breakfast this morning she continued her inappropriate performance and I told her it was time to talk. She tried to tell me it was because she was unused to our ways. But if she refused to adapt even a little bit to the way things are here, I knew she wouldn't be willing to live as my wife anywhere else besides Boston."

Grant stretched out his legs and folded his arms behind his neck. "So this morning, I put her on the train back to Boston."

"Oh, dear!" Danielle said softly, "And then here comes another blubbering female to your door in need of help." She laid her hand gently on his arm. "I'm sorry I had to bother you at such a crucial time, Grant. I feel awful!"

"No need to feel bad, Dani," he said placing his hand over hers. "It's given me a chance to take my mind off my circumstances. So, you can just look at it as giving me an 'out.'"

Danielle smiled softly, liking the way he'd addressed her as "Dani" during their entire conversation. Then realizing he was not aware of how significant that was to her, she suppressed the rising emotions in her heart. They sat quietly, both lost in their own thoughts, not realizing that their hands were still clasped.

Grant awoke dazed. It took him a few moments to get his bearings and to remember where he was. He heard a slight rustling and whispering voices. He rubbed his eyes and glanced around the room. He then realized he had fallen asleep during the wee hours while keeping watch over Butch Johnson. He quickly stood and reached for the patient's wrist to check his pulse. He waited anxiously, and when he felt the slow, steady beat, he breathed a sigh of relief. Several times during the night he thought they had lost Mr. Johnson, but that slow steady beat seemed to rebound and gave Grant a slight hope he might just make it.

It was still dark outside, so it was difficult to see. Again, whispering entered his consciousness. He listened intently. Yes, he did hear whispering voices. He squinted in the darkness, trying to see who else was in the room. Then he slowly rose and walked to the other side of the bed. What he saw smote him with compassion. Danielle and her mother were on their knees by the bedside pouring out their hearts to God. He reverently bowed his head as well.

"I know, Lord, that you have all things in control. So that's why I'm asking you to help my daddy," Danielle prayed, with a quaver in her voice. "I know my dad has been far from a perfect man, but You know how diligently mom has prayed for him. She kept believing You would change him and still believes that. Now, I'm asking You, if it be Your will, raise my daddy up and heal him. But, Lord, if You don't want to heal him, at least give him a chance to repent so things will be well with his soul."

Grant's heart was heavy as he watched them. Both women continued to pray, unaware that Grant was praying as well.

Suddenly Grant heard a slight rustle. He quickly turned back to the bed and saw that Mr. Johnson was plucking at the bed sheets. He knelt down and reached for his stethoscope, but the hands had stilled. He listened and leaned forward to listen again. He could not detect a heartbeat! "Please, Lord," he uttered unconsciously.

33

AN AMAZING RECOVERY

Throwing his stethoscope aside, he injected digitalis, then placed both hands over the man's sternum and began pumping, hoping to stimulate his heart. Danielle rushed to his side and asked urgently. "What's wrong?" Positioning Mr. Johnson's body, he said, "I can't detect a heartbeat, and I need your help. You'll need to resuscitate him while I pump his chest. I've seen this work before, so I'm going to give it a try." Grant quickly gave her further instructions and then looked at her and asked, "Ready?" She nodded emphatically. In the background, Susie continued to pray earnestly. They worked for several minutes, and then Grant felt the patient's neck for a pulse. He shook his head negatively, and they started again. They worked diligently for several minutes trying to initiate some response. Just as they started to begin another set of counts, Butch gasped and opened his eyes. The glazed eyes of a father looked into the startled eyes of his daughter.

"Daddy?" she asked softly. "Daddy, can you hear me?"

He continued to just stare at her. Grant reached for his stethoscope once again and listened to the man's heart.

"Daddy, can you hear me?" Danielle asked again.

A very slow grin spread across Mr. Johnson features. He continued to stare at Danielle with the silly grin on his face.

"Daddy, are you all right?" Danielle asked, peering intently at him.

Then his gruff, raspy voice, responded, "Well, if you'd just give me a chance to answer!"

The squeal that came from Danielle's lip was a delight indeed. She leaned over and gave him a soft kiss on the check. "Oh, thank you, Lord!" she breathed.

Mrs. Johnson came over and held her husband's hand against her cheek. Grant listened to a strong, steady heartbeat through the stethoscope.

"Good," he declared. "Very good indeed." Then he leaned close and asked. "Mr. Johnson, how do you feel?"

It took several moments before Mr. Johnson could focus on Grant, "I'm not sure," he answered hesitantly. "First of all, I might could tell ya better if I knew who you was."

His comment brought some relieved laughter to the room. "I'm Grant Hayes, sir," Grant answered. "I'm a doctor."

"Oh," came the gruff response. "Why do I need a doctor?"

"Dad, you were thrown from a horse and were badly injured. I brought Dr. Hayes here so he could help you," she explained. "Do you remember anything?"

Looking at the ceiling, a tear rolled unexpectedly down Mr. Johnson's cheek. "I remember hearing someone praying," he answered shakily. He grimaced from pain as he reached up to wipe the tear away. He continued, "It was like I was walking down a dark, dark hall. Everything looked so black. I didn't want to go down that hall and tried to turn around. But something was pulling me forward." Mr. Johnson looked up at his wife. "I didn't want to go."

"It's okay, dear," comforted Mrs. Johnson. "You're here with me now," she answered, patting his hand.

"Some force kept pulling me forward down that hall. Pulling and pulling. Then just when I thought I didn't have the energy to fight against the force any more, I heard you praying," he was holding his wife's hand so tightly that his knuckles turned white. He looked into her eyes and more tears spilled over. "After all these years of telling you to shut up your praying, all of a sudden I wanted to hear you pray more than anything in the world. And you just kept on praying." Mr. Johnson pulled his wife's hand close to his chest. "If you hadn't been praying for me, I would've been pulled down that black, black hall to who knows where."

"Everything's fine now, dear," Mrs. Johnson said, delighted that her faith and prayers were finally coming to fruition.

Then Mr. Johnson looked at his daughter. "And you were praying too, Dani girl. How could you pray for me when I've been so mean to you?" he asked.

"Because I want my daddy to be saved," Danielle answered simply.

Tears again flooded his eyes. "After all these years of fighting your religion, I suddenly want to know all about it," he proclaimed. "I want to do whatever it takes to keep me from going down that dark hall." Then he reached for Danielle's hand. "Can the two of you ever forgive me for being such an ornery old scalawag?"

From the shining countenance on both women's faces, Grant knew beyond a shadow of doubt that they would freely forgive him. Butch Johnson refused to wait any longer to pray, so mother and daughter prayed with him until they led him to the Savior. As he received the spirit of God into his life, a haze came into the room. Grant had heard his mother speak of a glory cloud before, and this must be what she had talked about. Although Grant had been around church all his life, the presence of the Lord that entered the room that day was like nothing he had ever felt before.

Grant gathered his medical instruments as the Johnsons sat engrossed in the miracle that had just happened in their family. Danielle and her mother sat on either side of Mr. Johnson and they talked as they had not talked for years.

"Hey there, son," Mr. Johnson roared, looking over at Grant.

"Yes, sir?"

"Forgive me for being an old rude cowboy," he said, "but I failed to say thank you for saving my life."

"You're welcome, sir," Grant said, feeling the pleasure of what being a doctor is all about.

"Hey, did I hear Dani say your last name's Hayes?" he asked.

"Yes, sir."

"Well, ain't that something?" he said. "Saved by a Hayes, someone I've always despised." He quickly added, "Until I found forgiveness, that is. I think I could love anybody right now."

They all laughed, remembering the wonder they felt when they found the Lord.

"Mr. Johnson, you need to take it very easy for a while. Your body was pretty broken up and with a head injury like yours, it's important that you remain still."

"Now, look here, son," Mr. Johnson answered, "God performed a miracle on me and I'm going to be right as rain." His gaze bored into Grant's. "Although I feel like . . . " he paused. "Well what d'you know? I don't feel right using cuss words anymore," he said in amazement.

While Danielle and Mrs. Johnson looked uncertain, Grant chuckled. "Yes, it's amazing what God can do in our lives." He snapped his bag shut and said, "Well, I best be on my way. I think I'll go home and see if I can catch a bit of shuteye."

"You certainly deserve it, that's for sure," Danielle said, getting up from the bed. "I'll see you out."

"Thanks again, doc," Mr. Johnson said brusquely. "See you at church. I plan to be there with bells on." He laughed loudly. "Might better be there for sure yourself, doc, as several may suffer heart attacks when they see me darken the church door."

"I'll be there just in case, Mr. Johnson," Grant smilingly answered.

Danielle and Grant walked together to the front door and he motioned for her to go ahead of him out onto the veranda.

She sighed contentedly and exclaimed, "Isn't it beautiful?"

"Yes, it is," Grant agreed, watching her.

Danielle turned to him and with sincerity said, "Thank you so much for saving my dad's life, Grant. And I'll never forget that you shared this important time with our family."

"I won't forget either," Grant responded looking down into her happy face. "It's wonderful to see you so happy, Dani. I'm glad things have worked out well for you all."

"Yes, they have, thank the Lord." She raised her hands and exclaimed, "But an even greater miracle than his physical recovery is his change of heart. I can hardly believe it, even though I saw it with my own eyes."

"You'll enjoy renewing your acquaintance with your dad," Grant said.

"Oh, Grant, I'm so sorry! Here you are all tired and worn out and I just can't seem to shut up," Danielle said, placing her hand softly on his arm. "Please go home and get some sleep. I'll be thinking about you."

Grant glanced at the hand on his arm and then looked into her face. "You'll be thinking about me, you say?" he teased.

"I meant . . . I meant that I hope you get rested up," she answered uncertainly.

"Well, then," he said, still looking intently at her, "on that note I'll be on my way." Before she could answer, he walked down the steps, mounted his horse, and rode away without looking back.

She stared at his retreating back, unexplained feelings bombarding her heart.

34

A Changed Man

Grant fell onto his bed, thankful for the chance to lie down. He had spent a few minutes telling his folks of the miracle he had witnessed. They were so astonished when he described the transformation of Butch Johnson. He smiled, thinking of his mother's doubts about the man. "Now, you may think me a doubting Thomas," she had said, "but you don't know the man, or his family the way we do."

His father had responded, "Now, Kate dear, you shouldn't be so pessimistic. Don't you think God can perform the impossible?"

"Yes," she declared haughtily, "but the Johnsons' attitude toward the neighbors and townspeople has always been impossible. Just when I think they might be changing and I go out of my way to make overtures to them, they pull something sneaky and someone in my family ends up getting hurt. I just hope he doesn't send his riders over here looking for Grant saying he messed up on his doctoring or something."

"Oh, now, dear heart," his father said, grinning, "you must believe, just like the Bible tells us to do."

"Yes, but my faith seems to be on a par with Thomas's; I'll believe it when I see it!" Kate declared. Then noticing that Grant could barely hold his head up, she commanded, "Okay, young man, off to bed. You've had a rough time today, starting with breaking your nonexistent engagement and putting your snooty girlfriend on the train and then having to deal with our renegade neighbors."

"Mom!" Grant protested. "Please try to be a little kinder."

"All right," she agreed grudgingly. "Just because you ask me. Now off you go."

Grant sighed, glad to be home. He dropped off to sleep thinking of a pair of sparkling green eyes.

During the middle of the week, Grant returned to the Johnsons' to check on Mr. Johnson. The head of the house informed him in a kind but very firm manner that there was no need to come back as he was healing just fine with the help of the Lord. Grant graciously accepted his decision and told him if he needed anything to let him know. Before he left, Mr. Johnson thanked him again for saving his life. Grant was disappointed that Danielle was not home. Mrs. Johnson said she'd run into town for a few supplies and would be sorry she'd missed seeing him. After bidding them both good day, he walked back to his horse, wondering at his sharp feeling of disappointment.

Grant and Fred spent the remainder of the week working in the yard, doing chores his mom seemed intent on getting done. Grant knew his mother was really just trying to get his mind off things, and as usual, her remedy was keeping busy. Straightening to wipe his sweaty brow, he looked across at Fred and said, "So how're you enjoying your vacation thus far?"

"Oh, it's marvelous!" Fred said, raising his hands heavenward. "You know, I don't think I've enjoyed myself like this in a long time."

"I'm sure!" Grant said with chagrin.

"But I feel like my hard work will be rewarded when we're able to visit with the young ladies tomorrow," Fred said with a smile. "Now that ought to make any man happy."

"I wonder if you'd be so chipper if Sharon Russell hadn't sent word about the get-together tomorrow night," Grant said.

"Well, I might've had to give myself more of a pep talk if I didn't have that to look forward to," Fred admitted, "but I'll dwell on that get-together. And you, my friend, will be quite impressed with what I'm able to accomplish while doing this task assigned to us by the invincible Mrs. Hayes."

Grant laughed. "I'm sure I will."

Fred looked at his friend, "Now that's a good sound to hear," he said.

"What sound?"

"Your laughter," Fred answered. "I haven't heard that in several days."

Grant smiled. "Sorry. I know I've been a bit of a grouch, but I'll do better. I promise."

"I know you will," Fred said. "And I understand. You've been through a tough time. You had every right to be out of sorts."

Kate came out onto the porch, followed by Gabrielle. "So are you all through?" she asked.

"Not quite, Mom." Grant and Fred picked up the pace. "But we're getting there."

"Well, you better hurry, or you two won't get finished in time to go to the get-together tomorrow night because I'll ground you."

"*Yes, ma'am*! We'll have this done in no time, ma'am," Fred said, bowing dramatically.

"Aw," Gabrielle complained, "you all get to go to another social? How come I never get to go?"

"Just wait, little one," Fred said, winking at her. "You'll be going to socials before you know it and will be the prettiest one there."

Gabrielle giggled. "Really?"

Fred leaned over his shovel, resting his hands on the handle. "Yes, really."

Gabrielle giggled and gave him a wave before skipping back into the house, happy as a lark.

"You really have a way with the ladies, don't you?" Grant asked.

"You find that surprising?" Fred asked peevishly. "I just didn't get the chance to court the women in Boston because they didn't have eyes for anyone but you when you were in the room.

Out here, well, I'm in a whole new element. The women actually notice me. And you know, my friend, I'm rather enjoying it."

Grant smiled. "Glad you like it here."

"Oh, I do. The women are much nicer here. *Everyone's* nicer here," Fred announced.

"That's our Texas hospitality," Grant commented.

"Well, I like it," Fred said. He dug for a few more minutes, then added, "It's not only the women I'm looking forward to seeing tomorrow, but I'm also looking forward to the church service. This newfound walk with God has made me a changed man."

"Yes, I'm not the only one who's easier to get along with," Grant teased.

"Let's just say, I'm glad I came to Texas." They worked for several minutes, and then Fred asked. "So how are you really doing, friend?"

"I'm fine, just fine," Grant answered.

"So you feel you made the right decision about calling it quits with Tina?" he persisted.

"Yes, I do," Grant responded. "Of course, thinking she'd be my wife and finding out otherwise is unsettling. But I feel I did the right thing."

"I too feel you did," Fred said. "I try to imagine what a shock it would be to think you knew Tina and then find out she was entirely different and you loved only an illusion."

They continued working and then Fred asked again. "So do you think you're over her?"

Grant paused reflectively and said, "You know, Fred, I don't feel at all devastated; in fact, it feels more like being let out of a jail cell. I realize that what I felt for her wasn't love at all."

"Wow!" Fred said. "That's something."

"Yes, it is," Grant agreed. "It must seem strange to others that I'm not more upset . . . I mean I feel bad about hurting her, but I don't think it'll take long for Miss Tina to recover. She'll just choose the next gent in line as the new fiancé."

"If that's the case, I'll venture to say I always thought Tina treated you like a servant. Most everyone saw it but you. He paused. "I admit she was quite a looker, but there's so much more to a relationship than beauty. My mother used to say that 'beauty is only skin deep,' and with Miss Tina that was definitely true."

"Why didn't you say something?" Grant asked.

"I didn't want to lose your friendship. You were so taken with her that I felt you might tell me to get lost," Fred explained.

"Well, we're past that now," Grant said. "You know, Fred, I'm concerned now because I'm not certain if I know what love is. I mean, how will I know if I love someone else?"

"Oh, I think you will," Fred assured him. "If you long to be with the lady, enjoy her company, love talking to her, and most of all think she's the most beautiful thing in the world, then you'll know."

"Well, my friend, that's pretty sage advice from one who admits to never having been in love," Grant said.

"Like I said, Texas has been good for me," he answered. The two friends laughed together and went back to their job assignments.

Sunday morning dawned brilliantly. The Hayes family enjoyed a delicious breakfast together and hurried to finish getting ready for church. Everyone was in good spirits. Much conversation and laughter could be heard as they climbed into their buggies to attend church. Gabrielle again asked to ride with Fred in the two-seater, so Grant climbed into the back of the other buggy to ride with his parents.

"Ahhh, if the beautiful sunshine is an indication of anything, this should prove to be wonderful day," Kate said, savoring the splendor of the morning. Alexander glanced back over his shoulder to catch his son's eye. "She always makes us feel good, doesn't she, son?"

"Yes, Dad, she always does," Grant agreed. The horses clipped along at a steady pace and they arrived to find others gathering as well for the morning service. Grant jumped down and assisted his mother. They walked arm in arm into the small sanctuary. He led her to an empty pew and paused to allow Gabrielle and Fred in as well. In a few moments, his father also joined them.

They were waiting for the service to begin when there was a rustling among the congregation. Grant heard a few gasps and turned around to see what was going on. His eyes met those of Danielle as she walked slowly into the building on her father's arm. Grant nodded at her reassuringly and she gave him a radiant smile of thanks. You could hear a pin drop; the silence was profound as the Johnson family walked down the aisle. Mrs. Johnson walked to a pew with Daniel and Danielle, and Mr. Johnson followed.

"Good morning, all God's people," Pastor Russell greeted, drawing attention back to the platform. "What a beautiful day to serve the Lord!"

"Amen!" the audience responded.

"Let's worship Him today in the beauty of holiness," he declared. "Take a hymnal and let's rejoice in the Lord together." Everyone sang exuberantly and praised the Lord with their voices. Following the song, Pastor Russell asked everyone to be seated.

"Do you believe God can work miracles?" he asked.

"Amen!" the congregation responded.

"Well, I really do today," Pastor Russell continued. "And I have something exciting to share with you. Butch Johnson has asked to address you for a few minutes this morning and I hope you'll receive what he says. So, Brother Johnson, please come forward."

Daniel and Danielle helped their father rise from the pew. Much whispering and sounds of surprise could be heard as they made their way down the aisle. Grant looked down the row at his mom and almost laughed at the expression on her face. Danielle glanced down at him when they reached the Hayes pew and quickly looked away.

Butch Johnson turned to his kids and shook his head, indicating he did not want their help, and then slowly ascended the two steps leading to the platform with the assistance of his makeshift crutches. He leaned on the pulpit and then began in his gruff voice, "Well, good morning. As I told the young doc here," he pointed at Grant, "he needed to be here today 'cause of the heart attacks some of you might have when I showed up today." Scattered uncomfortable laughter. "Well, I don't blame you for feelin' the way you do. I'll be the first to admit I've been a mean old codger, and I want to tell you all I'm sorry I've done wrong to most of you."

Mr. Johnson paused, emotion evident on his face. "I had a close call this week and I was plum scared out of my mind. Old Blackie spooked and I got thrown off of the wagon. I got hurt real bad and while I's unconscious, I had quite a journey." He rubbed his head. "I could feel a strong force pulling me down a long dark tunnel and although I didn't want to go and tried not to go, it kept draggin' me. I thought all was lost and then . . . " his voice broke and he bowed his head, rubbing his eyes. "Then I heard my wife praying." He paused again, trying to swallow his emotion. "Her prayers brought me back from the dark and I saw for the first time the kind of man I was . . . how other people saw me . . . how God saw me."

All eyes were riveted on him, and there was not a rustle or a whisper in the place. He straightened his stance and looked straight back at the audience. "I asked the preacher when he came to see me if I could speak today and he kindly let me. I want to say that I owe every one of ya'll an apology. I spent so much time drunk that I really don't know who all I've been mean to. So, I felt like church was a good place to start to make things right." He looked more intently at the people. "I'm sorry I wronged many of you here today. Please forgive me." Then he turned and loOkayed straight at the Hayes pew. "And I want to make a public apology to the Hayes family. I owe you the biggest apology of all for the way my family and I have acted toward you through the years. I crave your forgiveness." He waited, and Alexander Hayes acknowledged the family's acceptance by nodding his head. "That means a lot to me. Thanks from the bottom of my heart."

"Now I want to say a special thanks to the doc. He came to my house even after I'd held a rifle to his back and warned him not to come on my property again. And in spite of my meanness, he went out of his way to stay through the night with me and my family and he saved my life. Now that's a real Christian. Thanks, doc." Applause broke out all over the building and the congregation stood. Mr. Johnson finally held up his hand for silence.

"I want to say thank you to my wife and daughter who prayed God would change my life. Suzanne . . . " his voice broke and he could barely utter the words, " . . . believed I'd change and she never stopped loving me in spite of my actions. Love you, Suzanne, and thank God you never gave up on me." He paused, awkwardly wiping his tears. "Just a few more things and I'll get out of the way so the preacher can take back his pulpit. Since I've found my way into the kingdom, the Lord has delivered me from my desire to drink." The congregation applauded. He held up his hand once again to quiet them. "God broke the mean streak in me, thanks to His redeemin' power, and by His help, my family, 'stead of bein' remembered for pure meanness, will be remembered for kindness." Mr. Johnson peered into the upturned faces. "Thanks for listening. I just pray that the change in my life will affect others in this town of Progress."

There was not a dry eye in the house as everyone sat down and Butch Johnson descended the stairs with the help of his children He started back down the aisle but stopped at the Hayes pew. Alexander stood up and the two men clasped hands. Then Alexander reached out and hugged the changed man. To everyone's utter amazement, Mr. Johnson laid his head on Alexander's shoulder as his sobs filled the place. Kate stood up and reached out to place her hand on Mr. Johnson's shoulder, tears flowing from her eyes as well. Grant reached out and grasped Danielle's hand as their parents absolved the jealousy, the hurt, and the conflict that had been so much a part of their lives. The spirit of the Lord moved in the sanctuary in such a powerful way that there was no need for further words.

35

AN UNEXPECTED ATTACK

"Come on, man," Fred shouted from the bottom of the stairs. "You're keeping the ladies waiting."

Grant appeared at the top, "Well, well, we are a bit impatient this evening, aren't we? And, as far as keeping the ladies waiting, that's your problem, not mine."

"Well, well yourself!" Fred exclaimed, eyeing Grant's crisply ironed black denim pants and turquoise-colored shirt. "I must say you're looking quite dapper this evening."

"No more than usual," Grant countered, placing a black Stetson on his head.

"I beg to differ with you. Perhaps I could arrive first so they'll at least notice me," Fred argued.

Grant laughed, "Oh, Fred, you're incorrigible. Now can we go? Your banter is keeping the ladies."

"Yes, let's," Fred responded, slapping his friend on the back as they walked out the door together. They mounted their horses, and Fred asked, "Care for a race?"

"On the contrary, I'd prefer an easy, slow ride, giving me time to savor this beautiful evening," Grant countered.

"If I didn't know better, I'd think you were becoming quite the English gentleman," Fred teased as they started out.

"You've made an indelible imprint on my life," Grant said, shrugging.

Fred laughed and they continued sparring until they arrived at the church social. A friendly fire and tables laden with food welcomed them. Sharon Russell noticed their arrival and quickly excused herself from a group to greet them.

"Hello there," Fred said, bending to kiss her hand.

Sharon giggled and blushed becomingly. "Oh, you do go on, Fred Thomas! Now behave yourself and come join the others."

Grant smiled at the obvious attraction between the two. He followed them as they made their way to join the others. The group acknowledged their arrival and much laughter and easy conversation began. Several young ladies came to speak to Grant, and Fred caught his eye and winked. Grant politely conversed a few moments and then moved outside the circle. He looked around for Danielle and didn't see her anywhere. He noticed Daniel standing at one of the tables and made his way to speak to him.

"Hey, Daniel," Grant said. "How are you?"

Daniel looked up, and said hesitantly, "Uh, I'm doing okay, I guess." Then he paused, endeavoring to be polite and added, "And how're you?"

"I'm doing well," Grant answered. "Is Dani here tonight?"
Daniel looked around, "Yeah, she's here somewhere. I haven't seen her in the last little bit. She may've gone back into the church to get some more supplies or something."

"Thanks!" Grant said. "I'll head that direction. See you later."

At that moment, Danielle appeared in the doorway of the church, her arms laden with dishes. The evening shadows and the flickering fire enhanced her beauty. Grant caught his breath and then quickly ran to assist her.

"Hey, there," he said. "Trying to be Miss Hercules?"

Lost in thought, his sudden appearance gave her a start. The dishes started to slide and Grant reached out to stop the impending disaster. They worked a few minutes to straighten the stack.

"Sorry," Grant said when everything was again in place. "I didn't mean to startle you. I wanted to help you, not cause chaos."

Danielle met his eyes and then looked quickly away. "Oh, that's okay. I should've been paying more attention."

Grant frowned slightly at her reaction. Then he said, "Here let me at least carry part of your load since I almost made you lose it all."

Danielle gave a slight smile, but still would not meet his eyes. "I appreciate it," she said. "I was just trying to help Sharon get everything together so she wouldn't have so much to do."

"That's mighty kind of you, ma'am," Grant drawled, taking the majority of the items.

Danielle giggled, and Grant breathed a sigh of relief. "Are you all right, Dani?" he asked.

She glanced his way again and quickly looked away. "Oh, yes, I'm fine. Perhaps just a little tired after doctoring Daddy all week."

"I'm sure you are," Grant said sympathetically. "That was a very brave thing he did this morning in church, wasn't it?"

"Yes, it was," Danielle responded "I can hardly believe that after all this time, Dad has made such a turnaround." They walked cautiously to the tables and as Grant handed her the dishes, she arranged them expertly. "I mean, it's a miracle! He can't seem to do enough for Mama and is constantly saying, 'I love you, Dani girl!' It's been a dream come true for our family."

"That's great!" Grant answered. "Well, if anyone deserves it, you certainly do."

Danielle continued working and answered, "That's kind of you, Grant. I don't feel I deserve anything."

Her quiet demeanor still puzzled Grant, and he asked again, "You sure you're all right?"

"Oh, yes," she answered, waving her hand over the food. "I'm just fine."

"Well, well, what have we here? A private rendezvous?" Todd Herrington declared, placing his arm around Danielle's shoulder. "You know, darling, you shouldn't stand around talking intimately with another man. I don't like it one bit."

A moment of silence descended on the whole party. "Todd, please!" Danielle pleaded. "You've been drinking. Why don't you just go home and sober up?"

"Well, what better place to sober up than the house of the Lord?" his cackling laughter pierced the stillness of the night.

"Tell you what, my lovely," Todd said, swaying on his feet and getting right in Danielle's face, "why don't you just come with me and tuck me into bed like a good little girl."

"Todd, let go of me!" Danielle said, fighting off his advances.

Grant grabbed Todd's arm. "I don't think the lady's interested in your overtures," he said with steel in his voice.

"You stay out of this, city boy," Todd retorted. "This is none of your business."

"Oh, now that's where you're wrong," Grant said, placing himself between Todd and Danielle.

"Oh, yeah?" Todd said in a threatening manner.

"Yeah!" Grant said. He saw Daniel and a few others draw closer, but he held up his hand, letting them know he had everything under control. "Now you can either leave quietly or I'm sure my friends and I can forcibly make you leave. And we really don't want to do that."

Todd tried to stare Grant down, but Grant stood firm, returning his glare. Todd sneered, "You're Mr. Winner, all right. I mean, you just lost the most gorgeous female I've ever seen. That was sheer stupidity. So just because you lost *your* woman doesn't give you rights to *my* woman."

"That's enough, Todd," Grant said. "You've no right to be here in your condition." The two glared at each other. Then Todd, realizing he was at a disadvantage, staggered around Grant and reached to grabbed roughly at Danielle's arm, but she managed to pull away. "This isn't over, my sweet," he sneered. "You're going to be mine."

Grant took hold of Todd's arm and started walking him away from the group.

"I'm going!" Todd yelled, pulling out of Grant's grasp. "This is a bunch of do-gooders doing nothing." He staggered away into the darkness, his derisive laughter still echoing.

Grant quickly turned to Danielle and asked, "Are you all right?"

She smiled softly, "Seems you've been asking me that a lot this evening."

Grant paused, and then smiled. "Yes, it seems I have. Let me take a look at your arm." Realizing everyone had gathered around, he turned and reassured them, "I think the creature has fled into the night." Laughter relieved the tense atmosphere. Daniel came up to them. "You all right, sis?" he asked.

"Yes, Daniel," she answered. "I'm okay. Now go have a good time."

Grant looked at her forearm and commented, "Looks like the man caused some bruising."

"Oh, it's nothing," Danielle reassured him.

"Well, when you get home, it wouldn't hurt to put some ice on it," Grant persisted.

"Always the doctor," Danielle managed a tight smile.

"I just can't help myself," Grant said apologetically. Then their eyes locked for a moment

Danielle broke the gaze first, and uncertainly said, "Uh, I better get the rest of the stuff out here."

"Need help?" Grant asked, still shaken by the encounter.

"No, no," Danielle assured. "Thank you, but I believe I can handle the rest of it." She gave him a quick smile and walked off toward the church. Grant watched her for a moment and then turned to join the others.

"Hey, chum," Fred said, coming to meet him. "The battle's over, huh?"

"Seems so."

Just then, a piercing scream from inside the church interrupted their conversation.

36

A SURPRISE REALIZATION

Grant and Fred stared at each other only a second before they both rushed toward the church, the others following in their wake.

A few low lights were burning inside, but he didn't see Danielle. He rushed toward the back door of the church and burst through it. What he saw made his heart stop. "No!" he yelled, racing toward the two struggling figures.

"Please," Danielle pleaded. "Stop!"

Grant grabbed the offender and with an uncanny strength lifted him off his feet. The leering face of Todd Herrington met his gaze. He literally threw him across the churchyard and charged toward him. Everyone stood still in shock.

"You scumbag," Grant yelled, pulling Todd to his feet. "Let me show you what it's like to be treated roughly." He pulled his fist back to hit him, when someone stilled his arm.

"Hey, friend," Fred said calmly, "he's not worth it."

It took Grant several seconds to gain control of his anger. He looked back at Fred as if he did not recognize him. "Grant," Fred said again, "let him go. He's not worth the effort." Grant then turned to Todd and found him cowering before him. Grant then dropped him unceremoniously on the ground. "Get out!" he declared. "And if I find you bothering Dani again, you won't know what hit you."

Todd slowly staggered to his feet, sobered by the rough treatment. Looking frightened at the group gathered before him, he raced off into the night.

Grant quickly turned and made his way back to Danielle. She had managed to stand up, but one sleeve of her dress was torn almost completely off, and she was endeavoring to cover herself. When her frightened eyes met his, his heart almost stopped. He stood in front of her, shielding her from the group. "Fred," he said quietly, "see if you can find me a jacket of some sort and get everyone back to the party. I think she'd prefer some privacy right now."

Fred nodded reassuringly. "Sure, pal," he said, "I'll take care of it." He turned and immediately announced, "Okay, everyone, everything's fine. Let's don't let that scalawag ruin the fine party. Come along!" Fred herded everyone back to the churchyard.

Grant did not turn around immediately. "How are you, Dani?" he asked quietly in her direction. "I need to make sure you're okay, but I don't want to embarrass you. Would it be okay if I took a look?"

"Yes," she said, softly crying.

He turned and first of all, took her trembling hand in his. "You're going to be fine," he said reassuringly. "I don't think Todd will bother you again."

Grant lifted her arm and noticed additional bruising and a few scrapes oozing blood. He pushed tenderly on some areas along her arms and then took her chin in his hand. There was a graze along the right cheek, but on the whole she seemed to be okay except that her eyes were still pooling and she was trembling.

"Here, old chap," Fred said, coming up behind him. "Sharon found a jacket inside the church."

"Thanks much," Grant said, reaching back to take it, and placing it around Danielle.

"Do you need anything else?" he asked.

"If I could find a buggy," he asked, "would you like me to take you home?"

The kindness of his voice made her start crying. She simply said, "Yes, please."

"Will do," Fred said.

Grant continued to talk soothingly to Danielle and before long Fred returned with the information that he had obtained the loan of Pastor Russell's buggy and it was ready and waiting for them at the front of the church.

"So, are you up to walking to the buggy?" Grant asked.

"Yes, but please," she raised her chin, "I don't want anyone to think Todd Herrington won this round or any other." Grant smiled at her stubborn resolve, glad to see her normal behavior return.

"Okay, then, my lady," Grant said, offering her his arm. "Shall we make our final appearance?"

"Oh, yes," she said softly. She grimaced when she reached for his arm, but quickly covered the action. They walked slowly around to the front of the church and everyone gathered around them.

"Are you okay, Danielle?" Sharon asked, looking kindly at her.

"Yes, I'm just fine," Danielle reassured her. Then she said to all her friends, "Thank you, everyone, for your concern. After a bit of rest, I'll be as right as rain."

Everyone wished them well as Grant tenderly helped her into the buggy and after getting her settled, ran around to the other side to take his place.

"Ready?" he asked her.

"Yes," she said, but the shakes and tears had come back. "I guess I'm not as strong as I thought."

"After an encounter like you had, that's only normal. You're experiencing mild shock, so we've got to keep you warm. Encounters like this affect not only your body but your mind as well," Grant explained as they started off.

She giggled in spite of everything. "Well, it's nice to know I have an affected mind."

Grant looked down in admiration at her. "I'm glad to see your present circumstances haven't affected your humor."

She yawned. "That's one thing I hope is never affected," she said sleepily. "I always want to have humor in my life . . . "

Grant felt her head fall onto his shoulder. He looked down to find that she had fallen asleep. He took the reins with one hand and gently placed his arm around her to make her ride more comfortable. As the horse clipped-clopped through the night, Grant held Danielle with tender loving care.

He marveled at his rage when he had wanted to beat Todd to a pulp. To think anyone would harm Danielle was beyond what he would tolerate. It made him want to do everything in his power to protect her from anything that might harm her.

Then it hit him. He loved this beautiful young lady beyond distraction! He jerked unconsciously, which made Danielle move as well. He looked down at her and, thankfully, she settled back down.

He leaned his head against her soft blond curls. He loved her feisty manner and he loved their banter. He loved her humor and he loved her resilience. In fact, there were so many things about her that he loved, he could not name them all.

However, he remembered her manner this evening. She had been acting differently and he wasn't certain why. He sighed. Oh, well, he would think about all of that later. Right now he just wanted to get her home to safety and then he would make arrangements to have a talk with her when she was better. He chuckled silently, *And to think I was worried about being able to know if I loved someone.*

37

A Heart to Heart Talk

Full dark had fallen by the time Grant reached home. Because of the cloud cover, the light of the moon and the stars did not light his way. He was still deep in thought as he entered the house. A soft light in the parlor caught his attention and he smiled, thinking his mother had kept a lamp burning for him. He walked in to extinguish the burning lamp, and found his mother lying on the couch fast asleep. He shook his head and went to wake her.

"Mom," he said softly, patting her shoulder. "Mom, you need to go to bed."

Slowly she opened her eyes and stretched, "Grant, is that you?"

"Yes, Mom," Grant answered patiently.

Then she sat up and was instantly alert, "Are you all right?"

Grant laughed. "I think you could win first place in a waking-up contest. The second your eyes open, you come instantly awake."

"I stayed up to find out what's going on. Fred came home alone and said there'd been some kind of accident with Danielle and that you had to see her home. He said you'd tell me all about it when you got home, so I decided to wait up for you."

"Just like dear Fred to leave me to explain," he said, sitting down on the settee by his mom. "Todd Herrington showed up drunk at the church social tonight and began to menace

Danielle. We sent him on his way, and I thought the incident was over when we heard Danielle scream. We all rushed through the church and out the back to find he was, he was . . ." Grant paused.

"Yes?" Kate said, leaning forward.

Grant looked addled, and then he shook his head, as if to clear his mind. "Sorry," he said, "I can't seem to get it out of my mind."

"Well, then what happened?" she asked.

"Todd was holding her roughly and pawing at her. By the time I pulled him away, he had roughed her up pretty badly," Grant explained. "I hated to see her treated that way."

"I can imagine!" Kate explained.

"She let me check her bruises, and then she decided she wanted to go home, so I borrowed the Russell's buggy and took her home," he concluded, still deep in thought.

"Is there something wrong, son?" his mother asked, recognizing an underlying distraction.

"Well, while I was taking her home, I came to a startling realization," he said. Then he looked at his mother. "I love her, Mom," he simply said.

Kate sat quietly for a moment, and then smiled the way Grant always liked to see her smile. "You don't say!" she exclaimed.

Grant looked at her in surprise. "You mean that doesn't upset you?" he asked incredulously.

"Well, it might have a few days ago, but after what happened in church this morning, I could probably get used to the idea," Kate responded.

Grant laughed with relief. "You never fail to surprise me, Mom. I thought for sure you'd chastise me on why in the world I can't seem to find the right woman. And yet, here you are, smiling at me when I tell you that I think I love the daughter of one of your least favorite people."

"Yes," Kate said calmly. "God does work miracles, doesn't he?"

Grant burst into laughter, and then quickly covered his mouth when his mother glared at him.

"Shush!' she admonished. "You're going to wake the whole household." Then she took his hand, "Grant, I admit we've had great difficulties with the Johnson family. But just the few times I've been around Danielle, I liked the girl. She's amiable and polite and seems quite articulate."

"Well, I never!" Grant said in disbelief.

"I admit that I'll have some difficulty adjusting to the cranky old codger, but seeing how the power of God has changed him, anything is possible. God can help me to get along with him." Kate declared grudgingly.

They laughed together and sat quietly for a few moments in companionable silence. Then Kate said, "You know, I've always cared for Susie Smith from the minute I first saw her in my schoolroom. She was pretty, quiet, respectful, and so kind to everyone. You know, Grant, I should've considered the whole Johnson situation, instead of judging everyone by Butch and his sisters. And I should've been more considerate of Danielle instead of automatically assuming she was like her dad. I should just as well have assumed she might be like her mom."

"So I take it you won't mind me marrying the young lady in question?" Grant asked.

"No, I don't think I'll mind at all," Kate said patting his hand. Then she added slyly, "Anyone would be better than that Tina girl!"

"Okay, okay!" Grant said, holding his hands up in defeat. "I just wish you wouldn't keep reminding me of my shortcomings."

Kate giggled, "I'm just teasing you, dear." She hugged him close. "I love you, son, and more than anything in the world I want you to be happy."

Grant hugged her back and said, "I love you too, Mom. Your's and Dad's approval means everything to me."

"Then as Mr. Darcy advised Mr. Bingley, 'Then go to it!" Kate declared.

Grant threw his head back and laughed, and then quickly tried to cover his outburst. "Always coming up with advice from your favorite book!" Then he teasingly said, "But I believe I'll wait until the morrow to approach the subject with the young lady in question."

"I hope the young lady returns your affection."

Grant became serious as well. "So do I, Mom. I'm not quite certain of her feelings, but I hope to hear her say she loves me too."

"There you go, then!" Kate encouraged. "Now off to bed so that you'll be persuasive and beguiling."

The morning sun peeked over the horizon and flooded Grant's bedroom with light. On this particular morning, he was not gradually and slowly getting ready as was his normal mode. In fact, it was quite the opposite. He was, in his grandfather's words, "up and at it." He smiled, remembering his conversation with his mother when he arrived home last night. This morning he could rival her for the fastest waking-up person in the west.

His heart beat with anticipation and he felt excited about what the day might bring. He spent some time praying and reading his Bible. He wanted to seek God before he made his way to the Johnsons' Ranch. At about mid-morning, he felt he'd made his peace with God about the situation at hand.

Grant descended the stairs and found his father in the study surrounded by legal tomes and scattered papers.

"Good morning, son," Alexander said. "I was on my way to check on you since you failed to honor us with your presence at breakfast."

"I apologize that I missed the meal," Grant said, "but I'm just not very hungry this morning."

"Yes, your mom shared some of last night's conversation with me," Alexander said.

"I should've talked to you as well, Dad," Grant apologized.

"Oh no, my boy," Alexander assured him. "Your mom is usually better at giving advice about the romance side of things than I am." Then he came forward and grasped his shoulder. "I wish you the best, son. I remember how I felt when I finally decided to approach your mother. Although I believed she had feelings for me, I wasn't certain."

"Yes, sir," Grant agreed. "It's a step of faith on my part as well."

"All I can say is that the young lady has the chance of a lifetime to be with the finest young man anywhere," Alexander declared.

"Thanks, Dad," Grant said, shaking his father's hand. "And on that note, I'll be off to seek my future."

"Things will work out just fine, son," Alexander assured him, as he followed him out onto the veranda. Raising his hand in farewell, Grant rode away.

38

FINDING TRUE LOVE

Deep in thought and trying to form the right words in his mind, he arrived more quickly at the Johnson ranch than he realized. All seemed quiet as Grant walked onto the veranda and knocked on the door. He heard some movement inside and finally Mrs. Johnson opened the door. Her face lit up when she saw him.

"Dr. Hayes, I mean, Grant! What a surprise!" she exclaimed. "Won't you come in?"

Grant removed his hat, and said, "Thank you, ma'am."

"Who is it, Suzanne?" Butch's voice bellowed from the living room.

Mrs. Johnson grinned at him, and whispered, "He's a changed man, but he still has the same roaring voice." Then she led Grant into the living room. "It's Grant Hayes, dear."

"Wonderful! Come on in, doc, and have a seat," he invited.

"Thank you. I hope you're doing well," he said politely.

"Couldn't be better," declared Mr. Johnson. "And what can we do for you, doc?"

"Well, I was wondering if Danielle was home," he explained.

"As a matter of fact, she left about an hour ago," Mr. Johnson explained. "By the way, thank you for coming to her rescue last night."

"I second that!" Mr. Johnson roared, having never learned the art of modulating his voice. "Here I am all stoved up and can't take care of that young upstart myself."

"Now, dear," Mrs. Johnson said calmly. "You must remember your new salvation prohibits such action."

"Yeah, I know, but in this instance, the Lord might just forgive me."

"Just ignore him, Grant. He's a bit out of sorts this morning," Mrs. Johnson said.

"No, I'm not!" Mr. Johnson argued. "It's just my righteous indignation riled up! I read in the Bible it's perfectly okay to feel this way."

They laughed at his interpretation. "Anyway," Grant continued. "You say Danielle left about an hour ago."

"Yes. She said she needed some time to herself, so she packed a picnic lunch and went to her favorite hiding place," Mrs. Johnson explained.

"Do you think she'd mind me invading her favorite hiding place?" Grant asked. "I just wanted to check on her to see if she's doing okay."

"I don't think she'll mind," Mrs. Johnson said. "In fact, it would probably do her a world of good to have some companionship."

"Good," Grant said. "Then if you could direct me to where she is . . . " Mrs. Johnson and Grant went out onto the porch.

"Certainly. About a mile from here," she pointed, "is a grove of trees clustered around Dani's beloved pond. You can't miss it; those are the only trees in these fields."

"Okay, that sounds simple enough," Grant said. Then he turned to Mr. Johnson, who had come to the door. "I trust you'll take care of yourself, sir."

"I will," Mr. Johnson agreed. "And you remember one thing, boy. You're always welcome in our home."

"I appreciate that, sir," he responded. "Now I'll get out of your way." Grant lifted his hat in their direction before placing it back on his head. "Good day to you both!"

Grant mounted his horse and headed in the direction Mrs. Johnson had indicated, marveling at the change in Mr. Johnson. A few days ago he'd held a rifle to Grant's back because he dared set foot on Johnson land. Now he vowed Grant was welcome any time. He rode for approximately a mile and just as Mrs. Johnson had said, a cluster of trees appeared.

Grant carefully guided his horse through the trees. In just a few moments, he came upon Danielle looking his way with fear-filled eyes.

"Oh, my goodness!" she exclaimed breathlessly. "You scared me to death."

Grant dismounted and came toward her. "I'm so sorry. That wasn't my intention at all."

"Oh, don't mind me!" Danielle said. "I'm still a bit jumpy from last night." She looked questioningly up at him. "Are you just out riding?" she asked.

"No," Grant said. "As a matter of fact, I came looking for you."

"In that case," Danielle said, "won't you please join me?"

"Thank you, ma'am," Grant replied, surveying the picnic fare. "My, you've laid out quite a spread here, lady."

Danielle had spread a beautiful blue-and-green quilt on the ground in the shade. On it sat a plate of chicken salad sandwiches, a bowl of strawberries, and a tray of cream puffs. To the side of all of this was a crystal pitcher of lemonade, dripping moisture from the ice inside. The pond sparkled in the noonday sun.

"Yes, sir," Danielle said, fanning herself. "I felt I needed some down time and decided to pack a nice peaceful lunch."

"It looks delicious, but I can hardly fathom how a small lady such as you could consume so much food."

"Sir, are you hinting that you'd like a few morsels?"

"As a matter of fact, yes, I am," Grant said, laughing.

"Since you asked in such a gentlemanlike manner, here's a plate. Help yourself."

Danielle handed him a crystal plate and poured him a glass of lemonade.

"This is nice," Grant commented as he ate, savoring the food, the breeze, and the lovely company.

"Yes, this is my favorite spot," Danielle said, leaning back on her hands and looking up at the sky. "Whenever things used to get rough at home, I knew I could come here and find relief if only for a short time."

"I can see why," Grant agreed. "The pond is so peaceful and the trees provide a cool shade."

"Ummm," Danielle answered, with closed eyes. "The peace and quiet help to erase the stress."

Grant was unaware he was staring at Danielle, mesmerized by her beauty, until he saw she had opened one eye and peaked at him.

"You're awfully quiet. Is something wrong?" she asked. "Do I have a spot of cream on my face?"

Grant reddened, embarrassed that she caught him staring at her. "No, nothing's on your face, Dani," he said quietly. Then sensing something different about the intensity of his gaze, she asked again, "Are you sure there isn't something wrong?"

Grant stood up abruptly and turned his back to her. "Yes, as a matter of fact, something *is* wrong." He turned to face her and at that precise moment saw the color leave her face. Immediately he fell to one knee by her side. "I've frightened you and that certainly was not my intention." She continued to look at him uncertainly with huge eyes. He rubbed his thumb over the top of her hand. "I'm making a mess of things. Perhaps I'd better start over.

"First of all, I'm not upset with you. I'm just having a bit of difficulty expressing my feelings," Grant paused and settled himself more comfortably on the ground beside her, still holding her hand.

"I realized last night, Miss Danielle Johnson, that I love you beyond what I could ever imagine." At her quick intake of breath, he talked faster, "Now I know it's probably too soon to say that and I know it's probably coming as a complete surprise to you, but I find I can no longer hide my feelings." She continued to stare disbelievingly at him and he talked even faster, "But if you could just give me a chance, I think you could come to love me too. I won't rush you or force you to make any declaration. I just want to be around you and show you how deeply I care for you."

Still staring at him, but at last finding her voice, she croaked, "I can't do that!"

Grant's heart sank. "I'm sorry?" he asked, in a stressed voice.

Danielle swallowed and said, "I just don't think I can do that."

Grant looked at her in silence. "Oh . . . " He tried to hide his disappointment.

Her voice stronger now, she continued, "Grant, I don't think I can love you any more . . . because I've loved you to distraction as long as I can remember. So much that it hurts."

Grant caught his breath and then before she could say anything else, he wrapped her in his arms, muttering "Dani, Dani," over and over. "Oh, my love," he exclaimed.

She reveled in his tender expressions of love. "I've always dreamed of sweeping some man off his feet, and I think that just happened! This is a dream come true!"

He settled her in the circle of his arms and said, "A dream come true, you say? Why don't you tell me about it and boost my ego since you almost made me pass out from your 'I can't do that' statement."

She giggled and laid her head on his shoulder. "I had a crush on you in school and was heartbroken when you went away to Boston. Then when we met on the train, all those feelings flared up again. I thought all hope was lost when Tina arrived in town and I then decided to do my best to get over you. Even after you told me about her leaving, I still didn't think you considered me anything but a friend. So, I gave myself quite a talking to after Sunday service and vowed to stop my flirting and quell the friendly banter we enjoyed because it made me love you even more."

"So that's why you acted like you did at the party, then? Kind of distant and refusing to look me in the eye?" Grant questioned.

"Yes, I thought it would let you know that I didn't expect anything," Danielle responded.

"I'm glad we got that all straightened out," Grant said emphatically.

She sighed happily. "So what's next, Dr. Hayes?"

Grant kissed the top of her head, "Well, I haven't got that worked out yet, Dani . . . "

She interrupted dreamily. "I just love to hear you call me 'Dani.' Only my family calls me that."

"Well, get used to it," he said authoritatively. Then he continued, "I'm not certain what I, or rather, we'll do next. I need to finish up my residency and that means another year in Boston."

"I'd love to see Boston," she sighed.

"And I'm sure Boston would like to see you as well, Dani girl," Grant answered, peering down at her and getting lost in the love shining in her eyes. "You're making it difficult for me to keep my mind on the subject at hand," he scolded.

"Sorry," she said, quickly looking away.

"So, we'll begin our life in Boston, and then pray for the Lord's direction from there. What do you say?" Grant asked looking down at her.

"Sounds good to me," Danielle said. "As far as I'm concerned, Dr. Hayes, the Lord can direct us wherever He will, and I'll be happy as long as I'm with you."

He hugged her close once more and looked into her eyes, "So you'll marry me, then?" he persisted.

Danielle pulled away from him and said with mock sternness, "If you haven't figured out by now that my answer is yes, you really have a problem."

Grant roared with laughter and pulled her back to his side. "Okay, okay. my beautiful darling. I'll try to recognize the obvious from now on."

They leaned back against the tree, enjoying their newfound love.

"All I know is that the Savior guided me home," Grant mused, looking down once more into her liquid green eyes, "and I'm so glad He did because in the midst of Him guiding me home, He guided me straight to you."